Recall

M. VAN

Recall

M. VAN

42Links Publishing
Visit: www.42Links.net

Cover design by Ramona & Adrian Marc
Visit: www.artstation.com/amarc

Edited by Book helpline
Visit: www.bookhelpline.com

Chapter one

A warm breeze wafted up from far below and stirred a few strands of my hair. The airflow released by the relief valves littering the ground level trailed up along the high-rises and added to the already uncomfortable humid temperatures. Even as I stood on the roof of this tall building, the hot gushes of steam that rushed up from the vents originating from within the deepest regions of this planet's core dampened my skin.

I ignored the tangy heat as my gaze shifted over the tightly clustered buildings and narrow streets that crisscrossed their way into the center of the City of Umbras—one of the last four known remaining cities and part of the Combined Districts of Tenebrae.

Colorful arrays of lights bathed the buildings in a sugar-candy brightness for reasons unknown to me, except that the visual distortions helped to hide the fact that most of the structures had seen better days. This city was falling apart along with the rest of the planet. If it weren't for the deteriorating buildings or the wastelands just beyond the borders of the protective dome, then surely the sun taking its first steps toward the red giant phase hovering ninety-five million miles above our heads would give away that this planet was dying.

The massive shiny disk looked to be so close that it seemed as if it were on a collision course, but then the sun hadn't been that distant lifeline that it used to be for a long time.

Most of the sun's hydrogen inside its core had been exhausted and converted into helium. This helium caused the pressure in the core to rise, resulting in a massive increase in the sun's output of heat and luminosity. This left the city bathing in a bright reddish-orange hue.

It would probably still be over a billion years before the sun would start the red giant phase, but the effects had already been devastating. The planet had turned into a wasteland unable to sustain human life, and if it weren't for the dome shields protecting our cities, we all would have been gone a long time by now.

The communications device lodged in my ear beeped, and neon-green letters flashed across the lenses of the heads-up display strapped to my head. The black-tinted shades looked like goggles covering most of my face and were strapped around my head with a wide band to support its weight. They provided me with the information and advanced vision needed to complete the missions assigned to me.

I glanced up at the dome and switched to the enhanced-vision setting of my heads-up to see the individual energy particles that created the shield. Combined, those particles protected us from outside heat and radiation.

The com device beeped again, and I redirected my attention to the message that blinked across the screen of my heads-up: "Target en route, be advised." Sightseeing was over, and I took a deep breath, if only to pretend to calm my nerves.

As an artificial representation, calm nerves—or rather, anxiety—wasn't something I needed to worry about. Although the materials used by the bioprinter to construct this body were very much human—the synthesized brain programmed to control this vessel wasn't. Still, I saw no harm in pretending to be more than just a thing sometimes, and apparently neither did my CPU.

I straightened while my eyes roamed the multitude of colors that glistened in the windows of the tall blocks of concrete. The lights bounced off the glass in a colorful rainbow, creating the illusion of a beautiful city plastered over the crumbling layers of rock and cement. The rays spread across the city skyline until they hit the dome's grimy, soot-covered surface.

Exposure to millennia's worth of polluted steam rising from the inner workings of the planet caused the dome to be barely see-through, but in a way, that helped to hide the wastelands beyond and the reality of a dying planet. But the dirt wouldn't prevent the sun from bathing the city in a red haze.

I lined my sight on the end of an alley wedged between the buildings, where the bright spotlights couldn't reach ground level. My heads-up compensated for the darkness, switching to a green spectrum that opened a world of tossed-over garbage cans, discarded boxes, more trash, and a drifter or two. There was a twitch in the spectrum, going from black to green, and the heads-up zoomed in automatically.

Even at this distance, it wasn't hard to see the young man running down the alley as he headed straight for the building I was standing on. The young man panted frantically as he whipped his head to look over his shoulder before facing the front again. I took in the old, rundown garments and crappy shoes. Blood trickled down his shirt, and it left stains on the collar next to a tear in the fabric that revealed his hairless chest. He ran to me without having any inkling that I was there.

From a previous encounter of the night, I could piece together an image of the surprise that would seize the man's face the moment I revealed myself, or should I say the horror. The fright in his eyes, the quaver in his voice as he begged for my forgiveness, seemed unavoidable.

I did not enjoy this part of the job, not that I enjoyed any part of this job. But it's not as if I were supposed to have any emotional attachment to these things. It's not as if they'd haunt me in my dreams or gnaw at my conscience. I didn't have a conscience; I wasn't a conscientious being. After my shift, I would return to the Tenebrae Enforcer Department and have my mind wiped clean of the day's events.

My artificial brain would be hooked up to the central mainframe located in a room that had been dubbed "Memory Junction" by the human law enforcement officers, and whatever was about to happen would be erased from my mind—reset, back to original parameters, every fraction of my day gone.

The slapping of footsteps, the sound enhanced by my heads-up, increased as the young man got closer. Behind him, I could hear the heavy tread of my partner's boots. With my enhanced vision, I could tell the man's eyes were wide with fear as his hand reached to wipe a mop of hair from his forehead. His face looked strained, and his muscles worked throughout his body, while sweat mixed with the blood on his shirt.

I edged the tip of my boots closer to the edge of the ledge. A variation of information trickled down the lenses of my heads-up and was fed into my central processing unit. It ranged from the man's running speed to the distance from my position to the ground along with gravitational pull and intended trajectory. For a moment, I took it all in and then took that final step over the edge.

Except for the hair on my head and the barely exposed skin of my face, my body was protected from the muggy air rushing by. Letters scrolled across my lenses, informing me of my descent and viable options. I slightly spread my arms to balance my fall.

My bodysuit was made of an armor reduced to an atomic-scale honeycomb lattice that protected me from most assault weapons available, and the built-in exoskeleton could absorb most forces my limbs could be exposed to.

My boots clanked on a metal emergency

staircase bolted to the building normally used as an escape route. The structure moaned under my weight. As my knees flexed, I grabbed the railing and used my momentum to fling my legs over and continued my drop.

In the street below, the man still hadn't noticed me, and he reacted in shock when I landed in a crouched position right in front of him. His arms flailed as he struggled to stop his running pace. Before he could collide with me, I stretched my leg, swung it around without raising from my crouch, and connected with the man's shins.

The man still had some momentum going, and my kick sent him careening past me before he fell to the ground. Without effort, I kept my movement going into a one-hundred-and-eighty-degree turn to face the body crashing to the asphalt. He cried out when his bare flesh scraped the concrete, and he hit the ground.

Behind me, I heard my partner's footsteps slow to a steady walk. He knew I had control, although the young man in front of me didn't seem convinced of that. He scrambled to his feet, his mouth twisted into a sneer. An all-or-nothing battle cry bounced off the buildings as he shouted his defiance. The knife he held in his right hand shone bright green from behind my display.

I ducked underneath his swing, jabbed him with a fist in his stomach, and grabbed the arm holding the knife. The man grunted but didn't relent, and I planted a flat palm against his nose. Blood gushed down into his mouth and chin when I whirled around him, gripping the arm behind his back, wrenching until it snapped.

He fell to his knees, screaming in pain while I took the knife from his hand and dumped it into a nearby garbage can. For good measure, I kicked him. The blow forced him on his back, and I placed my thick-soled boot on his chest. His rib cage rose and fell with the man's ragged breath, and I waited for my partner to step in.

"Enforcer 959," my partner called out as he stepped closer. At the mention of my formal designation, I turned my head. My partner for that night had been Enforcer 877. Because of his lower number, he had seniority. It meant he had been built before me, but that didn't mean he had more experience. Like me, he had his brain wiped clean every night, and his skills were mere programming: just like mine.

Enforcer 877 looked disheveled, his face was streaked with grime, and he had removed his heads-up display. I sensed an almost shocked sensation, but since I couldn't feel shock, I dismissed it as a misfire in my circuitry. Still, I had never seen an enforcer without his heads-up, not that I would remember anyway. Even in this dark alley, his pupils were nonexistent, leaving his irises an overwhelming bright blue. Those blue eyes staring back at me caused an image to flash across my mind. The sharp-edged features of a young woman appeared vividly before my eyes and I had to blink twice to refocus.

The fact that I could even remember this image was an anomaly. Every night after our shifts as enforcers, we were expected to report back to the Tenebrae Enforcer Department headquarters, or TED, for short. There they wiped all nonessential information from our CPUs at Memory Junction. As far as I was aware—as far as anyone was aware—this process had a one hundred percent success rate. It had never failed, except for this one faint residual image that seemed stuck in my head.

The tech guy at the station had been unsuccessful in removing the image of the young woman. Eventually, I'd told him that I couldn't remember what he was talking about and had given him the impression that he had succeeded. For some reason, the picture and the fact that I knew about it remained stuck in my mainframe, but after the numerous failures to remove it, I had decided to act as if the issue were solved.

It had occurred to me that this could be some type of virus messing with my CPU. How else would I be able to remember why the tech guy hadn't succeeded in erasing it? But this weird secret inside my head made my circuits tingle, and I wanted to keep it for myself. None of this made any sense considering my construct, but that had only inflamed my decision.

As if to draw my attention, 877 lifted his heads-up display for me to see.

"He got the jump on me," he said. His low voice had a lot of bass and didn't sound robotic as one might expect. Nor did he look anything else but human. We all did. The bioprinter that constructed our bodies used a set of human templates. This meant enforcers could look the same, but with the headgear covering most of our faces, it hadn't occurred to me to compare. I wondered if I looked anything like 877.

My processor kicked in as my sensors scanned my partner: male, constructed two years ago, average height. As a rule, an enforcer was never allowed and technologically denied scanning his own body, so I couldn't be sure, but 877 seemed to be taller than me, which suggested he had come from a different template.

Enforcer 877's arm dropped to his side. "Handle the rest," he said unapologetically.

I turned to the man on the ground, wedged underneath my boot, and waited for the information to scroll across my screen. As the bright-green letters appeared, I read them aloud.

"Thomas D. Laevis, you have been arrested by Enforcer 959 in the employment of the Tenebrae Enforcer Department under suspicion of stealing, looting, aggressive behavior, and acts of noncitizenship." I paused for the information on my screen to accumulate. It sometimes took a while for an official to type out or dictate his verdict. Our programming didn't allow for us to make our own rulings, so there was always a human judge on call to oversee our work.

"Considering the evidence, you have been found guilty of all the charges read to you. Prepare to hear your verdict," I said.

There was another pause, and for some reason, I felt my throat clench. Maybe it had to do with the fact that I could guess the verdict. No other verdict had made it past mine or my partner's lips the entire night. The man at my feet also seemed to know what was to come. He squirmed and jerked under my boot, trying for a way out.

Finally, the screen started to flow again. It wasn't always the brightest officials on the other line at these hours of the night.

"Under the jurisdiction of the Combined Districts of Tenebrae you will be put to death so no further disruptions will come from your feeble mind. Enforcer 959, you have permission to validate the verdict."

The green letters blinked once before they disappeared from my screen and left me faced with the man beneath my boot. He had stopped squirming. He knew it was too late. Permission had been granted, and that allowed me to deliver his verdict in every which way I deemed necessary. This included shooting him in the back if he attempted to run.

A shiver ran up my spine, and I sensed a strange buzz at the back of my skull. It forced me to close my eyes for a second in an attempt to register the sensation. *Had I ever sensed anything like it? Could it be the thrilling vibe of the sixth kill of the night or maybe a couple of fried circuits?* I wondered if I should tell the tech guy at Memory Junction after I got back.

"Enforcer 959," 877 said. My eyes flashed open. I grabbed the weapon from my holster before the man on the ground could blink and fired twice. Two bullets embedded themselves in the man's forehead.

His body jerked, his eyes rolled back in their sockets, and the rise and fall of his chest ceased underneath my boot.

"Alert the Whitewashers," 877 said. I complied and alerted the cleanup crew that was supposed to dispose of the body.

"We need to stop at the station for a new heads-up display," he added.

Before following my partner out of the alley, I glanced down at the lifeless body sprawled at my feet. It occurred to me that the man wasn't a man at all. He looked too young to be a man. This body had belonged to a mere boy, and I had taken his life. The thought lingered for a moment as I stepped over the corpse and walked up to my partner.

Enforcer 877 watched as I strode up to him, staring at me with those bright blue eyes. Every time I looked at them, they had this weird effect on me, but I was not supposed to have any reaction to what I experienced—not at having killed that boy and not at 877's eyes.

That picture of the woman reentered my mind. It was the only thing I had to keep me occupied after the events of my day had been purged from my system and I sat in my chair inside Memory Junction. Now it seemed to invade my mind while I worked. *This wasn't good.*

These distractions could keep me from performing my duties to the utmost of my abilities. Still, for some reason, I had no compulsion to report the incident. If the tech guy found out, then fine, and he would purge the problem. If not, I would have something to occupy my nights.

Except for my training and information essential to performing my duties, all memories were removed, and I had analyzed what had remained to perfection. It had gotten kind of tedious, and I welcomed the variation in my thought patterns. But I hoped I would lose the memory of the boy by the end of my shift.

"Are you malfunctioning," 877 asked as I stopped in front of him. Without giving him an answer, I tapped the side of my heads-up device. Green letters scrolled down the screen, and I took them in before I replied.

"Error log is clear."

He cocked his head and watched me. His heads-up device had been damaged, and he couldn't confirm my findings with his own scan.

"You seemed to have a slight hesitation in your motor function. Perhaps your memory banks are reaching full capacity."

"Hesitation?" I asked. It seemed obvious what he meant. I had hesitated in carrying out the judge's verdict.

"Just an observation," he said, "I cannot confirm, but I will report the incident after we return to headquarters."

With that, he turned on his heels, and I followed him to the mouth of the alley.

Chapter two

At the end of the alley, it was as if we'd stepped into a different world. We had ventured into one of the few main streets that would lead all the way up to the center of the city, and it bustled with activity.

Because this was one of the main streets, it held a central Hymag line. The spirals that held the aerodynamically shaped transportation pod curled their way along the length of the street until they disappeared around a bend. Electromagnetic energy surged through the spirals, keeping the pod and its passengers secure as it propelled the transport at high velocity from A to B within the confines of the dome. These Hymag lines were a simplified version of the transport we used for travel between the remaining cities, and although these were a lot smaller, they still took up most of the street.

People who were unlikely to ever travel inside one of those Hymags maneuvered around and over the fast-moving pieces of technology as if the Hymags didn't exist at all. Hymags were reserved for the upper-class members of society, although that distinction would never be made by any government official.

The lesser privileged used metal scaffolds, constructed to climb over the spirals. These structures, aiding to cross the street, rose as high as a two-story building and gave the people living in this area access to the different parts of the city.

The people crowding the streets came in all varieties. Because of the humidity, most were dressed in flimsy garments that hung loosely around their bodies. The light-yellow clothing stood out against the hard-gray bricks where the rainbow lights decorating the buildings up top couldn't find their way down to the streets.

Although the area sat packed with people even at these late hours, traveling through the masses didn't take much of an effort on our part. We stood out in our black-armored uniforms with embedded exoskeletons and weapons. In these suits, we appeared taller and more impressive in general. Also, the green lights that reflected of our heads-up displays made us attract attention as if we had set off a beacon.

As soon as we were spotted, people almost froze on the spot. Years of interaction with the enforcers roaming the streets kept them from stopping, though. Through some unconscious, almost animal, instinct, they would step aside and make room for us to pass. Citizens feared us for what we could do to them, but tonight they seemed especially skittish.

Fortunately, most of the glares passed me and fell on 877. Like me, not many had seen an enforcer without his heads-up display covering most of his face.

As we walked side by side, an incoming message blinked across my screen. Because 877 had lost the use of his heads-up, I read our next assignment aloud as I received it.

"Severe breach of conduct, enforcers in distress —assistance requested immediately."

I glanced up at 877 as I relayed the location. It had been a busy night already, and it seemed it wasn't about to let up. Enforcer 877 looked down at the device he held in his hand. Although still formidable, he wouldn't be as effective in the field without the aid of his heads-up, and besides, it was against regulations. It wasn't just orders we received through the device; the heads-up also recorded everything that happened around us and could be used to validate our conduct.

"Have additional support responded to the call?" he asked in a hushed tone. I nodded.

"Two units have been dispatched," I said. This meant four enforcers had responded to the call. 877 and I would be five and six.

"That should suffice," he said, but I held up my hand before he could say anything else. Another message blinked across my screen.

"Additional support is demanded, and our presence is required," I said. Enforcer 877 gave me a placid look. Not a single muscle in his face moved as he seemed to calculate his next decision.

"You move in," he finally said. "I will join you once my HUD is replaced."

Left standing on my own, I watched as the crowd dispersed and made room for 877 to pass them as he ran in the direction from which we had come. He disappeared as the crowd dispersed and returned to what they had been doing in the first place.

A repeat of the message appeared on my screen, and I started to make my way toward the scene of the crime. It seemed a bit overkill to send a fifth enforcer to a breach of conduct case even if they were severe and an enforcer was in distress. Usually, only a handful of enforcers would be able to take on a crowd of five hundred.

I started to run, but even with people shouting ahead to warn others of my approach, my progress was less than what I was used to. Midrun, I glanced up past the array of colorful lights and sought a good spot to climb a building. Traffic was a lot less heavy up high than down here on the ground. I spotted a ladder suspended over a door inside a recess in the wall of one of the buildings.

It was another escape route, and the ladder would be lowered if the inhabitants needed a rapid exit. With the exoskeleton embedded in my suit, the jump to reach the ladder would be easy enough, but an image on one of the display screens of a nearby shop drew my attention.

A mere advertisement shouldn't have been able to distract me like that, but this image wasn't anything like the colorful, fast-paced commercials for taste enhancers to add a little more flavor to our diet of converted mushrooms and molds.

I stopped for a moment and glanced at the unmoving picture. I blinked and gasped. It was her—the woman whose picture sat stuck in my head. This was a different picture, but I was sure it was her.

There didn't appear to be a message or an advertisement attached to the image displayed. I checked the other screens in the window display, and they all showed the same standard news items that were always broadcasted across the feed.

Most of the mainstream information like the news was broadcast by ArtRep Enterprises across the feed and could be received by most any electronic device—if in range. ArtRep maintained the basic infrastructure and controlled the central network, although it was a known fact that anyone with enough knowledge of the system would be able to link up. Basically, anyone could tap into the vast communication network and download or upload anything they wanted or needed to know or share. But because ArtRep was also the same company that built us, *Artificial Representations*, caution was advised not to engage in any illegal activities. Heavy penalties were put in place to discourage people with malicious intent to hack the system and undermine the government, but that didn't stop them from trying. For some people, the flow of information was a powerful thing, and it was up to the ARs to stop them.

As I returned my gaze to the picture, it baffled me for a moment for as far as anything could even baffle me. I snapped out of it as my heads-up beeped and a reminder of the impending emergency blinked in the corner of my screen. Redirecting my focus, I moved into the recess in the wall and jumped to grab hold of the ladder. Hoisting myself up, I started my way up to the roof.

I pushed the woman's image from my mind and focused on jumping from rooftop to rooftop until I reached the location my heads-up had directed me to. Around me, the world looked peaceful, even with the residual gleam of the sun dominating the sky. The sun's increased illumination kept the nights from being what they used to be and blocked out everything else space had to offer. It was only from the history files embedded in my memory banks that I knew that, once, billions of stars had decorated our night skies, but none of those were visible anymore.

Below me, the streets seemed abandoned, and I checked the location given to me earlier. I had come to the right spot, but apparently, whatever had happened had played out without me, and the other enforcers must have dealt with the situation. Because the file hadn't been closed and I hadn't been issued any other orders, I presumed my presence was still required. If it hadn't, my heads-up would have informed me. I decided to investigate and descended to ground level.

Cautiously, I walked into the street and scanned the area. This was one of the side streets, far from any main streets and Hymag lines. High above me, spotlights blazed, lighting up the buildings, but the shop windows on the lower levels of those buildings looked dark and empty. Usually, shops, or government distribution outlets as they were officially known, were open 24/7 in this district. Except for two black multiperson speeders, the street sat deprived of vehicles.

Unable to detect anything with my heads-up display, I started to jog and scanned the side alleys as I ran. I maintained a steady pace until a figure stepped onto the otherwise empty street. This caught me by surprise because there hadn't been any signs of life indicated by my heads-up. This person must have been standing in a secluded spot that my scans had been unable to reach. Maybe he or she had hidden there during the reported turmoil.

As I closed the distance, I noticed the figure to be a woman. She stood in the middle of my path, wearing heavy boots, black pants, and a sturdy black jacket in good condition—too good for this neighborhood. Her clothing seemed odd and looked nothing like what residents of this city usually wore, although I recognized the style.

According to my memory bank, it appeared to be something people living in Subterra might wear. Subterra was one of the four remaining cities, but unlike the other three, it was built underground where temperatures were lower and heavier clothing would be required. It also wasn't a part of the Combined Districts of Tenebrae. With the growing unrest and government upheaval between the districts and Subterra, it seemed unlikely for a citizen of Subterra to find her way to the City of Umbras. One certainly wouldn't want to stand out as she was doing right now.

It wasn't as if Subterrans weren't allowed here, but you never knew who you'd come across. Umbras citizens had the tendency to hold some radical views, which might lead to situations that could be threatening to any Subterran.

A few strands of short blond hair poked out from under the cap that hid her eyes and most of her face. Black lines of what looked to be the remnants of a tattoo were visible as they strayed from her neck over to her collarbone, but I couldn't decipher the design.

As I got closer, she didn't move from my path. I had never encountered anyone who hadn't moved from my path, and my CPU seemed to have a hard time processing the anomaly. Even the citizens of Subterra knew of our existence. This was a rough neighborhood, tough, and perhaps these folks weren't as impressed by an enforcer as I might have been led to believe. The distance between the woman and me quickly evaporated, and I couldn't fathom why she wouldn't move.

I switched to a stride and stopped in front of her. She didn't react. Watching her for a moment, I contemplated my next move and searched the information available in my database, but it was as if it wasn't there anymore. Like the failure to detect the woman's presence, my heads-up display did not react now, either.

I was about to start another system check when a green light flashed so brightly it hurt my eyes, and my vision went white. Blinking, I fought to see and caught the woman lifting her gaze. As I realized what my eyes were seeing, I gasped at the stabbing pain attacking the back of my skull. Circuits went wild, shorting, then flaring, rendering the information on my screen a blur of green blobs. I stepped back, trying to keep my balance while that same woman from the picture stuck in my mainframe stared back at me.

As enforcers, our bodies were well protected by the best technology had to offer, but this pain wasn't external. This pain came from within, as if someone had set my CPU on fire, and I clamped my mouth shut to keep myself from screaming.

As the pain started to subside, I bent over to catch my breath, and as my vision settled, I noticed the woman hadn't moved an inch. Heat rose up my neck and crept into my cheeks as I straightened. In that same moment, I realized that feeling embarrassed was a human emotion that didn't belong to an artificial representation. Something was definitely off with my programming.

My heads-up display flashed again, blinding me once more, and I ripped it from my head. Unsettled by the exposure and my inability to react appropriately toward certain threats without the device, I swirled my head around to check my surroundings. Inhaling deeply, I decided to accept my abilities had been impaired. If anything did happen, I would have to deal with it on my own without the heads-up and without backup.

I turned my attention to the woman still standing motionless in front of me. It took me a moment to realize that there was moisture in her blue eyes. She blinked, and water rolled down her cheeks. For some reason, I recognized the pain radiating from behind those eyes. It seemed to grab me by the throat, and I figured another circuit must have gone down because I couldn't breathe. Her lower lip quivered as she opened her mouth, and for a moment I thought she might speak, but she didn't.

Still, she captured my full attention, and I barely heard the high-pitched hum of one of the multiperson speeders I had passed earlier as it started its engine.

The woman's eyes flickered for a beat from me to the speeder but then focused back on me. Her quivering lip rose at the corner for just a smidgen. It lifted some of the pain from her expression but then transformed into concern. I couldn't pull my gaze from her as the speeder pulled up next to us, and the black door of the vehicle flew open.

With a slight hesitation, the woman turned on her heel and slipped inside the speeder. My limbs seemed frozen to the ground, and I just stood there as I watched the aerodynamically shaped lines of the speeder disappear around a corner.

Chapter three

Darkness filled the room as I sat in my corner of Memory Junction and tried to remember what had happened. The tech guy had come, done his thing, and left a while ago. As expected, he had hooked me and all the other artificial representations up to the machine and started the memory-wipe process.

Because the steps he had to go through belonged to my basic procedural information database, I had followed his movements closely to check if he hadn't missed anything, and he hadn't. Therefore, it didn't make much sense that I was still sitting here in the dark, wondering about that image inside my head. Added to that, I sat there wondering about all the other things that had happened.

I still remembered the fear on that boy's face right before I'd ended his life. I remembered seeing the ad of that same woman I had later met on the abandoned street. *How could this be possible?* The tech guy was supposed to have rid me of all those memories, but instead, I sat there thinking about them.

Around me about a dozen artificial representations sat in their chairs, staring blankly at the ceiling. Memory Junction wasn't much of a room —just a bare space with white walls and a round desk in the middle decked with flat-screen monitors. Wires ran from the central computer and led to the chairs that were placed in a circle around the table. *Why wasn't I staring at that same ceiling?*

Green lights blinked on the heads-up displays in five-second intervals all around me and it started to unnerve me, which in itself felt unnerving. I had never felt unnerved in my short existence, or if I had, I couldn't remember it.

Thoughts of meeting that woman collided inside my head. I went over every detail of the meeting over and over. Her blond short cut hair hidden underneath her cap. The tattoo that barely revealed itself from under her collar. Those blue eyes boring into me as a tear rolled down her cheek. The twitch of her mouth as it briefly lifted into a smile before concern took over and pain filled her eyes again. Even though she looked older than she had in the image stuck in my head, it all felt so familiar, *but how could it? How could I feel anything?*

The tech guy would have downloaded the information gathered by my heads-up, but he hadn't mentioned any problems, so perhaps there weren't any, and it was all in my head, some glitch in my CPU. Although that didn't seem right. Something was going on, and I knew I should have spoken up, but that hadn't felt right either. This was my secret, and I wanted to keep it. Furthermore, I wanted to unravel it.

A beep sounded, and luminescent lights flickered

on inside the room. Surprised, I checked my heads-up and noticed it was night again. The door swung open, and a wide-eyed young man stepped into the room. The messy hair on the tech guy's head jumped in all directions as he raked a hand through it. He had a cup in his hand, and a heads-up device analyzer or HDA for short stuck between his teeth. The cylindrical device would normally be used in the field to analyze a faulty headset and considering its sensitivity; I wouldn't have advised chewing on it. This information must have gotten past the tech guy though.

Without acknowledging any of us sitting in the chairs, he strolled to the desk and hit a couple of keys on a pad before he even sat down.

There was a buzzing sound, and then all the chairs started to move into an upright position. Green lights blinked erratically on the heads-up displays around me, and my fellow artificial representations came to life. As if awoken from comatose sleeps, they stretched their limbs and bones cracked. With purpose, the ARs slipped from their seats and moved toward the door.

The green light on my own heads-up device blinked as well, and knowing what was expected of me, I mimicked the others and followed them outside, but there was no sense of the compulsion to do what was expected of me as there had been yesterday. *Why did I remember yesterday's expectations?* The thought set off a strange sensation that lingered inside my head.

My central processing unit was definitely malfunctioning, and I knew I should report it, but I had no desire to do so. Besides, reporting the malfunction might have me end up in the maintenance ward where some eager technician could decide to cut me open. I shivered at the thought—another strange sensation, but one that made me stand by my decision not to come forward.

I followed in line with my companion ARs. There were seven of us on this night shift, which seemed odd, but my mind was too distracted to linger on the fact. Seven enforcers were enough to hold up the law in a five-mile radius of city blocks, but also enough to keep us busy. I stood last in line behind the intake desk, where we were supposed to register before we started our patrols. A round-faced law enforcement officer with a mustache and a thinning hairline registered our thumbprints and assigned us our designated areas for the night.

As usual, the hallway buzzed with people. Human law enforcement officers in light-gray uniforms milled up and down the hall. Some carried the standard kind of delinquent by the shoulders to their pit stops hosted by the district jail: drug users, hookers, and I saw some members of a local gang that had terrorized the neighborhoods for years.

I moved up another place in the line and watched a man at the front desk explain how he had gotten a bloody nose to the officer assigned. At least that was what he seemed to be doing from the way he gestured wildly from his nose to his bloodied shirt.

The AR ahead of me pressed his thumb onto the tablet and was appointed a partner. I stepped up to the desk. Without much interest, the officer behind the desk held the tablet out to scan my thumb. He didn't look at me as he waited for the readout.

"Enforcers 959, you will be going out on a solo run tonight—congratulations," the officer said without a hint of sincerity. I glared at him, but he wouldn't have noticed with my eyes hidden behind tinted glass. It seemed obvious as the other six had paired up, and I was the only one that had remained. Still, I had no memory of ever going out on my own, although that wasn't a surprise.

I checked for information transmitted to my heads-up, but there was no information to check. In fact, the screen had gone blank. The officer behind the desk cleared his throat. He glanced at me curiously before a grin emerged on his face. As he lifted his oversized butt from his chair, he reached a hand out and tapped my heads-up with an outstretched finger. If I hadn't been wearing the tinted goggles, I was sure the officer would have frowned at my bulging eyes.

"Is that thing working?" he asked in a condescending manner. Most human officers did not have a lot of respect for ARs taking over their jobs for free and thought of us as mindless drones. He thought I wouldn't be able to function without the device strapped to my head, and he was probably right, although I wasn't going to tell him that. Playing along, I tapped the gadget and said, "No problem, sir, just a delay in the upload."

The officer watched me curiously as he sat down and then glanced at the tablet on his desk. He scrolled through a couple of pages that had my designated number printed on the headline.

"Everything checks out," he said. "You're clear to go."

"Yes, sir."

I turned and headed for the door at a fast pace. That tablet should have detected my heads-up wasn't working. With firm strides, I passed the front desk where the man with the bloody nose seemed to have gotten more agitated by the minute.

At the front door, I had to stop to let a couple of officers pass as they dragged a man who didn't seem to be bothered to use his legs. I held the door for the men as I felt a shudder rack my body. The sight of the street outside raised the hairs on the back of my neck. *Was I supposed to go out there without the aid of a heads-up? How could I do my job if I wasn't able to receive assignments or reach a judge if I needed a verdict?*

I was still holding the door as another officer entered. His brows furrowed as amusement filled his eyes. As the man stopped before me, my chest tightened, and I felt a tremble in the hand holding the door.

"Did they add doorman to the job?" he asked his partner jokingly as a second man stepped inside. Ignoring the shiver running down my spine and the two men, I managed to compose myself enough to walk out.

I moved down the steps of the old justice house and cornered into the darkness of an alley hidden in the wake of tall buildings on either side. I shied away from the colorful lights along with the facade plastered over this city, and I sought out the furthest and darkest corner where no one could see me.

I fought to breathe as I tried to release the tightness in my chest. Painful gulps of air forced their way down into my lungs without much relief. My mainframe screamed, sending electric shocks down my circuits. *This was not possible!* I couldn't think; I wasn't supposed to think; I was only supposed to react; I wasn't anything but a mere machine stuck inside a vessel constructed of the dead.

Pain similar to what I had felt standing in front of that woman yesterday jabbed at my eyes as if someone was poking at them with needles. With an awkward motion, I ripped the heads-up display from my head.

By the time the goggles hit the ground, I had sunk down the wall to sit next to them. My head pounded as a rush of images invaded my mind. My hands wrapped into fists clenching hard until my knuckles turned white and I pressed them to my temples. That picture, that tattoo, the pain in her eyes, images forced their way into my head. *Was this what a system overload felt like?* Pictures kept pouring into my mind. Steaming-hot drinks in paper cups with a green logo, a grimy-looking teddy bear, the sound of the ocean combined with screams of scattering gulls. I locked my head in a vice of arms and tried to squeeze out the images that didn't make any sense. Anything to ease the throbbing in my head.

A thought occurred, and it seemed as ridiculous as what was happening to me, but I wondered if these images could be memories. Maybe being hooked to these machines didn't wipe the memories I had acquired over the years, but just buried them.

As if something clicked with the thought, the storm inside my head calmed down, and my breathing relaxed. My brain started to function again, and I tried to analyze the images. None of them seemed to have anything related to what an artificial representation would encounter during their daily tasks.

Tiny outstretched arms reaching for a grimy-looking bear, but the vantage point was all wrong. It seemed as if I were the one reaching for the bear, and I even felt the desire to hold it. But this couldn't be. If I were the one reaching for that bear, I would have been a child—no more than four or five years old. *If these images were actual memories, then what would that mean?*

Through a haze of thoughts, I barely heard the footsteps approach until they were right in front of me. Still, I ignored them. For a second, I wondered about the look on a person's face at the sight of me, this figure dressed to intimidate and induce fear in the minds of others—garbed in black from head to toe, with those ominous goggles, now reduced to a pitiful pile, no more than a beggar. I would have ignored the passerby if he hadn't dropped something. A piece of paper slightly lingered on a breeze before it fluttered to the ground by my feet.

A five-credit note that would buy a person a new pair of shoes on the black market lay in front of me. I looked up to find the person, to point out to him what he had lost, even though I should probably arrest the person for carrying illegal currency.

The figure, also clad in black from his long overcoat to his black boots, kept a firm stride, with his hands clamped behind his back. He glanced over his broad shoulder, and I noticed the black hat and shades that hid his face. His clothes weren't local, and the color black hinted at him being an enforcer, but then his glasses weren't the enforcer kind—besides, enforcers wouldn't carry credits. Before he exited the alley, he looked over his shoulder again and threw me a two-fingered salute. I read it as a signal that dropping the note hadn't been an accident.

I stared at the piece of paper for a long moment while in the distance I heard vehicles passing by, men and women rushing to get home after a long day's work, fleeing the colorful mirage before the real darkness fell over them.

If my heads-up display had worked, I felt sure it would have told me all about the people passing this alley, but I also felt sure it wouldn't have told me anything about that tall, dark stranger.

With five credits in my pocket, I walked the streets as if I had a purpose, and maybe I did. After I had found what was hidden inside the note, it didn't take me long to get to my feet, although I had no idea why. Something compelled me to follow the instruction written on the note, and that shouldn't have been possible.

Could it be that someone had compromised my programming? But then how would that let me internally debate the issue? None of this made sense to me.

The heads-up display hid my eyes but didn't

provide me with any of the information I usually needed to get by in this maze of streets and alleys. Fortunately, the location written on the note was strangely familiar to me.

On the way, I had to handle a dispute over a stolen pack of unprocessed mushrooms. Although I hadn't received an actual official call to interfere and wouldn't be able to reach a judge, I figured I needed to step in, because it looked as if a kid was about to take a beating. Three broad-shouldered men had cornered a boy no more than eleven or twelve years old in the recess of a building. My mere approach seemed to calm the men's nerves, although they protested after I sentenced the kid with a misdemeanor and three weeks' probation.

Usually, trafficking unprocessed mushrooms could get you jailed for three weeks, but a twitch of my hand toward my weapon was enough for them to back off. The kid actually thanked me before bolting into the shadows of the night. The holdup hadn't taken long, though, and I had almost reached my designation.

Tide View Hospital towered over most of the buildings in the area. With a facade made of glass to increase the effect of the blazing candy-colored lights, it had become the ultimate contrast of beauty on the outside with the horrors within. The lights bounced off the building so brightly that it wasn't unusual for someone to wear sunglasses in the middle of the night.

As I stood in front of the building, I reached for the credit note inside my pocket and unfolded it.

Hidden in the folds of the credit note sat another note with a message scribbled on the surface: "She can help—Tide view—Dead man's hour."

Chapter four

The emergency room was bustling as I entered through the glass sliding doors. The waiting area sat packed, and staff was running up and down the halls. Gurneys lined the hallways with a diversity of people and a variety of injuries, from a kid with something stuck up his nose to ominous-looking thugs in disheveled clothes, cuffed to their beds and with law enforcement officers by their sides.

Some of them glanced up as they saw me, but nobody dared to approach. As an enforcer, I had full clearance and didn't have to answer to anyone in public. I only needed to obey the neon-green letters scrolling down the screen before my eyes.

Today there hadn't been any green letters, and thinking about it created this churning feeling in my gut. *What if someone realized I wasn't plugged in? Would they send someone after me? And if they caught me, would they chop me up into pieces to figure out the problem with my processor?*

I pushed the thought from my mind and straightened up. If they thought I was here on business, these officers wouldn't bother me. To them, we were a necessary evil they'd rather avoided, but showing a little courtesy never hurt.

An officer who sat next to a bald man in a torn sand-colored shirt looked up nervously. The buttons of his light-gray uniform struggled to keep the fabric in place, and the man almost choked on his fried fungi dough when I nodded my head to acknowledge him as I passed.

I moved through the halls to the central information desk and stopped to take another look at the note. It wasn't very specific, and I glanced around the area to see if I might spot the woman. For some reason, I knew it had to be her—the one whose picture seemed stuck in my head, but I had no evidence to support that. A clock on the wall indicated that it was two minutes till midnight.

The information desk sat empty, and I turned leisurely in a full circle. The white desk stood in the center of the room, and the projection of an enormous red question mark hovered over it. The sign gave the desk a predominant presence inside the room, but it didn't have any effect. No one seemed interested in asking or answering a question.

The rest of the large room was pristinely white, and I wouldn't have been surprised if the immaculate walls and ceiling hurt my eyes to look at without the heads-up. The place also looked very clean even though dozens of people milled around, and some of them were bleeding profusely.

If this hospital had the means to keep even public areas this clean, that would mean they'd have some serious government backing. Only the government could make decisions about who had access to technology like drones—one of which just sped by me. The thing looked like a square box that hovered over the ground, disinfecting anything that came in its path.

A man screamed, drawing my attention, and a doctor wearing a device on his head that looked like my heads-up rushed by toward him. As I followed the doctor's movement, another white coat drew my attention.

Turning my head, I just caught *her* crossing the hall and entering a room. With firm strides, I followed, and without hesitation or knocking, I opened the door. The room was dark, but my heads-up quickly adjusted and switched to the green filter, boosting the little light available. It seemed the damn thing hadn't died completely.

I didn't detect any immediate signs of movement and took another step inside. Without windows, the room had not much to offer. A desk with a chair stood on a shiny floor, and a stretcher sat crammed into the corner.

I checked for another exit as I made my way to the desk, but I couldn't detect it. She couldn't have vanished into thin air. My eyes roamed over the papers laying on the desk, revealing some information on a research study. A picture frame that sat on the desk drew me in. Before I knew it, I held it in my hand and gasped.

Pain and shock even worse than in that alley seized control of my body. It felt as if needles had sunk into my skull, exiting through my eyes. I ripped the heads-up from my face and tossed it on the desk.

My hands wrapped around my head, and I bit my lip to stifle the scream that brewed inside my chest.

I let my body drop until I fell into the chair. Head between my knees, I tried to gain my breath, but I couldn't get the image out of my head. That face, those eyes, it was her in that picture. It was her maybe ten years ago. Her eyes didn't hold the pain I had witnessed last night; sadness maybe, but not the sorrow that edged over into pain.

As a young girl of maybe fifteen, she looked strong as she held a protective arm around a skinny kid who looked a couple of years younger. That other little girl in the picture had darker skin, even darker eyes, and frizzy hair that seemed to live a life of its own. As I risked another look at both girls, a similar jolt of pain as before struck my head, and I dropped the picture onto the desk. I bent forward, burying my face in my hands hoping for the pain to subside.

It must have been because the pain started to lay off and my CPU started functioning again that I registered the lock clicking. My head shot up, my senses on full alert as I noticed someone in the room with me.

A figure stood at the closed door, and without my heads-up, it should have been hard to identify the person, but even in this dark room, I could tell it was her. My body went rigid as our eyes locked.

Hard, white hospital light filtered inside the room from under the door, enough to distinguish her features and barely enough to reach her eyes. Her arms lifted as if in surrender as she cautiously moved to the corner of the room.

In normal circumstances, my heads-up would have informed me to subdue the intruder and ask questions later, but my heads-up lay on the desk. But I wondered if I would have complied. As it was, I sat frozen in the chair.

With a click, a soft yellow light filled the room, forcing my eyes to blink to adjust for the shift. She had turned on a desk lamp that sat on a small table next to the stretcher. Without hesitation, she sat down on the makeshift bed, while her eyes never strayed from mine. A million things I didn't understand raced through my head, and I couldn't make much sense of them. Perhaps out of habit my eyes shifted to the heads-up lying on the desk.

"Don't," she said as I reached for the goggles. Her voice didn't reach over more than a mere whisper, but the urgency in her tone was evident. My hand hovered over the device, barely able to contain the need to pick it up. "Please don't," she said a bit more forcefully, but it still sounded like a plea. Hovering over the goggles, my hand balled into a fist, and I closed my eyes.

"I don't…" I started to say, but I fumbled the words and tried for something else, "Why am I here?"

"It'll be all explained—soon," she said. The softness in her voice forced me to look at her. Her lips curved into a smile, but she didn't seem able to hold it, and I could see the pain behind her eyes had returned. She let out a sigh of relief when my hand retreated from the device, but her shoulders tensed when instead my hand reached for the picture frame.

Her reaction told me she knew more about this picture besides the fact that she was in it.

"Why does my head feel like it's about to explode when I look at this picture?" I asked. I held up the frame without looking at it. She sighed in exasperation as if she were about to explain electromagnetic fusion to a two-year-old.

"It hurts because looking at it triggers a memory," she said.

"I don't have any memories," I said and shook my head. "Besides, I don't know these kids."

She leaned back, pushing her back against the wall and crossing her arms over her chest.

"Are you sure about that?" she said, raising an eyebrow, "You know, the kid on the left…that is me and—"

"I don't know you," I said harshly as I interrupted her.

"I see this enforcer business hasn't helped in the manners department," she said under her breath, but with enough bite that it hit a nerve with me. I wasn't about to sit here and be lectured by a citizen.

"My designation is 959, and I am an enforcer in the service of the Tenebrae Enforcer Department, property of ArtRep Enterprises, and your comment could be considered an insult punishable by law," I said. The words fell from my mouth as if I were on the streets, sighting some criminal.

As if she hadn't heard me or didn't care, the woman scoffed before she said, "Well, it's not nice to interrupt a person while they're talking." I glared at her, taken aback at her audacity. I had never heard of anyone dare to speak in such a careless manner to an enforcer.

She got up from the stretcher and strolled over to the desk where she sat down in the chair across from me and said, "I was supposed to take this slowly, but I guess they haven't been able to wipe the stubbornness from your mind." I narrowed my eyes at her, unsure of what she had meant. She grinned, but despite her cockiness, I could tell she seemed nervous by the way she bit her lower lip.

"My name is Saera," she said, "and the other girl's name is Maecy, or Maece, as she preferred, but I could never quite bring myself to call her that." Her grin almost widened into a smile as she seemed to reminisce in some distant memory. I had always wondered how that must feel. The pain inside my skull flared up again.

"This also happens to be your name," she said. I gripped the sides of my head and blinked. My eyes filled with tears, and it was hard to focus on anything.

"Memories can be a bitch, can't they," she said. The tone of her voice had changed and had gone soft as if she had decided to leave out the snarky parts to spare my feelings.

I wiped a hand over my eyes as the pain faded. My fingers came back wet, which added another new sensation to confuse my circuits, and I wiped the tears on my suit. I watched the woman carefully as I tried to decide how much of a threat she actually was. She seemed to be able to incapacitate me by saying a simple word—namely, the name of a child.

"I know it's hard to believe, but I know you—I

have known you ever since we were kids," she said. "You just can't remember right now."

"I have no memories," I said in defense, as if she didn't know that already. "You're just messing with my CPU." My processors kicked into overdrive. This had to be some ploy—a way to harm the current administration. "You're a rebel," I said, raising my voice as I jumped up from the chair. She dismissed my accusing glare and shook her head. Then she lifted her hands as if she didn't want to be perceived as a threat and stood.

"I'm just gonna turn on the overhead light," she said and pointed at the switch near the door. I nodded but stood ready to grab her if she decided to take off. She still had some explaining to do.

The lights flickered on, and I closed my eyes. As I opened them, the hard light stung for a moment, but then my eyes adjusted. I noticed Saera wore the white doctor's coat over the same garments she had worn yesterday. The black outfit and sturdy jacket let anyone identify her as a Subterra resident, and the doctor's coat didn't do much as a disguise.

Her blond hair was cropped short at her neck but was longer up top. Her blue eyes held a hard gaze and stood out against her pale skin. Her tough exterior might have come across as threatening if it weren't for the twitch of her mouth and her teeth digging into her lower lip.

Saera raised a hand and gestured behind me. I kept a cautious gaze on her, but she hinted again at whatever it was that seemed to be behind me.

"Just brace yourself," she said.

Leisurely, I started to turn, but I kept Saera within my peripheral vision. But all the diligence programmed into my CPU disappeared as I found myself staring into a mirror.

My head didn't hurt as much as it had before, but the mere sight of myself took me aback. I stumbled backward and landed on my butt on the desk. This was wrong—this was all wrong. The woman staring back at me in the mirror looked at least ten years older than the kid in the picture, and my hair was shorter and not as frizzy anymore, but the resemblance was uncanny.

I stood and moved to the mirror as if to examine myself for the first time. It felt as if it was the first time, although I must have noticed some of my features over the years—I had just forgotten. More accurately, it had been wiped from my mind.

I removed my gloves and inspected my hands. They seemed so strange, and my skin had a much darker shade than most of the population living in the City of Umbras. Amazed, I lifted my hand to touch my face. It looked nothing from what I had imagined. The only things I had to compare myself with were the other enforcers, and they had all been tall, broad-shouldered, and mostly male. I was clearly female, still an impressive presence in my armored suit, but also much leaner. *How had I not noticed this before, or perhaps I had and couldn't remember?*

Saera stepped closer to stand beside me and watched me through that same mirror.

"You've grown to be quite a stunner, sis," she

said, and for the first time, I witnessed a smile on her face that reached her eyes.

Shocked at her admission, I turned to face her and then abruptly turned back to the mirror to compare our unmistakable differences before looking back at Saera. Her skin was almost as white as the walls of this hospital. She flexed a muscle in her sharp-edged jaw as I peered into her blue eyes. I imagined those eyes could appear cold as ice, although they weren't now.

I shifted my gaze back to the mirror and inspected my jet-black hair and my dark hazel eyes that, even though my irises projected this weird glow, matched the color of my skin.

Facing Saera again, I said, "Us being sisters is as impossible as me having a…" I hesitated. I wanted to say past. Anything beyond of being an enforcer, but that picture might be the proof that I had.

"Listen," she said and hesitated as if she needed the time to think through her next words. "I want to explain, and I will, but I don't want your brain to fry or for you to suffer in agony. So if you want to know and if you're willing to trust me, then you'll have to come with me." Her hand reached out as if to touch me, but instead of letting her, I flinched and stepped back.

There was too much going on inside my head, and I didn't know which line of thoughts to trust. *Was this a trick? Had a virus slipped into my processing unit or was she telling the truth?* Her hand froze in midair, and the smile that had brightened her face faded. *But what if she were telling the truth? What would that mean?*

It would mean that I wasn't an artificial representation made by a bioprinter out of human remains with a computer stuck in my head. If this was true, then it was worth finding out, and if it wasn't, then I still had my enforcer abilities to get myself out of this. If needed, I could even arrest her.

"Will you come with me?" she asked. Her whispered words reflected doubt or maybe fear that I would refuse. I watched her for a moment as I would have if I was wearing my heads-up display. The device would have recognized any anomalies in her story by measuring the diameter and size of her pupil. Not many realized what a traitorous entity their bodies could become, but even without the gadget propped on my head, her story rang true to me—if only because of the nagging pain resonating from the back of my skull. I nodded and replied, "I'll come with you."

It wasn't hard to recognize the relief washing over her as Saera took a deep breath. I reached for the heads-up laying on the desk. Her hand took mine before I could grab the device or pull away from her.

"You don't need those," she said as she seemed to struggle for control of her voice. "You don't need anyone to tell you what to do." The touch combined with her soft-spoken but emotionally filled words didn't ease the strain in my muscles. I couldn't help it; my body had been wired for diligence for too long and seemed to react on its own. And yet her unknown familiarity embraced me in a warm blanket.

"I can't just leave it here," I said, not wanting to convey distrust but unwilling to part from the device that had guided me for as long as I knew.

"You should bring them," Saera said with a nod. "Just don't put them on."

Because Saera held on to my hand, I grabbed the heads-up from the desk with the other and then let her guide me to the door.

Chapter five

Maece

Saera stopped at the door and looked slightly up to face me. She stood a little shorter than me, and from the scan I had made the previous night, I remembered her to be five foot seven. Her frame was lean and borderline thin. One hand held on to mine while the other rummaged through a pocket of her white doctor's coat. I noticed a tattoo on the back of the hand holding mine. Flames drawn in black ink extending from under her sleeve seemed to engulf her hand. I wondered if these markings on her hand had anything to do or were connected with the ink I had spotted on her neck and collarbone.

Thinking about the possible shape and size of the tattoo created an uncomfortable sensation in the back of my head. Afraid to set off another painful memory, I shook the thought from my mind. Saera, unaware of my discomfort, pulled out a pair of dark shades and held them out to me.

"You'll stand out too much otherwise," she said. I glanced at the heads-up in my hand and secured it with a clip to my belt.

"It's not as if I won't stand out in this," I said, gesturing at my armored suit. "Black isn't exactly an inconspicuous color in these parts of town." In the same movement, I gestured at her clothes that, besides the white doctor's coat, were as black as mine.

"We won't be in sight long enough for anyone to notice," she said.

"So then why do I need to wear these?" I asked as I took the tinted glasses from her. Her mouth twitched into a mischievous grin as she said,

"Your eyes kind of freak me out."

"Ow," I said, placing the glasses on my nose.

"Don't worry," she added without a hint of embarrassment. "They'll turn back eventually...I hope." Without further notice, she opened the door, and I followed Saera into the hallway.

Even with the new shades, I felt strangely naked without the heads-up hiding my face as Saera led me by the hand. Walking through the hall, I noticed nothing much had changed. Doctors and nurses kept themselves busy with patients, cleaning drones mopped the floors, and the information desk still sat unattended.

Three doors down from the room we had exited, Saera crossed the hall and opened a door that led to a staircase. I closed the door behind us. Saera shot me a quick glance, and the determination in her expression was obvious as she led me by the hand down the stairs.

The steps seemed to go on and on, and we had to be at least four floors beneath the surface when Saera stopped in front of a metal door. She hesitated with one hand on the nob.

"Listen," she said and hesitated again before she turned to me. "These people you're going to meet, they might seem intimidating, but they're pretty nice." She looked at me expectantly, but I had no idea what to say. "I know it doesn't make sense now, but you have to believe that I'm trying to do what's best," she added. With that, she squeezed the hand she was still holding and opened the door.

I followed Saera into a dark hallway. Emergency lights hanging at large intervals were the only thing that kept us from being completely surrounded by darkness. Walking in the semidark without the help of my heads-up felt ominous, and the sunglasses bridged on my nose didn't help either. Something could jump at us without either of us having seen it coming. Still, I ignored the urge to unclip the goggles from my belt and decided to rely on my natural senses instead.

We made several left and right turns, and as we exited another door, it became obvious we must have left the hospital grounds. The dark but impeccable hallways turned into tunnels that seemed to have been carved right from the stone holding up the walls around us.

Gravel crunched underneath my boots, and the staccato of sound started to annoy me. Saera stopped when we reached a part of the tunnel where the lights guiding us ended. For the first time since we'd started our trek, she released my hand. Then she removed her white doctor's coat and clicked something on her wrist. A highly focused beam of light shot out from the device and cut a path through the darkness.

"I could try the HUD," I said as she reached for my hand. "It still has the night-vision function."

She took my hand and shook her head. "You can't use that thing anymore," she said.

"Why not?"

"Because it helps to keep your memories in check," she replied. I glanced at her while we started to walk again and thought about it.

"How does that work?" I asked. She flashed her light into my face, and I flinched.

"How the hell should I know," she said.

"It could be that the HUD emits a signal that travels via the optic nerve to the visual cortex and from there is able to reach different parts of my brain," I said. "That might be possible, couldn't it?"

Saera sighed, which might have been out of frustration.

"What's wrong?" I asked.

"Why can't you just accept that it is what it is, Maecy," she replied, sounding frustrated. "This is exactly the kind of thing that has you venturing into shitty situations like this."

Pain erupted inside my skull and shot down my spine. The sensation overwhelmed me, and I dropped to my knees. Saera kneeled next to me while I clamped my teeth to stifle a scream.

"I'm sorry," she said as she wrapped an arm around me. "I shouldn't have said that. I wasn't thinking."

I gulped air into my lungs and waited for the painful moment to pass. Saera tightened her grip around me.

"I have to tell you," I said between gasps. "I'm not…getting…any of this."

She squeezed my shoulder and shifted back to sit on her haunches. The light strapped to her wrist bounced off the wall before it settled on the gravel at our feet.

"I won't pretend to know how the technology exactly works, but it has something to do with memories," she said. "Everything that takes place in the present is fine, but things that happened in the past will trigger this pain you feel."

"So how come your face doesn't trigger these flashes of pain anymore?" I asked as I fought to catch my breath.

"I don't know exactly, but this guy I know, Kyran, has something to do with it," she said, "and it's been two years. A lot has changed."

Almost as an afterthought, she said, "I have changed." I watched her as she seemed to disappear in her own thoughts. Shadows darkened most of her pale face, and she looked almost see-through as if some fading hologram. I glanced around and could only feel darkness pressing down on me inside this underground tunnel.

All of this—ignoring a broken heads-up, accepting a strange meeting in a hospital and now following this woman into the bowels of the earth—seemed so alien to me and yet so familiar. Even if I wanted to, I couldn't go back to my life as an enforcer, because what if there was a chance I could be more than that—more than an artificial representation. I needed to know, and following Saera felt like something I had always done, although in avoiding the imminent pain, I tried not to think about it too much.

Besides, heading back to TED would probably mean wiping my memory, and all of this would disappear or worse. If they'd determined something was wrong with me, they'd put me out of commission and throw me in a waste disposal furnace.

"Come on. They're waiting for us," Saera said as she climbed to her feet.

"Who is they?" I asked. She held out a hand to help me up.

"People that can help you," she said, "but I think we should probably keep the talking to a minimum. I don't want to say the wrong thing and fry your brain again."

I opened my mouth to ask another question, but she gave me a look that stopped the words from exiting my mouth. Instead, I placed a hand on the back of my neck and stretched the muscles there. My head throbbed, but the pain had become bearable. Still, it seemed wise to keep our mouths shut for the rest of the way, wherever it was that she was taking me.

It felt as if we had walked for hours when a door stopped our progress. I looked over my shoulder to see only blackness and knew it would be difficult if I needed to get out of these tunnels on my own. The route we had taken to get here had us going around several corners, and although I had counted them, I knew it would be a near-impossible task to find my way back.

Saera traced her light over the door, which seemed to be made of solid steel. She held the beam steady on an apparently insignificant part of the wall next to the door and then placed her hand flat against it. I watched as the area around her hand lit up. Something clicked and then a voice that made me jump sounded from out of nowhere.

"She came," a hoarse male voice said.

"As you can see," Saera replied. Her words immediately triggered my eyes to trace the walls for surveillance equipment, but it was too dark for me to identify anything, and Saera kept her light pointed at the ground. She was clearly not interested in finding the device.

"Any trouble," the voice said.

"None," Saera replied. For a while, the voice stayed silent, and I shot Saera a glance. She shrugged.

With a click the tunnel bathed in a green mist while lasers traced our bodies, covering every millimeter. The scan ended within seconds, and then the voice came to life again. "You may enter."

"Your friend's not very talkative," I said just as a whoosh of air pulled at strands of my hair. I expected the door to swing open, but instead, the wall seemed to start moving up. It took me a moment to realize that it wasn't the wall that was moving up, but that we were going down.

My stomach churned as the platform we were standing on seemed to drop at an enormous pace, and subconsciously I took a step toward the middle. With the knowledge rendered from my information database, I had identified this form of transport as a magnetic lift and knew there was nothing to worry about. The idea that this information might come out of some residue memory instead of programming did have me a little worried.

"Your friend's scan doesn't work very well," I said to distract myself from the discomforting feeling that lingered in my stomach. "I'm very much armed."

"It wasn't a weapons scan," she replied over the hum of the magnetic lift, "and these guys aren't my friends, not exactly."

"So…there is a chance of being taken by thugs or rebels," I said as I watched the walls rise.

Saera frowned, pursed her lips, and said, "Could be possible…but I doubt it."

"That's comforting," I replied. She grinned as the lift started to slow and then nodded toward the exit that seemed to rise from the ground as the lift ground to a halt.

Saera had to shield her eyes from the light falling on us, but I was still wearing the glasses she had given me. The shades would also have protected me from looking overly amazed if my mouth hadn't fallen open.

The lift opened to a giant cavern, although the word didn't do justice to the structure. A dome, carved out of the stone, not unlike the dome protecting the city, housed over a round platform in the middle.

From where we stood, a stone bridge led across a ditch wide enough that it couldn't be jumped and deep enough that I couldn't see the bottom. Three more bridges connected with the platform on opposite sides, but they didn't seem to lead to other lifts.

Instead, they lead to entryways that were round and at least twenty feet in diameter. It wasn't hard to figure out their purpose once I saw a Hymag parked at the edge of the platform, although it stood at a strange angle toward any of the exits. The transport was bigger than the ones that they used up top, and I was sure there would be some sort of trick to get the thing out of here. *How else would they have gotten it inside?*

A rush of cold air touched the skin on my face, and a shiver ran down my spine that reverberated through my entire body.

"You'll get used to the cold again," Saera said before she abruptly placed a hand over her mouth, stopping herself from saying anything else. I closed my eyes and braced myself for another jolt of pain. When it didn't come, I cocked my head to a side and shrugged—nothing happened. As if to be sure, Saera waited for another beat and then said, "Shutting up now."

I grinned and noticed a man standing at the other end of the bridge.

"Is he waiting for us?" I asked. Saera glanced at the man and let out a sigh.

"Yep," she said as she grabbed my arm and pulled me along with her, "let's get this over with."

The man stood tall, shoulders straight and hands folded behind his back as if he stood in a military lineup, but even though everything about him screamed authority, he looked relaxed. His clothes were a formfitting black, accentuated by the many weapons strapped to his sides. As we drew closer, I noticed that he had some gray streaks peeking through at the temples of his dark, neatly trimmed hair. His facial hair looked like an abandoned goatee with a touch of gray.

My boots clomped on the stone bridge as we walked across. It was hard to keep my attention on the man waiting for us. Besides the fact that I had never seen a structure this impressive underground—at least not that I remembered—a lot was happening behind him.

It reminded me of the control rooms back at Tenebrae ED where all the feeds strung across the city converged into the central mainframe. Every image collected on the streets and inside official buildings found their way across the feed into that database where they were tagged, analyzed, and filed. It also included all the data collected by enforcer headgear.

Like the control room, massive screens hung in a circle and hovered over dozens of workstations. Several people dressed in black sat at tables, tapping virtual keys or flipping switches. The men and women working the stations looked young but capable, as if they had worked those stations their whole lives. They appeared almost soldier-like in their efficiency, but I didn't think they were. To me, his operation resembled more of an enforcer or law enforcement operation, although I hadn't seen anyone that fitted that description either.

Dark eyes peered up at us as we descended the final steps off the bridge. Creases sat around those eyes, and although it seemed as if this man hadn't laughed a day in his life, he looked handsome in a rugged kind of way. Moving closer, I snuck a peek at my hand as I felt the urge to compare. The man's skin was darker, definitely darker than Saera's, but not nearly as dark as mine.

Perhaps it had something to do with not wearing the heads-up, but it felt strange to come face to face with all these different faces without the green backdrop of what the device usually strapped to my head provided. Then again, how many faces would have been left behind after having my mind wiped clear of any memories every day? Standing level with him, I had to look up to face him.

His gaze flicked over me, but otherwise, his expression stayed impassive. Then he turned to Saera, and his expression became somewhat friendlier. As if I wasn't even there, he said, "The doctor is waiting."

Without waiting for a reply, he turned and gestured for us to follow him. Questioningly, I turned to Saera, but she shook her head. My heart raced as if I had run five blocks chasing some criminal. I noticed my hands were trembling, and I balled them into a fist. These sensations running through my body were new as far as I knew, and I didn't like them. I had never felt like this without physical exertion, and even then, I had barely noticed them. It reminded me of the body wedged under my boot before I'd pulled the trigger, and it occurred to me what this thing wreaking havoc inside me might have been. *Could this be what fear felt like?*

Our not-so-talkative companion stopped at a workstation and spoke to one of the younger men dressed in black. Then he pointed at us. I couldn't hear what was said, but the young man nodded his understanding before he left his station.

"This way," our guide said, and to me, it seemed like a signal to stop.

"No," I said. Saera looked at me with raised eyebrows. Whatever-his-name-was just cocked his head and folded his hands behind his back. I realized that this could be the same man who had dropped that five credits at my side.

"I want to know what's going on here and what's with the doctor," I demanded.

"Please, Ma…" Saera started to say but stopped herself.

"I get it," I said, starting to get annoyed, which to me felt like another new emotion I didn't like. "You can't talk about the past because it'll fry my brain, but could someone please tell me what is going on right now!"

They both looked at me as if I were speaking in a different language. Well, Saera did. The man just looked impassive.

"I don't even know this guy's name," I said, pointing at the man but looking at Saera. "For that matter, I don't even know you except for what you have told me."

"But you did come," Saera said, "and that's because something inside told you to trust me."

Saera's gaze held a hopefulness that balanced on the edge of desperation.

I opened my mouth to reply when our silent friend spoke up.

"Harp," he said.

I had just enough time to look at him before a jab of pain erupted inside my skull and ran down my spine. Falling to my knees, I grabbed my head and groaned in agony. Saera grabbed my arm and knelt beside me.

"You didn't have to do that," she said. Her voice barely reached me, but I noticed the man had stepped closer. I tried to focus on my breathing as he too knelt by my side. As the pain faded, I released my head and looked up to stare into the man's dark gaze.

"I hope knowing my name was worth it," he said as he placed a hand on his knee. His words sent another jolt of pain down my neck but nothing near what I had felt before.

"We have two problems," he said, speaking in a low, hoarse voice. In it, I recognized the voice from the hallway before that green mist scanned us. "One, memories trigger a relapse in your frontal lobe and cause the sensation you just felt."

"Sensation," I said, irked.

"Then there is problem number two, which we can't address until we solve number one," he said near my ear. "Now, if you'll oblige us with your cooperation, then we'll be able to enlighten you."

I sensed a degree of spite in his voice, but considering the throbbing in my head, I decided to leave it for what it was.

Harp grabbed me by the arm and pulled me to my feet. Saera rose along with me but avoided my gaze.

"Now, please, if you would be kind enough to follow me," Harp said.

Chapter six

Reece

I watched as the crowd went wild after Billy Tender slammed his opponent's fist into the table, nearly creating a crack in the piece of furniture. Unlike the name might have suggested, there was nothing tender about the man otherwise known as Rockslide. He was at least six foot three, all muscle, and with a bald head that seemed to have been carved out of granite. Rockslide sneered as he raised a fist in the air and called out for his next opponent, or should I say, victim.

That seemed to trigger an idea in my head, and I grinned as I glanced down at the short, stocky man standing in front of me. Riffy clapped his hands and seemed to enjoy the night's entertainment. The Bolder bar was one of the few places in the city where simple folk like my friends and I could enjoy the finer things in life, like arm wrestling.

Sure, this place, filled with mostly drunk and half-drunk miners and power plant workers, would probably not be suitable for everyone, but it felt like home to us.

I grabbed Riffy, who stood with his back to me, by the shoulders and bent to shout into his ear.

"Dude, you could totally take him down," I said, holding back a grin. Riffy turned and looked up to face me. His grayish eyes had gone wide and stared at me in shock. Along with his chubby cheeks, it made his baby face look even more adorable.

Keeping my face straight, I smacked his shoulder in encouragement. "You got this." His eyes went even wider than I would have thought possible as I started to raise my hand to signal Rockslide that I had found him another competitor. Riffy grabbed my arm and pulled it down.

"Are you insane?" he exclaimed.

I took a quick head count and noticed that most of the sturdier-looking men had retreated to their tables or hung around the bar, keeping their heads down. Rockslide had noticed the same as his eyes roamed across the cavern, daring anyone to meet his gaze. I nodded and faced Riffy.

"Look at him," I said, turning Riffy around to face Rockslide. The big man sitting at the flat slab of stone that substituted for a table started to gulp something down and then slammed the cup on the table. "He's been doing that all night; the guy is wasted. He is just prey, waiting for you."

"I don't know, Reece," Riffy started to protest, and his shoulders tensed. This time I grabbed both his shoulders and shook him slightly from behind.

"You are Riffy Adall, fearless warrior and a force to be reckoned with," I said. "This guy is no match for you."

"Yeah," he replied. His voice was filled with hesitation, but I could sense his confidence building.

Luckily, his back was facing me, because I couldn't hold a straight face. I grinned as I leaned in and said, "You've got this, big man."

"Yeah," Riffy said again, but this time his words were fueled with confidence. "I can do this."

"You can do this," I added for good measure.

"Yeah," Riffy shouted. It seemed the stupidity of what he was about to do had reduced his vocabulary, but it didn't stop him from clapping his hands and stepping out of the circle surrounding the spectacle. With firm strides, Riffy made his way to the table. As he walked, he shrugged off his jacket and tossed it in the chair across from Rockslide.

The bald giant's head perked up, and he eyed Riffy as he stood before him, arms crossed in a shirt that was way too tight and accented my best bud's oversized belly. At that point, I kind of lost it and started laughing as I glanced down to my left.

Kelle looked unimpressed as she glared up at me and then rolled her eyes. The tiny woman had silently watched my exchange with Riffy but over the years had stopped bothering to keep us from doing anything stupid.

"What?" I asked, bearing a sheepish grin. Without a reply, she shook her head and turned on her heels. As Kelle left me standing at the edge of the crowds hovering around the table, I glanced at Riffy. Sweat plastered his forehead, and as he took his seat, he looked up in search of support. I gave him my thumbs-up but then left the group of spectators and followed Kelle.

The bar wasn't much to look at. As with a lot of buildings on the outskirts of the city, the insides were carved out of solid rock, and it had the standard round, cave-like features. But it wasn't for lack of trying.

The owner of the bar had done his best to add a little atmosphere with some softer lighting and had dressed the walls in tapestries to lessen the depressing effect of the gray-blue stone. He also had a couple of seating areas carved out of the stone that would ensure some form of privacy for its occupants. I slipped into one of those spaces as I followed Kelle and joined her at our table.

"Come on," I said as I made myself comfortable. "You have to admit that was funny."

Kelle raised an eyebrow but didn't reply. She sighed and rubbed a hand over her jet-black hair that stood about three millimeters from her skull. With her porcelain features, Kelle looked fragile at the age of twenty, but she was a force to be reckoned with. She was the silent, brooding type, and the intensity in her dark eyes could bring a man to his knees.

Behind me, I heard a high-pitched, feminine-sounding squeak, followed by a thud and a crack. I glanced out the recess and toward the table where the arm-wrestling match took place, but couldn't see past the onlookers.

"Are you still pissed at me?" I asked as I turned back to face Kelle. Showing teeth, I poured all my charm into a smile, but it did not seem to have the desired effect on her. She gave me an annoyed look that spoke volumes. She was still very much pissed at me.

Kelle raised her hand and pointed a finger at me. Normally this would not have bothered me, but since she'd used her right hand, it made me shift uncomfortably in my seat.

It had been several years since Kelle had lost her right arm in a Hymag incident and had it replaced with a mechanical prosthesis. There was something of a cross between adorable and badass in watching this tiny woman with this robotic arm. The fact was that, with it, she could knock a person senseless without even breaking a sweat. She would probably be able to beat Rockslide if she could ever get herself to care about something that seemed a waste of time to her.

I gathered some sweat of my own under my armpits as I gazed at the metal appendix that doubled as an index finger.

"You should have told me what she was planning," Kelle said. Her voice was calm, but the look in her eyes told me she was ready to spit fire.

"And she would have kicked my ass," I replied in my defense.

"Would you rather I kick it?" she said.

I had trouble holding her gaze, and I felt relief as I heard another shriek coming from the other side of the bar. Kelle shifted her head to look in that direction, and I followed her gaze. Riffy was holding on longer than I would have expected.

The scene had not changed, though, and I could

only see the backs of the onlookers. As I returned my attention to Kelle, she had lowered her hand and closed her eyes as if she needed to gather herself. I managed to keep my mouth shut and gave her a moment. Fortunately, I didn't have to wait long.

"Have you heard anything?" Kelle asked. She looked worried behind that stoic mask she tried to hold up, but I knew better than to mention it.

"Nope," I said and stuck two fingers up in the air. The elderly woman behind the bar nodded and then pulled a bottle from one of the shelves.

"Son of a…" Kelle muttered, swallowing the rest of the sentence. I lifted my feet and rested them on the table.

"Don't worry," I said. "They know what they're doing." Kelle shook her head, and I had to admit I shared her concerns, but all we could do was wait it out.

"For a pretty boy, your mommy has taught you lousy manners," the elderly lady who had joined us from behind the bar said as she swatted my feet from the table.

"Hey," I replied as I gained my bearing. I glared up at the lady, ready to shoot her a sly remark. My mouth got stuck halfway. The old woman winked at me. Stunned, I closed my mouth and felt my cheeks flush. Kelle must have noticed, because she snorted something that vaguely resembled a laugh.

"Here ya go," the woman said as she placed a bottle of mushroom ale on the table along with two glasses. "Drink up."

I sputtered a thank-you as she winked at me

again. A cold shiver ran down my spine, and I shook myself as soon as she turned her back to me.

"Now that was weird," I said in a low voice. Kelle grinned, but soon enough her face returned to its brooding self.

As I started pouring drinks, a shrill beep sounded, and I glanced at the device strapped to my wrist. Kelle's eyes perked up, and she eyed me expectantly as I checked the device. I wasn't expecting any other calls, so I kind of knew beforehand that this was the message we were waiting for.

"It's long distance," I said, raising my butt out of my seat. "I'll be right back." Kelle nodded, and I caught her throwing back a shot of ale before I could make my way to the bar's exit.

At this point, I too could use a shot to wash away the anxiety brewing in my gut. I slipped out of the bar and closed my jacket as I stepped into the street. It seemed mostly empty, but my eye caught sight of a very drunk-looking man. He wobbled across the street until he suddenly stopped.

Fortunately, I was far enough away to only hear him retch and not see the details of the vomit spewing from his mouth. His day had been either old or very young, depending on your point of view.

I glanced up with a futile hope that someday I would do that and see the stars, but as it was, my eyes fell on the gray-blue color of solid rock. It stretched over the underground city of Subterra as far as the eye could see.

It seemed that to me that that drunk and those idiots back at the bar were the only ones up at this ungodly hour. An eerie quiet hung around me as I walked to one of the signal enhancers at the corner down the street.

Any communication with life beyond the city walls needed signal enhancement. The rock and the metals embedded within were just too dense for any signal to penetrate. That's why we used signal boosters. These devices used old-fashioned cables to send a signal to a relay station, and it could travel further distances from there. Distances like, say, a city up top or a secret rebel base.

Feeling unnerved, I stepped within the range of the booster so it would be able to pick up the signal of my wrist device and tapped my ear. Then I waited as the device connected to the feed. It took about a minute before I received a reply.

"Reece, is that you?" a hesitant voice on the other end said. A grin formed on my face.

"Ty, my nerdy little beauty," I said, hoping to sound chirpy. "What's up?" The thought of Tyrel's face glowing as red as the glow of the expanding sun hovering over the planet released some of the tension I felt. We had been waiting for the call for a while and I sort of dreaded the outcome.

"Hi…Reece," Tyrel said in her shy voice, and I could just imagine her sitting red-faced behind her desk. Then she cleared her throat, and it occurred to me she might not be the only one on the line. I decided to reign in my enthusiasm and let her speak. "Harp wanted me to tell you that we've made contact."

I swallowed hard, placing my hands on the signal booster for some much-needed support and waited for Tyrel to elaborate.

"She's here."

My heart skipped a beat, and I punched the air around me. I wanted to shout out a firm yes but knew it was still too early for that. This was just the first part of what we needed to accomplish. Still, I couldn't help but feel as if we had claimed a victory. Pulling myself together, I drew in a deep breath and asked, "How did she seem?"

"I…I don't know," Tyrel said. The tension in her voice was palpable, and it wasn't anything to boost anyone's confidence.

"What about Saera, what did she say?"

"I haven't spoken to anyone," Tyrel said. "I don't know anything except that she's here and with the doctor to deal with the memory thing."

I nodded, not sure if I would be able to use my voice and keep up the cheery facade.

Tyrel took this as her cue to continue. "Harp has sent a Hymag to pick you guys up, so I guess you'll find out soon enough."

"Okay," I said, feeling a combination of defeat and determination. "We'll be there soon."

Before I could end the connection, Tyrel added, "Say hi to Riffy for me. And Kelle, of course."

"Of course," I replied and felt the giddiness return. "See ya soon."

I disconnected the call and exhaled. The air underground was stale but chilly as I glanced up and ran my eyes over the structures carved from solid rock. A faint light peeked from one or two windows, but most were dark where the residents lay fast asleep, unaware of the changes this night might bring. I dug my hands into my pockets and started back toward the bar and wondered about Riffy's and especially Kelle's reaction when I brought them the news.

Chapter seven

Maece

Harp guided us down a staircase, and we passed a couple of doors along a hallway until we reached what looked like a lab underneath the platform.

Centered in the middle of the lab stood a chair. The arm and leg restraints mounted to the chair didn't ease my nerves. Another man dressed in black approached us as he weaved between a row of tables, although nothing about him resembled the men and women working upstairs. This man was short with a protruding belly, and most of his hair had retreated to the sides.

"Well, I'll be damned," he said as he approached. "You did it! You actually did it. This is so exciting." The man had a high-pitched voice that seemed to rise with excitement. He stuck out his hand in greeting. "I'm so pleased to meet you, Ms.—"

Saera and Harp both called out to stop the man from finishing his sentence.

"Don't!" Saera yelled.

"Doctor," Harp's voice boomed. The doctor froze on the spot. His hand stuck in midair as his wide eyes roamed over us, flicking from one person to another.

"Why don't you first do your thing, and then we'll get to know each other?" Harp said. The doctor nodded his head vigorously as he retreated his hand to his chest where he started to fiddle with his jacket.

"Em…why…eh…please sit," the doctor said in an almost comical stutter. Then he gestured at me before his finger pointed at the chair. I glanced at Saera, and she must have noticed my hesitation.

"This is the easy part," she said. The reluctant smile she gave me didn't boost my confidence, and another look at the arm and leg restraints kept me frozen on the spot.

The doctor shifted an uneasy gaze from me to Harp, to Saera and back to me again. He opened his mouth to speak, but Saera beat him to it.

"Hey," she said as she stepped closer.

But before she could add anything else, I said, "I can't be sure of anything." I continued in an accusing tone, "Not about your reasons or your intentions. Hell, I can't even be sure that you won't cut out my CPU or brain, or whatever." I pointed an accusing finger at Harp. "And don't you think calling out some name that makes the insides of my head feel like it's on fire is going to convince me."

Harp let out a sigh and dropped his chin to his chest. He looked to be losing his patience with me, but I couldn't have cared less. Saera, on the other hand, stood calmly in front of me with an expression of understanding on her face.

"You're right," she said. "We can't give you that

assurance, and I could tell you that the doctor intends to do everything he can to help you, but then why would you trust me, right?"

"Oh, absolutely," the doctor started to sputter, "and I'll explain what I'm doing every step along the way."

I ignored the doctor's interruption and kept my gaze on Saera. Her pleading eyes shimmered with unshed tears.

"I can assure you that this procedure is very safe," the doctor added. I briefly glanced at the man who seemed to be sincere, but I didn't know him—so he could have been lying to my face for all I knew.

"I know this must be daunting, but we have no other way," Saera said and then hesitated. She bit her lower lip as she searched for the right words. "I don't know how else to convince you." She moved a hand through her hair and shifted her head. I didn't need to follow her gaze to know she was looking at Harp for support.

A second later, her shoulders slumped as she faced me again, but she kept her eyes directed at the floor. She took in a deep breath, and as she raised her chin, she said, "Trust me, please."

Her words came out a mere whisper, and it wasn't so much her words, but the look on Saera's face that had me deciding to put aside my doubts. For some reason that I couldn't understand, Saera had already gained my trust. *And what was it I had to lose?*

By now TED most have interpreted my inability to comply with their orders as an error, and I doubted I'd be able to return to my duties as an enforcer—

besides would I want to? Not if what these people had told me turned out to be the truth, and so, with a nod, I complied.

A sigh of relief passed Saera's lips as I sat down in the chair, and the doctor came to stand beside me. He had a little trouble fastening the restraint around my arms and legs. The built-in exoskeleton of my suit made the span of my wrists and ankles wider, but he managed. I wondered if the restraints would hold me, though, if I really wanted to get out. Actually, I knew they wouldn't.

"Could you remove the glasses," the doctor asked as he walked over to a table with a bunch of equipment. Saera came over and stood by my side. She removed the shades and wiped a strand of hair from my face.

"Your eyes still freak me out," she said with a half-smile.

"Thanks for the pep talk," I replied.

"Oh, don't worry about that," the doctor said as he approached with what looked like a giant needle. "Once we redeem the balance in your postcentral gyrus along with your occipital lobe, then the amount of pigment in your irises should return to normal."

"How does that work?" I asked. The doctor lay the needle on a tray next to my chair and started working on a large electronic device that was suspended over my head.

"Well," he said as he jerked and pulled at the device, "I could tell you, but you wouldn't understand."

Saera chuckled and glanced at Harp, but then

her smile quickly disappeared.

"Let's go," Harp said in that minimalistic way of his. Saera squeezed my arm.

"We'll be right next door, watching you through those," she said. She pointed at a barely visible monitoring device that hung in the corner.

I watched as she followed Harp into the next room when I noticed the doctor hovering over me with his needle.

"Whoa…wait a min…" I started to say, but as soon as I felt the sting of the needle, everything faded to dark.

I lay on my stomach on a cot as I opened my eyelids and stared straight into Saera's eyes. She sat on the ground next to my cot, knees pulled to her chest and her back against the wall.

"Hey, shorty," she said and scooted closer.

"Huh," I grunted, lifting my head an inch off the pillow, "what happened?"

"They fixed part of your brain," she replied with a broad smile on her face. This surprised me; I hadn't seen her smile like that before. It was as if something had lifted off her shoulders, and it showed on her face. I raised myself onto my elbows and wiped a sleeve along my mouth to get rid of some drool.

"Only part of my brain," I asked.

Her lips formed into a thin line. "Well, your head won't hurt anymore if I call you Maecy," she said.

I frowned. "So why didn't you call me that just now, besides the fact that I'm taller than you?"

The question made her smile grow wider again.

"Well, you weren't when we met, and because you hated it when I called you shorty."

"I recalled you saying that I hated it when you called me Maecy," I replied.

"Nah, I think you secretly loved it."

"Maybe you should explain to me this sisterly relationship you mentioned because I'm not getting it," I said and let my head fall back on the pillow.

Ignoring me, she crawled up off the floor, grabbed my legs, and forced them over the side as she sat herself down on the cot next to me.

"Hey," I protested.

"The doc said I was supposed to get you out of bed as soon as you were awake."

She jerked at my arm, and I tried to wrench it from her grip.

"I'm still sleeping," I said, but she refused to release my arm. After a moment, I relented and sat up. Our eyes locked and I held her gaze.

"Your eyes changed back to normal," she said.

I thought about it for a moment. "I don't even remember how they normally looked," I said. "I don't even know if what you're telling me is the truth."

"I know," she said, and I could hear the tiniest of cracks in her voice. "But…" Her voice trailed off as she fiddled with something in the pocket of her pants. She pulled out a small pad and flicked it on.

After tapping the device, a folder opened, and a bunch of images rolled down the screen. She searched for a while, and seemingly satisfied, she held the device out for me to see.

The image displayed was one of her and me

sitting on the edge of a platform with a Hymag parked behind us. We looked younger than we did now, but it could only have been a few years. We both had big smiles plastered across our faces while Saera pointed at the person taking the image.

For a second, I braced myself in fear of the pain that would certainly rack my brain upon seeing myself in an image from the past, but nothing happened. I managed to relax, but the strangeness of seeing myself in a situation that I couldn't remember ever happening remained.

With her finger, Saera scrolled to the next image and then pressed down on the pad. The moving picture of a scowling Harp started to play and panned over to where Saera and I were still sitting and laughing on the edge of the platform, but it was Harp's voice we heard.

"Would you please get your asses over here," he said, sounding fierce, but as the image recorder shifted back, I saw an actual smile on his face. A second later Harp's arm swung out and swatted at the person recording the rare moment.

"I didn't know he had it in him," I said as Saera stopped playback. Saera shoved a playful elbow into my side and grinned.

"Just so you can be sure that you did know us when you were older," she said. "The rest will follow shortly."

Saera stood and held out a hand.

"Come on," she said. "It's time you find out who you're supposed to be."

I took her hand and stood. My feet had barely

found their balance as she took me into an embrace and whispered near my ear, "I'm really glad you're back. I've missed you."

I didn't know how to reply. Unlike her, I didn't know what I had missed. Not wanting to appear ungrateful, I hugged her back. Even though the gesture should have felt foreign, it came naturally to me. Without another word, she released me, took my hand, and guided me to the door.

We stepped into the hallway from earlier and crossed it before entering the lab. The doctor wasn't around, but Harp stood at one of the tables and stared at a monitor hanging on the wall. The screen had been divided into four sections, and while three of them had static pictures, the lower left screen displayed moving images.

I stopped at the sight of myself strapped in the chair. My body shook and convulsed while the doctor stood by my side and tapped the screen of the pad in his hands. Although I had no memory of what had happened, my blood ran cold. Saera must have noticed because she spoke up.

"Colrin," she said in a tiny voice. Even before he reacted, I knew Harp would turn around. Colrin was Harp's first name, and somehow I knew. I remembered it. He glanced at us and then tapped the man sitting behind the desk on the shoulder, and the man instantly stopped the replay. Saera squeezed my hand she was still holding and guided me past the chair and across the room.

Harp stepped closer and narrowed his eyes at me. "You okay?" he asked. Raising an eyebrow at the offer of concern, I nodded in acknowledgment. He seemed content with that and turned to the man sitting behind the desk.

"Kyran, I believe you've met Maece," he said. "Maece, this is Kyran—he'll be guiding us through memory lane today."

As Kyran stood and offered me his hand, I recognized him as the wide-eyed tech guy from Memory Junction with the wild hair.

"You work at TED," I said as I accepted his hand. He grinned and removed the HDA clamped between his teeth.

"Just part-time," he said. "It's a pleasure to meet you, Ms. Lux."

I felt three pairs of eyes on me as if they were waiting for another brain-frying incident or gauging my reaction to my last name. This all seemed too weird. A moment ago, I had never even thought the name and now felt as if it belonged to me.

Kyran grinned again and turned to Harp.

"The doc knows his thing," he said.

"That's why I hired him," Harp said. "Now get to it."

Kyran gestured at a couple of chairs. "You're gonna need them," he said and sat behind the desk. Saera and I both took a chair and sat down on either side of Kyran. None of them offered a seat to Harp, so neither did I. He folded his arms behind his back and stood behind me, which felt a bit intimidating.

Kyran's fingers hovered over the table, and a range of colorful lights flashed up. He maneuvered his hands as if he was operating one of those tablets I had seen him use at TED. Around us, the lights in the room dimmed, and we focused on the screen hanging on the wall.

"Let's start with a little backstory," he said as he pressed a key, and one of the four sections on the screen flickered to life.

Kyran wasn't kidding when he announced starting off with a little backstory. The screen showed us images of how the Combined Districts of Tenebrae came to be. News footage compiled over the years revealed the story of how scientists had worked at creating wormholes to expedite our ability to conquer the vastness of space.

As a race, we had traveled to distant corners of the universe for millennia but never managed to find anything but planets or gas giants unable to sustain human life. Of course, efforts had been made to build colonies on the moon, and an outpost had even been built on Mars, but there wasn't much desire among the population to live on a deserted rock, even if they were equipped with massive artificial gardens.

Back then they believed wormhole travel would be our only chance to encounter an environment like the one we knew and to find new worlds to expand the reach of the human race. Unfortunately, their efforts hadn't gone as planned. After numerous successful attempts, it seemed as if those same scientists had bitten off more than they could chew when they accidentally created a wormhole too close to the sun's core. This caused the sun to vent most of its fuel into space connected through the wormhole.

Things quickly turned from bad to worse. The incident had hastened the sun's transition toward the red giant phase, causing the star to burn brighter. Ice caps permanently melted, and before long oceans turned into vast wastelands.

Fortunately, they managed to close the bridge in time, or else the sun would have transitioned into a red giant billions of years before it was supposed to. Planets like Mercury and Venus and perhaps even the earth would have been engulfed by the expanded sun. If nothing else, the close proximity to the massive disk would have scorched the planet, and even our dome shields wouldn't have been able to protect us from the harsh environment.

Most of this information already existed inside my head and was considered common knowledge, although I wondered if it had been planted by TED or if they were some residual memories someone had decided to leave inside my head. Saera, sitting at Kyran's right side, yawned.

"I know this is tedious," Kyran said, glancing at Saera, "but your sister's mind is still a bit fragile, and we need to input these things in the right order, so she won't get confused—we've developed this protocol for a reason."

"Why bother," Saera replied trying to contain another yawn. "She's already confused." Before I could react, Harp reached out and smacked her on the head. It wasn't hard or anything, but Saera reacted as if he'd been punched her in the face.

"Aaauw," she said, drawing out the sound.

"Pay attention," Harp said and returned to his

imposing stance. I just raised an eyebrow, but felt curious as to what kind of relationship Saera had with Harp and, related to that, how did I fit in?

Kyran grinned for a second, but his face turned grim as he hit another key and said, "A lot of people died back then because only the major cities had access to the shields that protected us from the radiation and rapidly changing environment—not to mention the destruction of the colony on the moon."

"Yeah, yeah," Saera piped in, "the world turned to shit and civilization along with it, and while we know there might be other settlements out there, our communication with them is nonexistent."

"Saera," Harp said in warning.

"I know, we have to be gentle with Maecy's brain," she said sounding annoyed, "but can't you just ask her how much she knows and move on from there." This time Saera folded her arms across her chest and slouched in her chair.

Kyran and Harp both glared at her but then redirected their gazes at me.

"That would probably do," Kyran said as he shrugged and looked up at Harp.

For a moment, Harp held a thoughtful expression and then said, "Maece, would you tell us what you know?"

His use of the name, which Saera had told me I preferred, made me wonder if he cared. This not knowing was becoming old very quickly, and I shrugged before I nodded in compliance. The faster we got through their "undoing-a-brain-wipe" protocol, the faster they would get to telling the stuff I needed to know.

"In the beginning, hundreds of cities protected by energy fields had survived, and the ones that could tried to work together. On this continent, among other things, they built a vast underground Hymag system that allowed them to travel between cities without the need of shields, but over the millennia as our situation grew direr, war and distrust gained the upper hand," I said.

I continued to explain that the only reason that the Combined Districts of Tenebrae, which consisted of the cities Umbras, Nebula, and Opacare, had managed to persevere was because of the Subterran people.

"Which I'm not going to describe in detail because you're all from there," I said.

Saera grinned. "See, that took about two minutes."

Their lack of discord over my statement of them being Subterran seemed to prove my point. Although their black, sturdy-looking clothing had ultimately betrayed them.

As Saera had pointed out, I too was getting impatient. It felt as if they were giving me the runaround, and I still had no idea why I was here. If the little information Saera had given me was true, and from the images she had shown me before I dared to guess that it was, then I could understand her intentions. She wanted her sister back, even though that statement seemed ridiculous to me. We were so different in appearance. *How could I ever be her sister?*

"Now can we stop playing around," I said, "so you can tell me what's going on. Please."

Chapter eight

Maece

"Your stupid ass volunteered," Saera said, "and everything went sour after that."

Harp shot Saera a hard look. On other occasions, Saera had seemed more subservient toward Harp, but this time she stood her ground. She held Harp's gaze and seemed determined to get her point across.

"For what?" I asked as I had no idea what they were talking about.

"Perhaps, I should explain," Kyran said as he got up from his seat. "I might be the only one able to keep the emotions from running wild."

He took a seat on the table so he could face us, and all sorts of lights flashed to life as his butt rested on the glass-like surface, but nothing happened on the screen behind him. Kyran glanced up at Harp as he prodded his feet on the chair he had just abandoned. Harp nodded in agreement.

"As Saera just said, you volunteered to go on a fact-finding mission," Kyran started, "to keep us updated on anything interesting ArtRep Enterprises was up to." He continued to say that officially we weren't sanctioned by the Subterran government. "Unofficially, we're tasked to investigate anything that might be of use to our leadership."

"Who's we?" I asked.

All eyes shifted in Harp's direction, telling me where to find my answer.

Harp didn't even blink as he explained, "We are a private branch that works in service of the Subterran people."

"You're rebels," I said without hesitation.

"That depends on your point of view," Harp added.

After raking a hand through his wild hair, Kyran said, "For diplomatic purposes, we've existed as so-called rebels for years, without any government affiliation. This way they have someone to do their dirty work and at the same time have someone to blame in case of some conflict with our neighboring cities. A special council has been put in place to supervise our actions, and they report back to the government, so the government is still a component in the organization of things."

With his statement about this council, Harp shot Kyran a sharp glance as if he had just divulged a piece of information that he shouldn't have. This made Kyran shift uncomfortably on the table, and several lights flashed as he did. He cleared his throat and added in a hushed tone, "No one is supposed to know that."

Saera rolled her eyes at Kyran before she said, "As part of Harp's team, you volunteered to aid in the investigation."

"So, that's when I joined the rebels?" I ask.

"No, you've been part of this for a long time, along with—" Kyran started to say until Saera planted a fist against his shoulder.

"Kyran," she said in warning.

"What?" Kyran replied.

"You gotta give her the space to figure these things out on her own," she said. Kyran shot her a confused look and then turned to Harp.

"But I thought you said—"

Before Kyran could finish, Harp intervened, "Just give it time." As he spoke, Harp placed the emphasis on the first word and then gave Kyran a hard look.

Kyran looked a bit hurt as I studied the faces around me. Saera's brow furrowed as she shifted her attention from one man to the other. She looked confused about something, but Harp held that same placid expression as he always seemed to do.

Before long, I felt like a spectacle as all eyes in the room turned to me, and I shifted my gaze to the ground. This was a lot of information to take in. A few hours ago, I was still an enforcer working to uphold the law, and now these people were telling me that I belonged to a group that went against that same law.

Tenebrae saw Subterran rebels as a vexatious group that needed to be put down with an iron fist. I had no memories about this, but I wondered how many of them must have died by my hand. If it wasn't for some sixth sense buried deep inside me that told me to trust these people, or at least Saera, I might have bolted from the room. They must have known of the things I'd had to do as an enforcer, and they still had decided to pull me out.

Being Saera's sister, or even being part of one of Harp's teams, might have been a reason to pull me out, but would these reasons have been valid enough if it meant compromising the entire operation? *Was there some other reason for them to have pulled me out?*

Something in their story didn't add up.

"I don't understand," I said. "You said it had been two years." I pointed a finger at Saera. The gesture wasn't meant to point the blame at her. I just wanted to make clear that she had been the one who had told me.

But I wished I hadn't after I saw the guilt flash in her eyes. She opened her mouth, but even without knowing what that look meant, I cut her off and said, "How did I end up as an enforcer and why did you let them use me as their personal killing machine?" My voice wavered, and I had to swallow hard as the image of that boy wedged underneath my boots flashed across my mind.

"Something went wrong, and you disappeared off the grid," she said. "For a long time, we thought you were dead." Her voice was barely audible while she had the briefest of eye contact with Harp. That pained look that by now I had seen more often than I would have liked on Saera's face resurfaced.

"How come..." I said, softening my tone. "I mean...why now?"

"We don't know what happened exactly, but they

must have captured you somehow. Like Saera said, we thought you were dead until she saw you on a broadcast—you were working security at some celebrity event," Kyran said as his fingers fiddled with the HDA on the table. As I observed his nervous tick, I noticed his cheeks were a bit flushed, and his eyes seemed to take in everything except me.

He coughed before he added, "Besides the obvious reasons, Saera came to Harp with this information, and we were able to put the plan of getting you back in motion." For a moment longer, I wondered why Kyran kept avoiding me but then set it aside as I realized what he had said.

"Other reasons than the obvious ones?" I asked, sensing there had to be more going on. "Obvious besides him being my boss." Because that was the only obvious reason to me, although I could tell there had to be a connection between Saera and Harp. Kyran looked at me for a moment and then blinked as if the pieces had fallen together for him.

"Oh, right," he said, "and because he's your dad of course… or something like that."

"Kyran!" Saera called out sounding annoyed.

"What?" he asked unaware of what he'd done wrong. Saera made a noice that resembled a soft growl before she let out a long breath. After a moments of hesitation Saera cleared her throat and then said, "He, uh…" She paused, but then threw a heartfelt smile in Harp's direction. His face remained impassive, staying in the exact pose that it always seemed to be stuck in, but there was something in his eyes. I think it could have been pride.

"Besides working for him, he's...like our dad," she said. "He sort of adopted us, but that's a long story, and it is better remembered."

I had to remind myself to close my mouth as I stared at them both. Along with about a dozen other questions running through my mind, Saera prompted one question that seemed most important to ask.

"Will I?"

"Will I, what?" Kyran asked.

"Remember," I asked hesitantly. "Remember my life from before."

Both men looked at me as if I were some lost puppy. Well, at least Kyran did; Harp held his usual expression. Saera shook her head vigorously.

"You said it was possible," she said, pointing an accusing finger at Harp. The big man shifted his feet and conveyed some form of unease for the first time since I had met him.

"I told you it had been done before, but it wouldn't be probable."

"Bullshit," Saera exclaimed, "that's not what you said. You said this was the same thing that had happened to Spiro."

"Saera, please." Harp spoke in a low and calm voice. "It's not—"

Unwilling to let him finish his sentence she said, "No, not 'Saera, please.' I've been patient enough waiting for almost a year for Kyran to get her mind ready so we could get her back, and now that we finally have her back you're telling me she will never remember us—then what the hell did we do it for?"

I stared at Saera in surprise at her outburst and

felt a little hurt at the idea that I wasn't enough. Tears started to fill Saera's eyes, but she wasn't done yet.

"They might as well have killed her."

Her words suggested that I hadn't been worth saving without the memories of my previous life. Then it occurred to me that I didn't even know this woman, except for what they had told me, and that wasn't much. So why did I care?

"Enough."

Harp's voice reverberated inside the tiny space. The silence that followed felt taxing until Saera sighed in frustration and got up from her chair. Our eyes met for the briefest of moments, and I saw shock wash over her as if she'd just realized what she had said. Even though I couldn't remember what our relationship had been like before, I had felt the sting when she mentioned that I might as well be dead. Her cheeks flushed before she turned on her heels and stormed from the room.

I stood, feeling the urge to barge after her, but Harp, reading my intentions, stepped in my way.

"I know this doesn't make much sense now, but trust me when I say that I will do anything in my power to get your memories back, and if technology doesn't permit it, then I will personally tell you everything I know," he said as he placed a hand on my shoulder, "but please, stay and let Kyran explain. I'll go and talk to Saera." Although these had been the most words I had heard him speak since we'd met, it was his eyes that did most of the talking.

Those dark eyes bored into me with a tenderness that I had never seen. Deciding to trust his judgment,

I nodded in agreement. He dipped his head in satisfaction and then glanced at Kyran, who sat motionless on the table. Apparently, words were overrated in these parts, because without saying anything, Harp turned and walked out the door.

Stunned, I watched the door click shut behind him. Kyran let out a long, hissy sigh, and I turned to face him. His mouth twitched upward, and he said, "Tricky thing, having a family."

"Right," I said with a little grunt before I realized that I was part of that family. At least, I had been.

Kyran scooted from the table and gestured at the chair.

"Come on, let's get you a little bit more up to speed."

"Who's Spiro?" I asked before Kyran's fingers could reach the keyboard. His head twitched, but he didn't look at me.

"I'm not sure that is mine to tell," he said. He sounded nervous as he rattled off the words.

"Oh please," I said in exasperation. *Here we go again*, was all I could think.

"Sorry," Kyran said with an apologetic shrug and returned his focus to the keyboard. Frustration seized control over me, and I forcefully dropped myself into the chair while Kyran tapped a couple of keys on the glass surface of the table.

Lights flashed, and images appeared on the screen, showing documents on everything having to do with the investigation into a company called ArtRep.

Through those papers, I learned that ArtRep was

the company that provided all three cities residing within Tenebrae borders with artificial representations. They also controlled anything that had to do with technology, communication, and power generation. Kyran explained that Subterra had always been a more peaceful society, and they never had a need for artificial law enforcement.

"Those are the main ArtRep buildings in Umbras," Kyran said. "Do you recognize them?"

I watched the picture on the screen of the giant skyscrapers that seemed as if they almost touched the dome shield. Two of them seemed to be of similar height, but the third towered over both. As I scrutinized the tall buildings and the rainbow of colors that bounced off their reflective surfaces, I realized that I did recognize them.

"I've been there," I said sifting through my memories. "I...I had to stand by a door outside a room where a meeting was held."

Kyran grinned and nodded in satisfaction.

"How come I can remember this?" I asked. "Shouldn't this have been deleted at Memory Junction?"

Kyran's grin grew wider before he said, "As you know, I have a second job. I've been working at Memory Junction for a while." I glared at him, but he just chuckled. He had been working at TED because of me, and it seemed he'd been tinkering with my brain.

"So why can I only remember you from last night?" I asked.

"Well, because that wouldn't be smart," he said,

giving me a sideways glance that told me my question had been stupid. "I could only tweak your memories here and there or introduce you to certain ideas—to trick you into thinking for yourself. Only in the last couple of weeks, I left some of the recent memories intact, and I added that picture so you could get used to it and seeing Saera wouldn't completely fry your brain."

"Thanks, I guess," I replied. My mouth remained open, but the words seemed to have gotten stuck in my throat. A question had bothered me ever since we'd started this trek down memory lane, and even though I had asked it, I had yet to receive an answer. I glanced at the ground and swallowed hard before I gained the courage to look up at Kyran.

"How did I end up there?" I asked and paused for a second. "I mean…was I…"

Kyran's cheeks flushed while his gaze shifted to the screen and he grabbed the HDA off the table.

"Please don't force me to tell you why you were there," Kyran said and then jammed the HDA between his teeth. Stunned at his words, I could only glare at him. Kyran must have realized what he had just said because the color of his face neared a shade of purple.

"Why I was there?" I asked and hated the quaver I sensed in my voice. As if he hadn't just implied that there had been a reason behind me ending up as an enforcer and that it hadn't been because I was captured, Kyran kept his gaze on the screen. He didn't even dare to look at me anymore. "Kyran, please, you know more than you're saying, and I think you know more than even Saera does."

Kyran cleared his throat but kept his eyes fixed on the screen as he said, "I shouldn't have said anything—it's not my place. You should ask Harp."

The tension in Kyran's body was palpable, and it was obvious I wouldn't get any answers from him. I would have to ask Harp, although I had a feeling I wouldn't get the answers I needed from him either. Harp hadn't been the most forthcoming person with information, although he had promised me to tell me everything if my memories didn't come back.

As if our last words hadn't been spoken aloud, Kyran tapped his fingers on the glass surface and pulled up a timeline on the screen.

"This is the guy we're keeping an eye on," he said after he'd removed the HDA from his mouth and pointed a finger toward the image of scribbled lines and numbers. Then he showed me a picture of an elderly man with short, gray hair and a wrinkled face. Gray eyes complimented the color of his hair. "This is when Harand Sulos became the new CEO of ArtRep Enterprises."

On different charts, Kyran pointed at lines indicating numbers of how ArtRep's influence had grown ever since this Harand character had taken charge of running the company.

"Many think he managed to fall into grace with the Tenebrae government by managing to increase the energy output," Kyran said, "not only to maintain the shields, but also providing storage facilities that could be used as backup—we have no idea how he managed it tough."

"ArtRep also builds AR's," I said, "that would probably contribute to his influence on the government."

"Yep," Kyran added, "we have pretty good indications that he has the government in his pocket."

Men like Harand Sulos would reside in the tallest buildings in the center of the city, protected by the best shields, enjoying all the comforts this planet still had to offer, and no one dared to go against them.

"So, he's responsible for turning me into an enforcer," I said. Kyran shrugged as he answered.

"I guess."

"But why?" I asked as I pinched the bridge of my nose, "I mean… why not use the bioprinters and create an actual AR?" Kyran glanced at the screens in contemplation.

"Maybe this is cheaper," he said, "who knows."

I slumped in my seat, crossed my legs at the ankles, and let out a deep sigh. All this information was starting to give me a headache, but that didn't quench my curiosity. Maybe because I hadn't been able to think for myself or been able to show any kind of interest in anything, but for some reason, I wanted to know all.

"How did they do it?" I asked. "How do they turn a person into a compliant killing machine, and why can't it be undone?"

"It's not that it can't be undone or else you wouldn't be sitting here. With the memory thing, it's just…" Kyran said but trailed off after a glance at my face. "They use this," he said instead.

An image of my head appeared on the screen

above. Within seconds the composition of it changed, and it became a see-through mesh of wires. It looked like an organic electrical system. He zoomed in where different parts of the brain started to light up. Kyran pointed at the part that lit up yellow.

"Do you see that black spot?" he asked as an area at the back of my neck lit up on the screen. I nodded but didn't reply. "That thing is a highly sophisticated piece of tech planted in your cerebellum from where it sends signals to the different parts of your brain. This, for one, is how they block your memories, but what it also does is override your unconscious and subconscious mind."

"To what purpose?"

"To keep you subservient and easy to control, of course," he said. Kyran shot off a monologue that included all different kinds of medical and scientific explanations about how they had done it and how it was difficult to undo it, but about thirty seconds into his rant, I zoned out. That eagerness to quench my curiosity faded.

After a while, Kyran looked at me as if he wanted me to confirm that I understood. I raised an eyebrow and then cleared my throat.

"You stopped the signal it was sending, which made it possible to talk about the past, but that piece of metal stuck in the back of my head is blocking those old memories from reaching the surface," I said in a recap, "and getting the thing out might become problematic because of…something that could potentially kill me."

"Something like that," he said as he pressed a

combination of keys. The screen overhead turned black, and Kyran turned to face me. He eyed me thoughtfully as he grabbed the HDA from the table again and stuck it between his teeth.

"How can I be sure that what you are telling me is the truth?" I said. I focused intently on Kyran's face in the hope of reading him better. It didn't seem possible to read anything of Harp's body language, and although Saera appeared more open, I wasn't getting the information I needed. "You said it yourself —you tweaked my memories."

A faint smile formed on Kyran's face as he said, "Why did you decide to go with Saera in the first place?"

His eyes didn't venture away from mine as I thought of an answer. My reasoning hadn't made sense to me at the time, and it still didn't. On an intellectual level, I knew Kyran could have been the reason for planting my trust in Saera, but for some reason, I knew he hadn't. Ghostly memories like that one with the grimy bear felt too real, and even though Saera hadn't been in that one, I somehow felt her presence in it. I shook my head at Kyran, unable to come up with a viable answer.

"Gut feeling, hah," he said with a grin. I nodded my reply as I felt an uncomfortable tightness in my chest.

"I never had the privilege to work with you. I'm the new guy," he added, "but from what the others have told me, you used to be a pretty tight gang before you…eh…went missing." He fumbled the last part, and as soon as the words had left his mouth,

Kyran's face flushed red again. Unsure of the importance of his hesitation, I focused on the bit of detail he had revealed.

"The others?" I asked.

Kyran grimaced and then shook his head. "Not my place to tell," he said, "but I think you'll find out that your family is even more dysfunctional than you're already guessing, but they truly are your family." The HDA interfered with his speech, but I could tell he meant it. "Maybe you should go find them, because we're pretty much finished here."

I eyed him a moment longer in the hope he would say something more. That hope quickly faded as he stood and turned to leave the room.

"Yeah, I think I will," I said under my breath as I gazed across the empty room.

Chapter nine

Maece

I walked up the steps leading to the platform. I stopped at the top, and for a moment, I peered across the circular area. The effort that had gone into creating the domed structure must have been immense, but then that was what the Subterrans did —building underground cities.

They'd started doing it even before the sun had failed. As a people, they had never had the urge to venture into space or had any use for the latest in technology. Sure, they used the technology needed to man the food production facilities, power, and oxygen plants, but as their ancestors before, they had a knack for what they used to call *farming* in the old days.

This was always frowned upon by the other major cities until those dissolved into husks filled with empty structure after their energy fields had failed.

The remaining cities of Tenebrae had to deal with hundreds of thousands of refugees, and Subterra offered to help. Of course, Tenebrae took the generous offer, but their definition of a refugee was a bit different from what the Subterrans had in mind. For Tenebrae, this was an opportunity to gain access to Subterra's food production facilities and power stations, and instead of sending refugees, they started sending soldiers.

The war that followed was brutal, and many lost their lives on both sides. All this happened over five decades ago, but the relationship between the two societies never fully mended. So this was probably the reason for this Subterran presence underneath the City of Umbras, and I wondered if the city leadership overhead had any idea of its existence.

I watched the people milling around the central control area with the screens hovering over the desks and took my first steps toward them. Some of them eyed me as I approached, although they attempted to hide it. I tried to ignore them, but some of them made their curiosity obvious by stopping midstride or looking down from their screens.

My boots clunked on the rock surface, echoing inside this hollow space as I strolled past the Hymag hovering idly inside its spiral cage, and I noticed my reflection. In the mirror, an image of a creature built to induce fear stared back at me. The heavy boots, exoskeleton suit, and weapons seemed to be doing their job—even inside a facility filled with what looked like highly trained personnel.

I avoided looking at my face as if it might be the reason for the strange looks I was getting, although I figured it might be the only thing about me that looked normal now.

I spotted Saera and Harp standing at the edge of the platform in what seemed like a heated conversation. However, only Saera gestured wildly with her arms, and her face looked flushed. Harp, on the other hand, seemed to be listening patiently with his hands folded behind his back.

I started in their direction and glanced around the open space. Several heads diverted their gazes instantly, and then I wondered if it even was the way I looked that had them interested or that perhaps the doings of this strange family was what had captured their attention. Gossip was something that would survive as long as humanity would.

As I neared, Saera spotted me, and she fell silent.

Harp nodded and said, "Good of you to join us. I presume your all caught up?"

"On general history and how my brain got screwed up," I said and recognized the cynicism in my voice. It seemed that stopping that signal from interfering with certain parts of my brain made me able to tap into my personality. If only now I could figure how to get the memories back that had formed that personality without dying. "Yeah, I'm all set up."

"Good," Harp said. "Follow me, and I'll explain our plan." He turned and started walking toward the men and women sitting behind the desks.

I glanced at Saera as she sighed; I guessed out of frustration. Her cheeks were still flushed from the conversation, but as our eyes met her face colored a dark crimson. Unable to hold my gaze, Saera lowered her head to stare at her boots.

"Are you okay?" I asked.

Her lips formed a thin line as she looked up at me. She shifted uncomfortably before she spoke. "I…

ehh…about what I said before…" She hesitated as her eyes darted from left to right. It was clear that she attempted to apologize for her previously spoken words and although they had stung, I didn't enjoy watching her squirm like this. My absence and presumed death had hurt Saera a lot more, and I could understand that she wanted her sister back. I wasn't sure if I could ever be that person again, but I wasn't about to make it harder on her. I reached out a hand and touched her shoulder.

"It's okay," I said and offered a friendly smile. "I didn't take it too personal because, let's face it, I don't even know who I am."

Saera let out a soft chuckle and tilted her head to give me a crooked grin. I released her shoulder, and we stood in silence for a moment.

The low murmur of activity drew my attention, and I glanced at the workstations where Harp stood. Nodding toward him, I asked, "What's going on?"

Saera placed her hands on her hips and shook her head.

"He thinks, or rather, he hopes," she said, "that ArtRep has a way to remove the neuro regulator from your head without getting you dead."

"Presuming you mean the little black spot that Kyran showed me, I'm guessing that is good news."

"Yeah, well," she said and hesitated, "don't get me wrong. I want that thing out of your head, but at this point, it is still a guess as to what it would do to you."

"But I'm guessing Harp wouldn't be risking a dangerous mission just because of that." I asked.

"Probably not," Saera said with a sigh, "he has gathered a lot of information about ArtRep ever since we found you and Kyran infiltrated TED, but Harp isn't sharing. Now that he has your HUD at his disposal, he intents to use it."

I raised an eyebrow, and Saera must have read the confusion on my face.

"Your HUD has a far wider range and can be used to get us into all sorts of nifty places," she said.

"To do what?" I asked.

"To gain intel."

"I get that," I said, "but on what and why?" I sounded annoyed and I think my voice might have been too loud, because Saera tugged at my arm and pulled me closer.

"I'm not sure," she said at a whisper, "but I've overheard Harp talk to this guy named Monroe—he's this alderman and part of the council." Saera paused and eyed me for a second as if she were checking if I remembered the man's name. At the blank stare I shot her, she continued.

"I have a feeling something big is up and it's going to affect all of us, but I don't think Harp has enough evidence to convince the government."

I let the information sink in while close by the Hymag spirals hummed to life. The transport was getting ready to depart. The magnetic charge that was released in the process sent a tingle down my body and raised the hairs on the back of my neck.

"There is enough tension as it is between the people aboveground and us," she said in a louder voice to drown out the sound of the Hymag powering up. "Ever since the war, they occupy several of our power stations, and in return, we aren't that forthcoming in sharing our mushroom and fungi output. It's better not to accuse anyone up top without the proper evidence."

We took a couple of steps toward the central hub of operations where all the desks and monitors stood. As we moved out of reach of the magnetic field generated by the spirals holding the transportation device, I said, "So, I'm supposed to fetch the proof about something I know nothing about to convince the government of something…"

"Kind of," Saera said with a grimace.

"Right," I said as I thought it over, but I didn't feel particularly irked or bothered by that notion. The worried look on Saera's face told me she had doubts about my reaction, and I decided to lighten the mood. With a thoughtful expression, I said, "As long as I can remember what I find out, right."

Saera just stared at me, unblinking. Without a hint of amusement, she grabbed my arm and pulled me in the direction of the others.

"Oh, come on. That had to be a little funny," I said as she tugged on my arm. "Without memories, it's hard to figure out my personality, so I'm trying things out." I gauged her face, but it didn't move a muscle. "It's not as if I can count on Harp for a smile."

This seemed to hit a nerve, because she smiled, and as she peered at me from the corner of her eyes, I could see the joy in them. I giggled, but as soon as I heard the strange sound escape from my mouth, I slapped a hand over it. This triggered Saera, and she broke out into a full laugh.

As if I had achieved some major victory, I felt the tension fall from my shoulders, replaced by relief. In light of the situation, the sensation was difficult to explain even to myself, but somehow, it felt as if I belonged here.

Harp was waiting for us, standing in his usual pose: chin up, shoulders straight, and hands folded behind his back. He didn't look amused, and our smiles faded in an instant.

"This is Tyrel. Please give her your heads-up display," he said. A young woman stepped out from behind Harp with a shy smile. Her hair, tied in a ponytail, was dyed in different shades of red and green, but judging from her dark-colored eyes, I assumed her to be a natural brunette.

I started unclasping the goggles from my belt because I didn't want Harp to think I didn't trust him, but his question made me curious.

"Why?" I asked.

"Tyrel here will fix it," Harp said.

The girl's eyes widened, and her shyness was shoved to the background. "The device isn't broken, sir," she said in a high-pitched voice. "We just intercepted the signal and disrupted the optical collimator to prevent it from reaching the-"

"Ty," Harp said, interrupting her in a loud voice. Tyrel's mouth snapped shut, and her shyness returned.

"Will it keep ArtRep from tapping into the

signal?"

The girl nodded her head vigorously without uttering another word.

"Then go fix it," Harp said.

Tyrel's teeth tugged at her lower lip and creases formed on her young face, but she didn't retort. Instead, she said, "Yes, sir."

Harp took the device from me and handed it to Tyrel. Without another word, she turned on her heels and headed for her workstation. Then Harp turned to me and said, "You're going back to TED." He said it with such an intent that I almost choked on my saliva.

"Wha…what?" I said and felt my cheeks burn up as a result of the embarrassing stutter. Harp stared at me with that indecipherable gaze that would have left me guessing, while Saera shook her head and smirked.

"You'll be infiltrating and help us tap into TED's mainframe," Harp said as if it was the most logical scenario. It probably would have been if perhaps I had known these people a little better. I bit the inside of my cheek, feeling nervous. A couple of hours ago, I wouldn't even have questioned the order and would have executed it blindly. Now, it felt daunting.

"Why?" I asked. The word had already fallen from my mouth as I realized its stupidity. Saera had explained why—they wanted to know what ArtRep was up to.

"Even though Kyran has had access to TED's systems for a while now, he'd only been able to retrieve a limited amount of information," Harp said.

"With the help of your heads-up, he'll be able to get us inside the central mainframe."

"And you hope to gain information on what ArtRep is up to," I said.

"And to get that thing out of your head," Saera said vehemently.

Harp stood motionless for a moment before his gaze shifted from me to Saera. His face didn't give anything away, but his silence made me feel uncomfortable.

"Right?" Saera said, searching for confirmation. A sudden tension settled over me, and I wondered if Saera had felt it too. The awkward feeling lingered for several more heartbeats until Harp replied by dipping his chin in a slow nod.

Not sure on what had just transpired, I decided to move on, but I kept an eye on Harp's stoic expression as I asked, "I assume you have a plan to explain why I've been off the grid for so long?" The department must have gotten suspicious after by not complying with their orders.

"You haven't been off the grid," Harp said. I cocked my head and waited for an explanation that wouldn't come. Instead, he peered over my shoulder, and I followed his gaze to see Kyran walking toward us. Then he held a finger to his ear, and it seemed as if he was listening to someone talking directly into it.

"Copy that," he said and turned to address a man sitting at one of the desks. Before Kyran could reach us, Saera took my arm and pulled me out of direct earshot.

"He's not good with technology," she said in a

whisper near my ear.

"Who?" I asked in a similarly hushed voice.

"Colrin," she said, unable to contain a grin. "Don't get me wrong. He's a great leader, and he knows how to work with the stuff, but he's like an infant when it comes to explaining how tech works."

I glanced at Harp, who had pulled Kyran in for a conversation with the man sitting behind the desk.

"That's why he doesn't say much?" I asked.

"Oh no, he doesn't like talking in general, but he gets grumpy when he's asked questions he doesn't know the answer to," she said. "So, if you have questions, keep to the what and ask the how when Kyran or Tyrel are around."

The joy on her face was evident, but there was something endearing in the way she tried to safeguard Harp from the awkward moments.

"Whenever you're ready," Harp called out. Both our heads shot in his direction, and his gaze told us to move it.

We joined him at a station that sat empty until Kyran took up the seat behind the monitor and pulled up a map of the city overhead.

"This is you," he said to me. I shrugged as I didn't understand what he meant. Kyran grinned and said, "This is you patrolling right now." He pulled up some screens filled with code and continued his explanation. "I hijacked your signal a long time ago, and now I'm using it so that it seems as if you've been running around town all night."

"How does that work?" I asked. "I get tasked to do things all the time, and I have to report back."

"Well, it seems you've been hard at work," Kyran said. "You solved a lot of crimes tonight, and by the time they figure out that those people are still alive, you'll be long gone."

"Okay," I said a bit hesitantly, "so I can just walk into TED on my own like I've always done?"

"If that was the plan," Harp said. I turned to face him, but his gaze shifted to Saera.

"I'll be your prisoner for the night," she said.

Chapter ten

Maece

The old justice house seemed quiet as I peered at it through the green spectrum setting of my goggles. Tyrel had given them back to me after she had finished fiddling with them. Two enormous statues stood like sentries in full enforcer gear at the base of the steps that led up to a set of massive steel doors. Six columns stood in a line to carry part of the building's roof.

The building was brand-new, but it looked as if it had stood in that spot for centuries. They had modeled the structure after a building someone had found in one of the old archives. It had been a digital picture, copied countless times, which made it impossible to determine its date and origin, but the design was expected to be thousands of years old.

"What do you see?" Saera said, tapping me on the shoulder.

"The usual," I replied.

"Which is?" she asked, sounding impatient. I switched the green spectrum back to normal and turned to face Saera.

"The night shift has returned already, and the day shift just left," I said. "A couple of regular law enforcement officers just entered, but it seems quiet."

Saera bit her lower lip as she peeked around the corner. The alley I had chosen to hide from view was at least two hundred and fifty feet down the street from the old justice house, and I doubted she could make out much. Her jaw flexed with tension, but her eyes were focused.

The sight of Saera made my stomach churn. It was one thing to put your own life on the line but another to drag someone else down with you. I exhaled a long slow breath before I said, "Why are we doing this again?"

Saera eyed me curiously as if she were determining if my question had been sincere or not.

"I wish there'd be any other way," she said in an apologetic tone, "but you and that enforcer gear of yours are the only things that can get us inside that building to steal the information we—"

"I know. I know," I said before she explained again about gaining intel on ArtRep and how we needed to find a way to get that thing out of my head. The constant reminder that I had some device stuck in my head that could potentially kill me wasn't appealing.

"Are you ready?" I asked. I wanted to sound steady and in control, but my voice betrayed me with a slight tremor. Saera must have noticed because she shot me a glance. Instead of a hard look filled with warning, she threw me a nervous smile.

"With your skills and my brains, we should be

fine," she said and turned. She held her hands out, and I cuffed them behind her back.

"Not too tight?" I asked.

Turning, she faintly smiled and said, "They're fine."

"Listen," I started to say, "to make this look good, I might have to—"

"Get a little rough," she said, cutting me off. "This isn't the first time I've been arrested, although this is the first time by you. Usually, it was because of you."

Startled by her words, I shifted the goggles up to my head so I could see her with my own eyes. "What does that mean?" I asked. Saera closed her eyes and sighed audibly.

"Sorry," she said, "I keep forgetting about the memory thing. Forget about it." She started to turn toward the edge of the alley, but I took her by the shoulder and pulled her back, so our eyes were level again.

"You can't just drop something like that on me and then pretend it didn't happen."

"Maecy, this isn't the time or the place."

"Fine," I said in a hard voice and placed the HUD over my face. I took her arm and started around the corner.

"Maecy," she said and pulled us to a stop. "It's not that I don't want to tell you, but I think it's better if you remember these things on your own, so they won't get tainted."

"Tainted?"

"You know, colored by another person's

memories," Saera replied.

"How would that happen?" I asked.

"Because we've sorted it out…" she said hesitantly, "but…"

She hesitated again. Not sure I would be able to make any sense of Saera's vagueness, I took a quick scan of her vitals. Saera's heart rate was elevated, but that didn't stop the blood draining from her face. I detected the increase of moisture in her eyes, and I decided to lighten the mood.

"Have I been that much of a handful?" I asked. She nodded and rested her chin on her chest, but not before I caught nervous grin that had quickly faded. Taking a breath, she looked up, and even if I hadn't worn the heads-up device, I would have been able to tell she was fighting tears.

"I can't explain why, but telling you who you were…we were or should be…it'll never work," she said, and I heard the crack in her voice. "Does that make sense?"

I pondered her words for a moment as I took in her pale face. The fact that we looked as different as we did could count as an interesting turn of events in how we'd become sisters in the first place. But considering her explanation, it seemed our history could be even more complicated than I would have guessed.

"I think so," I replied. Saera chuckled nervously.

"You can arrest me now," she said.

We climbed the steps leading up to the giant doors. With a steady grip on Saera's arm, I held her close.

My heads-up device was working overtime, scanning anything and everything. It still felt a bit weird that I wasn't receiving any incoming orders or verdicts from judges. Instead, Harp and Kyran were connected through the heads-up's long-distance communications array, and rather than information scrolling down the screen, I had a direct link with them into my ear. If they wanted me to know something, they could just tell me. Saera had a similar device implanted in her ear that linked with my heads-up, and I hoped Kyran was right when he told me that TED scans wouldn't pick them up.

I walked up to the front desk and jerked Saera's arm, pushing her forward until her body hit the desk. She whimpered, and I hoped I hadn't hurt her. This was how enforcers treated their prisoners, and I needed it to look convincing. What I hadn't thought of was my strength. The enhancements made to my body by ArtRep along with the exoskeleton suit made me physically stronger, and I had never thought about the effect on people. Thinking wasn't something that had come with the job description.

"Intake," I said, sticking to my part. The officer grunted, dropped a chunk of fried fungi beef into a bowl, and wiped his fingers on a napkin. Then he glanced at his pad and slid his still-greasy fingers over the slick surface. From the old leftovers on the pad, I could tell this officer liked to indulge in greasy foods. Looking up from his pad, he glanced at Saera.

"Subterran," he said. I nodded my answer.

"Nice catch. ArtRep will be pleased," he said with a smirk. "Take her to MJ105."

This wasn't standard procedure. A criminal taken off the streets would never be taken to Memory Junction, but as we had gone over the plan, Harp had told us that it would be likely to happen. He had seemed convinced that this would prompt a change in procedure and it turned out he was right. How he had come to know all this remained a mystery even though I had asked him. Harp turned out to be very masterful at evading questions

I jerked Saera's arm and forced her to walk. Fortunately, she complied and didn't speak up, which could have ended badly for her. If I wanted to stay true to my part, I should have at least knocked her to the ground if she had done that.

As we passed the main intake area, I noticed her watching me from the corner of her eye. I wished I knew what she was thinking—whether she wondered what I had done to all those other prisoners that I had brought in over the years or that after seeing me in enforcer mode if she sensed doubt about whether I could ever become the Maece she once knew.

The crowd of officers, enforcers, and the people dubbed thugs thinned once we passed the main intake area, and I guided Saera down a long corridor. The place looked and felt like the hospital. The floor had a soft gray tint, and the walls were white. It had an impeccable appearance with a hint of chemicals wafting in the air.

We passed the main entrance to Memory Junction, and several doors were marked with a green light. This meant the rooms were occupied by enforcers getting their minds wiped. The thought made a shiver go down my spine. As if she sensed my discomfort, Saera glanced up and whispered, "We're almost there."

The main reason Harp had sent Saera along as my pretend Subterran prisoner was because he believed that I otherwise would never have gotten past those first few doors marked with the green lights. Although the room that the officer at the desk had directed me to was located within Memory Junction, it wasn't an area where I usually would have ventured—except when assigned guard duty and apparently escorting a Subterran prisoner.

Spotting an enforcer stepping around the corner, I withheld my reply. Saera noticed him too and lowered her head. The green light on the enforcer's headset blinked on, ready to scan Saera. There would be no reason for the enforcer to scan me or the other way around, although my heads-up had been scanning from the moment we stepped inside the building. Tyrel had disabled the light and had added an extra command to switch it on if needed. I had kept the light off because there had been no reason to scan 877.

Like mine, the enforcer's face was mostly hidden behind his heads-up, but I had clearly seen these features the night before. As 877's light blinked, I focused on my breathing. Besides the standard information concerning height and facial feature, the heads-up was perfectly equipped to pick up a person's heart rate, and at this point, my heart was hammering inside my chest. It was as if with every step drawing closer to 877, my heart rate shot up.

To my right, I noticed the door marked MJ105. It was the room where I was supposed to take Saera. I took a long, slow breath. After completing Saera's scan, 877 would have been informed of our destination and reason for being there. Even though he wouldn't have remembered me from last night, I had to tell myself to breathe. As he passed by, it was as if he hadn't even noticed us.

I had known it to be unlikely for an enforcer to scan another enforcer if there wasn't any direct indication of something being wrong, but I still felt relief wash over me.

Lingering at the door that would lead us into MJ105, I waited until 877 disappeared from view. Instead of going inside, we went around the same corner 877 had come from, and I was glad to see it abandoned. Three doors into the hall, Saera stopped in front of a sleek metal door that lacked any markings or designation. "This is it," she whispered.

She was right, of course, because she had seen the same plans as I had. We had found the location of the central mainframe, and with any luck, Kyran would be able to access the information Harp was looking for. Hoping to find something that would help get the device extracted from my head felt like pushing that luck, and I set the thought aside.

My eyes roamed the empty hall, searching for any kind of disturbance. I scanned for sounds that might become a problem for us, but as far as I could tell, there were no footsteps or voices. I tapped my heads-up. Without me having said anything, Kyran's voice rattled off in my ear.

"I'm on it," he said. I flinched at the sound of his loud voice. Saera grinned.

"It's as if he's inside my head," I whispered.

"And loud," she replied. There was still a bit of a grin detectible on her face, but the way her head shifted from left to right told me she was as apprehensive as me.

"Kyran," I said in a whisper.

"Yeah, yeah, hurry—I know." His voice sounded as if it would alert the entire station of our presence, and I almost told him to tone it down. I heard him tapping his virtual keyboard while he spoke.

"I need two more minutes to deactivate surveillance so you won't be detected going inside or being inside."

"Two minutes," Saera said, sounding agitated. "Are you kidding me? We can't just stand here like some dumb-ass puppets. What if someone comes?"

"I don't know. Think of something," Kyran replied, "but I need you to stay in that exact spot or else I'll lose the connection. Now shut up and let me work."

Saera and I shared a glance. She didn't like this any more than I did. We were easy targets standing here in this pretty, white hallway, but the way this worked was that inside the old justice building every area was divided into its own security network. This meant that if anyone tried to hack the system, they didn't just need to hack one system, but several correlating systems, and triggering one meant triggering all of them.

Inside my heads-up, a message blinked red, and I

swirled my head around. Footsteps sounded down the hall and not just one set. These were at least five, and from their tread, it was obvious that these were enforcers coming our way.

"Kyran, get this door open," I whispered as softly as I could but in an urgent manner.

"I know. I know," he replied. "Almost there."

It wasn't long until the sound of boots barreling down on us wasn't just something my heads-up registered. Saera heard and glared at me, wide-eyed. She fidgeted with her hands bound behind her back, and the metal clinked. Her head shot to the right where the sounds were coming from, and I could read the fear on her face. If they caught us here, I wouldn't have any explanation to get us out.

The other enforcers would probably assume something had gone wrong with my programming, and by checking the building's system, they would know Saera was supposed to be around the corner and down the hall in room MJ105.

"Get these off me," Saera whispered.

"Shh," I hissed.

"Maece," she said. Her using my actual name proved she must have been terrified, but I couldn't let her freak out, which was what my scans had started to indicate. I placed my hand on her neck and pulled her close so I could whisper in her ear.

"They'll hear you." My words were barely audible, but a slight nod of her head told me she understood. Leaving Saera's cuffs on would be her best chance. Worst case, they would take her to ArtRep, and then maybe Harp and Kyran could find a way to help her.

The sound of boots clomping down the hall became louder, and they could appear around the corner at any second. I tapped my ear twice, hoping Kyran would understand the urgency I couldn't spell out. He didn't reply, and I feared the worst. I pulled Saera close and positioned my body in front of her so I would be the first thing the enforcers saw.

Engaging them would probably be useless, especially if there were five of them. Frantically, my head shifted from left to right as if scanning the hallway one more time would reveal something I had missed in my previous scans. As if suddenly some escape route would appear. I glanced at Saera, who looked as I felt—mortified.

Chapter eleven

Maece

Boots pounding, left, right, left, right—they became an eerie drone in my head until, finally, Kyran's voice replaced the eeriness with a promise of safety.

"Go," he whispered as if even he was afraid the approaching enforcers' scans would pick up on his voice. Without checking if Saera had heard, I pushed the door open and pulled her inside behind me. The sound of boots was so close now that they must have come around the corner and stepped into our hallway. Hoping they hadn't noticed, I eased the door shut until it clicked and waited. Holding my breath, I listened. Saera stood silently by my side, watching that dreaded door.

Once the footsteps had passed, we both let out long sighs. As I met Saera's eyes for a moment, the relief I felt was mirrored in her face. The corners of my lips threatened to rise into a smile, and I couldn't help it. I grabbed hold of Saera and hugged her.

"That was close," she said, sounding breathy, but she smiled as I pushed her at arm's length. My headsup display indicated spiking adrenaline levels, and she had an elevated heart rate. Other than that, she seemed fine. I opened my mouth to ask if my indications were right, but she beat me to it.

"I'm okay, so you can stop scanning me now," she said a bit snappy, but her grin told me it was fine.

"Let's get on with it then," I replied as I released Saera from her bonds and glanced around.

A glass wall separated the room into two distinct sections. The one we were standing in had that all-familiar white sterile feel that I had seen inside the hospital and walking down the halls outside the door behind me. On the other side of the glass, the walls seemed to be dressed in a sleek black coating. Except those weren't walls. Lights blinked in intervals on the five man-sized mainframe computers. Thick columns of cables lowered from the ceiling and connected to the five towers propped against the wall.

"Now what?" Saera asked. I had asked myself the same question when I didn't notice a visible entrance into the mainframe area.

"Please don't tell me I have to blow something up?" I asked Kyran on the other side of the line. I glanced along the edges of the glass, suspecting that even explosives would have a hard time cracking this barrier, which my scan confirmed. Five-inch armored glass stood between us and the information we needed. Kyran's voice sounded amused as it came over my coms. "Don't worry. I wasn't about to."

"Then what?" Saera said, scrutinizing the barrier in front of us.

"Maece, move to the left and wave your hand in front of the glass," he said. The area he had indicated didn't look any different from the rest of the glass wall, but I did as he asked. At least I'd intended to, but I froze as Kyran's urgent voice bellowed in my head. "But don't touch it!"

My foot hovered in midair as if my nerves had locked it into place.

"You idiot," Saera retorted, clearly not amused by Kyran's method of warning. "You nearly gave me a heart attack."

My boot landed with a thud on the tiled floor, and I let out the breath I was holding.

"Sorry," Kyran said in a softer tone, "but touching it might set off an alarm."

"And activating it won't?" I asked. Kyran and Harp were sitting far away and deep underground, but the sound of Kyran's fingers tapping reverberated as drums in my head.

"I've been working inside that place for a while," Kyran replied, "and I created a back door. Just stay where you are. I'm opening a connection with the help of your heads-up."

"Let me guess: something Tyrel fixed?" Saera said.

Kyran didn't reply over the feed, but instead, Harp's raspy voice filled my head.

"Stop bugging Kyran and let him work."

I glanced at Saera standing next to me and shrugged. She crossed her arms over her chest and watched as I waved my hand at the glass wall. A portion of the glass darkened until it wasn't see-through anymore. Several colorful icons popped up on the created screen, and text windows opened.

Green letters filled the different windows, scrolling up and down too fast for the normal eye to read.

"We're risking our lives for that crap," Saera mumbled.

"Hang on," I said and used my heads-up to slow the data until it became comprehensible. "I'm getting background information on ArtRep."

"Well," Saera said impatiently. I ignored her, reading through the text as fast as I could.

"What?" she said, and I presumed it had something to do with my mouth falling open.

"They're...so many of them," I said under my breath.

"Of what?" Saera asked again.

"Harp, are you getting this?" I asked.

"Yeah," he said in a clipped tone.

Saera punched me in the shoulder, and my gaze shifted to her. She glared at me wide-eyed.

"The ARs," I said. "We're not talking about a few hundred serving TED. There's thousands of them, and every one of them is Subterran."

Saera blinked as if her brain had trouble processing the information. Her eyes shifted from me to the screen and back again.

"What do you mean they're all Subterran?" she said.

"The ARs, none of them were constructed in a bioprinter," Kyran piped in, "enhanced maybe, but not constructed. They are all Subterran."

"How is that possible?" she said, the disbelief in her palpable.

"But..." I said and hesitated, "if there are so

many of them, where did they all come from and why isn't anyone missing them?"

Saera shook her head without having an answer for me and I returned my gaze to the screen. Along with a picture, the screen filled with information on Harand Sulos, the CEO of ArtRep Enterprises. Empty eyes stared back at me from the old man's picture.

"Most of them came from the power plants still occupied by Tenebrae since the war," Kyran said, "but there seems to be a network that operates from one or two hospitals located on the edges of Subterran territory."

"Let me guess: Icordia," Saera said. I glanced at her sideways as the name rang a bell. She noticed and said, "Don't worry. Not something you would want to remember."

I had a feeling that whatever happened to lead me to work as an enforcer for the Tenebrae Enforcer Department most have started at that hospital. A sensation, rather than a memory, sent a shiver down my spine.

"They've been using our own people against us," Harp said as the numbers of what seemed to be some sort of payment scrolled across the screen.

"I don't get it," Kyran said. "What the hell are these?" I could understand his trouble interpreting the information. *What would a Subterran gain by selling off their own? Selling how?* The only currency left on this planet, at least as far as we could tell, was unprocessed mushrooms and fungi. The Subterran government used these products to trade with the combined districts. Mushrooms and fungi were used to reproduce nutrient assets for our daily diets and had become a vital component for survival. As the main supplier of these products, Subterra had a surplus, and it didn't seem logical that this was the currency the numbers represented.

Within Subterran borders, food and other essentials, like clothes and sanitary products, were equally divided among its citizens, and for the most part, people seemed content with that.

The Combined Districts of Tenebrae had a similar approach in which they decided who received what. Dependent on background or class, this meant some received more than others. For the less fortunate, this entailed that they received just enough to survive, but when had surviving ever been enough? Especially when most had to make do with so little while the few lived in luxury.

In a society where the government dictates where you live, what you eat, and what you own, people tend to become inventive. For as long as humans had roamed this planet there had always been those who'd sought opportunities to make a profit. For that reason, black market dealings had created their own form of currency in the form of credit notes, but these were mostly IOUs and weren't worth much in the real world.

What was it that Tenebrae had to offer a Subterran citizen? All I could think of were perhaps some pretty lights and other forms of technology that most Subterrans didn't care for.

Saera's eyes seemed to glaze over after I told her

about the weird currency trail, and I thought her mind must have drifted off until she said, "Energy, they produce magnetic power and lots of it."

"What good would that do anyone," I said pointedly, "I assume Subterrans' self-reliance hasn't changed since I've been gone."

"Then why don't you come up with something," she said as she narrowed her eyes at me.

"I wouldn't rule it out," Harp said over the coms. Saera smirked and I would have rolled my eyes if she'd been able to see them.

"Oh shit," Kyran said.

"What?" Saera and I simultaneously replied.

"Eh..." Kyran started to say but hesitated. The line went silent for a moment as if the two of them had cut us off. Saera lifted her shoulders as I searched her face for answers. Then Kyran's voice reentered my head.

"Are you sure," he asked, and I presumed he was talking to Harp.

"Tell them," Harp said sharply.

With that, Kyran cleared his throat and said, "Maece, do you remember that device I mentioned that they have inserted into your cerebellum?"

"That..." I started to say, but hesitated and then swallowed. It wasn't that I didn't know what he was talking about, but Kyran's voice sounded ominous, and I felt sure I wasn't going to like what he had to say. "That thing that is blocking my memories," I managed to add.

"Yeah," he said. Another moment of silence fell, and an impatient Saera placed her hands on her sides.

"Kyran," she said in a loud voice.

"It's…it's a self-destruct."

It had gone silent inside the room and on the coms as if we needed time to let the information sink in. On automatic, my hand went to the back of my neck and rubbed the spot where I imagined the device to be.

"But you disabled the one in Maecy's head, right," Saera said. Silence followed, and not getting the answer as quickly as she wanted, she bellowed, "Kyran!"

Her voice came out loud, and my head shot toward the door. Nothing stirred, and I hoped no one had heard her. I grabbed her arm and jerked it.

"Why don't you hang a sign on the door that says we're in here," I said in a firm but low voice.

"We didn't even know to look for it," Kyran said, but Saera ignored him. She glared at me with the utmost disbelief. Perhaps she had expected me to freak out, but Kyran's information about the explosive didn't come as a shock to me. It had occurred to me on one of those long times spent in Memory Junction. At the time, I saw myself as a ruthless killing machine, and it didn't seem logical to not have something to control us ARs. I couldn't remember why the thought had even come up. It could have had something to do with Kyran's tinkering inside my brain, but somehow the thought had resonated.

"Why aren't you more upset?" she asked, crossing her arms over her chest again.

"I don't know."

Saera narrowed her eyes at me, and I felt glad for the heads-up covering my face. This way she couldn't read my reaction, and I had a feeling she could read me like the back of her hand.

On the other side of the line, Kyran sighed audibly.

"What?" I asked.

"Sulos is the only one who can give the order," Kyran replied. "He's the one who built in the kill switch. That's why no one knew about this—none of the unimportant people anyway."

"Like you," Saera said.

"Harand Sulos," I said, once again ignoring Saera, "CEO of ArtRep."

"The one and only," Harp said. I had almost forgotten he was still on the line.

"Then we must kill Sulos," Saera said.

"Saera," Harp spoke in a monitoring tone.

"They're Subterran," she said. Her voice rose an octave. "And he can kill them with the flick of a switch, including Maecy."

"We can't act on this, not until we analyze the information," Harp said. His voice had changed, almost sounding soothing, but I could tell it didn't affect Saera. Her clenched jaw twitched, and from my scan, I could tell her heart rate was faster than before.

"If they figure out Maecy is off the grid, they'll inform Sulos, and he'll flip the switch," she said.

"I'm aware of the risk," Harp replied, "but Kyran and Tyrel know what they're doing." Saera's hand twitched at her side, and along with the wild look in her eyes, I had a feeling she was about to do something stupid.

"Saera, please," I said, reaching out to her.

"No," she said adamantly, wrenching herself away from me, "and stop scanning me."

On the other end, I could still hear Kyran's fingers move across the keypads, and from the corner of my eye, I saw new data scroll across the screen.

"We have to act before it's too late," Saera added and took a step back. "We need to kill Sulos."

"No," Harp said harshly, "we cannot risk a war, but a plan is in place." He didn't give an explanation, but from the look on Saera's face, clarification wasn't necessary. Her flushed face and wide eyes told it all. She was pissed, and although the information we had just received hadn't been pretty, it seemed something else was going on.

Something in Saera's expression changed, and she lifted a hand to her forehead. She seemed anxious.

"What plan?" she asked. Her voice sounded surprisingly calm, even though nerves caused her to bite her lower lip.

"I'm sending in the team," Harp said. Saera looked confused as she shook her head.

"But that won't work," she said.

"I know it's not your standard routine, but they can handle this," Harp replied.

"No," Saera said in a loud voice that made me check the door again. "I'm not going to let you do this. I'm not going to sit and wait so you can screw me over again."

The anger in her voice was directed at Harp, but I had no way of knowing what it was about. Saera's eyes filled with tears, which could be either hurt or frustration or maybe both. Something inside me told me it was hurt. The same hurt I had seen in her eyes before. The hurt I had seen that night we had met for the first time since I could remember.

Although it didn't make any sense to me, I felt a need to console her, to be a source of comfort, but I didn't know how. I took a step toward her, trying to close the gap she had created between us, but Kyran's voice forced me to stop.

"Maece, whatever you're doing, stop! I'm losing the feed."

I had moved away from the glass, and the distance interfered with the heads-up connection. As I stepped back into place, Saera moved closer to the door.

"I'll go," she said. "If needed, I'll kill Sulos myself."

"You stay with Maece," Harp said in a hard tone that sounded almost threatening. "I'm sending the team, and that's final."

"If you think I'm just going to sit by and wait for Maecy's head to explode while you send someone else I love to their death, then you don't know me very well," she replied and took another step toward the door. "I'll go. Besides, we're already here and can be at the ArtRep buildings a lot sooner."

"Saera," Harp said. His voice had returned to his calm self.

"No," she replied, "I'm going."

"You are still under my command," he said. "Now let them do their jobs." Ignoring Harp's order, Saera moved to the door.

"Saera, what are you doing," I asked and heard the fear in my voice. I had no idea what they'd been talking about, but I sensed it wasn't good. Our gazes locked, but I couldn't reach her. It was as if the dark mask hiding my face wouldn't allow me to get through to her.

Her hand lifted to open the door. Inside my head, I heard Kyran's strained voice.

"Are you seeing this?"

"Maece, don't you move from that spot," Harp said in a hard voice. "We need this intel."

"Please just wait," I said. My voice was barely audible but filled with desperation. If she exited this room without me, she would die for sure, and even though my lack of memories didn't allow me to know her, in my heart, I knew I did. More than that, if the pounding in my chest and the tears stinging behind my eyes were any indications. I lifted my hand in a gesture to just wait. She seemed to comply, and I grabbed the opportunity to gaze at the screen.

I sucked in a breath as my quick scan absorbed the green text running down the screen.

"This can't be right," I said under my breath. "He couldn't do this."

The moment the words left my mouth I regretted them. They had nothing to do with what Kyran had found about the explosive in my head or had anything to do with Harp, but Saera might have understood them that way, because before I could even turn to her the door had opened, and she stepped through.

Chapter twelve

Maece

"Saera," I called after her, but it wasn't any use. The door closed behind her, and she was gone.

"I'm going after h—" I started to say, but Harp's booming voice invaded my head.

"No," he yelled, "you stay put." The way he stressed it made me stand frozen on the spot. "You've seen what's in these files."

I glanced at the screen, fists clenched. Pictures of starving men and women filled my head. Children carrying heavy loads with bodies like skin over bones. The images were too painful to look at, and I returned my gaze to the door. Sound scans didn't indicate anything wrong, which meant enforcers hadn't found Saera yet. My feet twitched as I shifted toward the door.

"Maece, please," Harp said in a pleading voice. "You cannot ignore this. This is more important than you, me, or Saera."

My fingers started to hurt as I squeezed my fists harder. This was unbearable.

"How long?" I asked.

"Almost there," Kyran answered. As he said it, I heard the first sounds of trouble outside the door. Her voice was muffled, but I could clearly make out the words: *"Let go!"*

That was it—that was all it took. With four quick strides, I was at the door. Harp and Kyran were shouting at me over the coms, but Saera's muffled voice drowned them out. I drowned them out. Acting on pure instinct, I opened the door and observed the space beyond. The immediate hall was empty; with the help of the heads-up. it was easy to locate Saera by the sounds she made. Using the added power allowed by the exoskeleton, I ran in the direction we had originally come from.

I reached the connecting hallway at full speed with no intention of slowing down and spotted Saera around the corner in the clutches of an AR. I reminded myself that they weren't ARs. These were people, Subterrans and not artificial representations. The enforcer had her pinned against the wall and was reading Saera her rights. With her cheek pressed against the plastered surface, she faced me, and I saw some of the fear in her eyes replaced by relief.

The enforcer noticed my approach. His visor shifted slightly, and I could imagine the data scrolling down his screen, calculating the reason a fellow enforcer would be running toward him at full speed while he already had control of the situation. I might have been able to detect surprise in his eyes if I'd been able to see them. My heads-up analyzed his body, which had no indication of an elevated heart rate or excessive working glands. His hand moved to his hip and slid over his holstered weapon. Apparently, the risk-assessment software had determined me to be hostile.

With the help of the heads-up, it was as if everything slowed down by a factor of ten. The enforcer's hand lifted the weapon from its holster raising until he found me in its sight. Data slid across my screen, calculating the perfect angle for the enforcer to shoot. The second the weapon reached its perfect aim, I dropped to a knee, using the moment I had gained and the slick tiles to slide along the floor. The weapon fired, and I felt the energy blast heat the air as I slid underneath it until my boot connected with the back of the enforcer's knee.

The leg buckled and the enforcer lost his balance, releasing Saera in the process. On my knees by his feet, I reached up to grab his belt and jerked him down. His body fell backward, but before his head could hit the ground, I moved to straddle his chest. As he lay sprawled on his back, I wrenched the heads-up from his head. Gray eyes enhanced by the added glow stared back at me in surprise, just as I had expected.

Not waiting for a response, I raised the device and crashed it down on his skull. The first hit didn't have the desired effect. Although dazed, his gray eyes still peered back at me, and I hit him again. Blood spilled from a cut on the left side of his head as his eyes closed. I hit him one more time and then threw the glasses down the hall. They connected with the wall and shattered into pieces. Enforcers wouldn't dare to go on without their heads-up, and him chasing after a new device could buy us some time.

Within seconds I was on my feet and reached for Saera's hand. She took it, but instead of me leading her, she tugged at my arm.

"This way," she said.

Side by side we ran down the hall until I noticed company at our backs. Midrun I glanced over my shoulder and saw two enforcers following, weapons raised. I let myself fall back in step behind Saera to cover her. The first blast slammed into me, causing me to stumble forward. From where the round had struck me, searing heat faded out through the atomic-scale-honeycomb-latticed armor of my suit. It protected me from most weapons, including the ones used by the enforcers, although they stung like hell. The suit did protect me from most weapons, but not all. As soon as the order came in the enforcers would change their ammo, and we'd be in danger of becoming red blobs on a wall.

I regained my footing as Saera glanced back. She opened her mouth to speak, but I cut her off before she could utter a word.

"Go!" I shouted. She complied and sprinted ahead of me. To keep her in front of me, I held back. The suit could help me to be a lot faster, but Saera couldn't afford to be hit by one of those magnetic pulses. It would render her unconscious and might even kill her.

Behind us, boots pounded in pursuit, but I dismissed them. I scanned the hallway ahead of us and found what I was looking for.

"Next door on the right," I yelled. "Take it."

A few steps later, Saera's body shifted as she slammed into the door, opening it in the same instance. She disappeared into the staircase just as I registered the click made by the trigger of a short-range magnetic-blast weapon. I ducked, keeping my head low, but the round hit me in the shoulder, and I slammed into the doorpost. I clenched my teeth to stifle a scream, but couldn't prevent a groan from escaping.

On the steps going down, Saera stopped and turned to wait for me. I appreciated the expression of concern, but I needed her to move.

"Keep going," I said through clenched teeth. Finding my balance, I turned, grabbing my own weapon in the same move and fired twice. I hit the first enforcer square in the chest, and he stumbled, reaching for the wall to find support. The other one anticipated my shot and ducked. I fired again and caught him in the knee. His leg wavered, and he went down.

From the corner of my eye, I saw a door open. Shock ran through me as I saw the green light of an occupied enforcer chamber lit above the door. Without waiting to see how many would venture from the room, I stepped into the staircase and slammed the door shut behind me. I started for the stairs leading down, but then Saera came bolting up my way. An energy blast connecting with the wall above her head made her yelp, and she grunted with the effort of keeping her momentum going.

"This is turning out to be a bad idea," she said,

taking the steps two at a time.

"And you only think of this now," I replied. I let her pass so she would be ahead again and had just started up the stairs as the door behind me cracked open.

"Stop," a female voice called out, but I didn't slow to check who the enforcer turned out to be. I probably wouldn't remember her anyway. I crossed the next landing in one large stride and then followed Saera's lead taking the steps two at a time.

She opened the door to the second floor and went through. A black-clad figure crossed my vision while I felt another blast hit my suit. It had caught me in the upper leg, forcing my knee to hit the second landing. I used my hand to catch my weight and then let myself fall to my shoulder and rolled onto my back as I raised my weapon.

Ignoring the shock at seeing the enforcer hovering over me so close, I fired several times. The soft round features of a woman's jaw poked out from under the heads-up display. Two blasts hit her, and she faltered backward, tripping on the top step and falling. She fell into the arms of the enforcer coming up the stairs behind her.

Outside in the hall, I heard a different kind of weapons fire. It wasn't the incinerating explosion of an enforcer kill charge, but more of a smaller caliber magnetic weapon. I scrambled to my feet, stumbling past the door. I kept looking right and left until I found Saera. Without having seen it, my heads-up informed me of a white hallway similar to the one downstairs that started to fill up with at least three enforcers and a couple of regular officers. My heads-up equally informed me that they seemed to be holding their position, advising of a possible friendly fire incident. It appeared they didn't want to shoot the enforcer who was now charging Saera.

She fired the weapon in her hand, but the large figure running at her didn't even flinch. I started running after them, hoping I would get to the enforcer before he got to Saera. To my surprise, Saera didn't back off. She took a fighting stance, one foot forward and knees bent. The enforcer rushing at her raised his arms to grab her, but she ducked, catching the brunt of his weight on her back and then flipped him over.

The body of the large man landed with a thump on the tile floor as I reached Saera's side. A wide grin spread across her face as if telling me I wasn't the only one who could kick ass. I managed to reply with a faint smile, but my focus was on the man lying on the floor. His body jerked as I fired my weapon at him, grabbed the heads-up from his face, and tossed it down the hall.

"Come on!" Saera shouted and grabbed my shoulder. My heads-up made me aware of weapons clicking ready, and I rose to my feet. I ran after Saera to the end of the hall and toward a dead end.

Chapter thirteen

Reece

I had no sense of motion as the Hymag sped along its magnetic lines. There wasn't any use for windows inside this box because there wouldn't be anything to see outside except rocks.

"The pilot says we should reach the post underneath Umbras in a few minutes," I said as I made my way back to my seat. I plopped down on the bench next to Riffy and across from Kelle. Riffy moaned as I patted him on the shoulder.

"Ouch," he said, sounding like a little kid.

"I'm so proud of you," I said, placing my head on his shoulder and snuggling into him.

He shoved me and growled, "Get away from me."

I grinned and glanced at Kelle. She had been the one to gather Riffy up off the floor after Rockslide had beat him in the arm-wrestling match. The man had done honor to his name, ramming Riffy's arm down on the old stone table. It had broken Riffy's wrist, but before gathering our equipment, we had plenty of time for a stop at the hospital, where they had his arm fixed in a jiffy.

Riffy probably would have been able to do it himself, but the doctor had his wrist set and mended within minutes, and except for a little muscle ache, he was fine. Waiting for the doctor had taken longer than the time it took to fix Riffy's injury, but at least we'd been in time to catch our ride.

Besides, the news I had brought them had quickly shifted their attention. It wouldn't be long before our little band of misfits would be complete again, and that was what we all had been waiting for.

Even Kelle, sitting across from me, seemed to have perked up with the news. Not that it showed on her face, but the tiniest twinkle in her eyes betrayed it.

"I can't believe Tyrel didn't tell you anything more than she did," Riffy said and huffed.

"I think Harp might have been standing next to her," I replied.

"That would explain it," Kelle said, raising an eyebrow.

"I still can't believe it took this long to get her out," Riffy said.

I glanced at him sideways and said, "There isn't much you do believe, is there."

Riffy shoved his elbow into my side, and I groaned. "Guess the arm isn't bothering you anymore."

"I just hope they're okay," Kelle said. Her thoughtful gaze shot straight past me to the front of the Hymag where the cockpit was located.

"I second that," I replied, retreating into my own thoughts.

It had been so long since I had seen Maece that I wondered what she would look like. She must have changed over the years. I had seen a couple of recent images in the files Harp had kept on her, but in them, she always wore that dreadful heads-up display.

Saera hadn't been much fun to be around ever since Maece had disappeared. Especially after she had found out that Maece had volunteered to help Harp and had disappeared on one of his missions. I blew out a breath and caught Kelle staring at me. Trying to smile at her failed, and so I added, "They're okay, both of them."

The pilot indicated our arrival, and as soon as he did, the door to the Hymag slid open. At the exit, I watched how clamps extracted themselves from the transport pod and attached to the platform. Metal groaned as the clamps locked on and maneuvered the transport to its parking spot. I stepped onto the circular platform where I usually took the time to take in the immense space and the craftsmanship that went into building this underground hideout, but something drew my attention to the central control station.

All desks were manned, and images flashed across the large screens hovering over them. I spotted Harp standing in his usual pose with his hands behind his back, his eyes glued to one of the screens. This wouldn't have been out of the ordinary if it weren't for his fist clenching and unclenching behind his back.

I glanced down at Kelle, who I knew would have

noticed the same thing, and she shrugged. Riffy just stood by my side, gazing across the room as if he was seeing it for the first time, with a glazed-over expression. I shook my head, grabbed my gear, and started to make my way to the control station.

As if he had eyes on his back, Harp shifted his head to watch our approach.

"Harp," I said, stopping at his side.

"Reece," he replied. Then he nodded at the others.

"What's going on?" I asked. Harp sighed and shook his head.

"I never should have involved Saera," he said. His voice carried obvious contempt as he added, "That's what's up." Then he walked to one of the other desks as if we weren't even there.

Kelle shifted uncomfortably at my side, and I placed a hand on her shoulder.

"It was his own stupid idea," she muttered under her breath.

I noticed Kyran and joined him at his workstation. His eyes were glued to the screen in front of him. It wasn't hard to guess what had him so enticed. The overwhelming green images fed to the screens by an enforcer's heads-up display flittered in front of our eyes. Kelle stepped closer as we both saw Saera bolting up a flight of stairs and dodging a magnetic blast. Her mouth moved as her face filled the screen, talking to the person wearing the heads-up. I took in a sharp breath as I realized who she was talking to.

I felt the slightest pressure on my upper arm and

looked down to see Kelle standing next to me with a concerned expression on her face.

"Holy crap," Riffy said, glancing up at the screen, "is that both of them?" I nodded, not fully able to verbalize my thoughts, but I doubt he needed the confirmation.

"Goddammit," Kelle said under her breath as we watched Saera holding her ground while a six foot tall, broad-shouldered mountain of a man wearing heavy armor charged her. My left hand balled into a fist as the right one subconsciously maneuvered to the weapon strapped to my thigh.

Anger started to gather inside my chest, and I knew exactly who to blame. My eyes shot toward Harp, still standing in his trademark pose. He should have called us in sooner. We could have backed them up.

"Jesus," Kelle added as the enforcer hit the deck, followed by a sigh of relief. She shifted uncomfortably on her feet, surely feeling as helpless as I did. Riffy's gaze had dropped to the floor, occasionally drifting up, peeking through squinted eyes at the screen, with a face torn into a grimace.

Maece's heads-up revealed an almost white image as the intense glow from the sun penetrating the dome reached the green spectrum of her goggles. As her arms whirled to disarm an officer aiming his weapon at Saera, her vision again trailed to the window engulfed by the bright light. At that moment, I knew that the years that had passed had done nothing to sever the connection we had shared, because I knew exactly what she was thinking.

"They're gonna jump," I said, barely audibly. Kelle, who had heard, pulled both her hands over the fuzz of black hair on her head, keeping them there as we watched the scene unfold.

"What?" Riffy asked.

Kyran dropped the HDA that he had been chewing on from his mouth, pressing buttons as he shouted into his mouthpiece, "They changed ammo."

Unable to stop myself, I gripped Kyran's shoulder, willing him to do something as the screen showed what I knew to be Maece's hand pulling Saera down to the ground.

Chapter fourteen

Maece

The intense glow of the sun penetrating the dome lit up the window at the end of the hall as we ran toward it. A door on the left opened, and a gun-wielding law enforcement officer stepped out. Saera dove to the ground as he took his shot. She hunched into a roll, and a chunk of tile exploded into pieces near her foot.

The officer's eyes followed Saera's roll across the floor until she emerged in a crouched position in front of him. He aimed his weapon again, ready to fire, but by that time, I had reached him and slammed the palm of my hand under the arm wielding the weapon. The gun flew from his hand, and the surprise in his gaze was evident until I punched his jaw. Following the motion through, I connected my elbow with his temple. He fell back inside the room from which he had appeared.

I grabbed Saera's jacket and pulled her to her feet. Behind us, voices yelled, but if it wasn't for the heads-up display, I wouldn't have registered them. I did hear Kyran's voice boom inside my head as it came over the coms.

"They changed ammo!" he shouted. He had barely spoken the words when green letters on my screen added a warning. Incoming, it read. Still holding Saera's collar, I jerked her down this time as I let us fall to the ground. I maneuvered my body over hers to protect her with my suit as a massive explosion rocketed the hall. I gritted my teeth, and Saera screamed as the heat of the residual flames rushed over us.

The once-white hall filled with gray smoke, and black soot covered the walls where the blast had hit. I fought a cough as I scrambled to my feet. Smaller caliber ammo fire erupted behind us, but none of the strikes came close to us. In a quick glance, I noticed the gray smoke filling the hall was worse behind us—nearly black. It must have thrown off their aim.

I shoved Saera ahead of me. At the same moment, a searing pain erupted between my shoulder blades, telling me that the smoke hadn't interfered with the enforcers' aim. The suit deflected most of the energy, and I felt the heat run along my back into my limbs. I gasped and felt Saera's arm wrap around me for support.

We had all but reached the end of the hall as Saera threw me a worried glance.

"The window!" I yelled over the sound of magnetic weapons fire.

"What!" Saera shouted.

"Trust me," I replied with a grin. My heads-up had already scanned the window and had noted that the glass had cracked in the explosion. I had feared the armored glass would have been hard to break, but I guessed the enforcer had done us a favor by setting off that blast. The device strapped to my face had also calculated the best angle to hit the glass and trajectory toward the ground.

Grabbing Saera, I drew power from the exoskeleton suit and jumped. Saera tensed in my arms as I held on to her tightly. The glass exploded into a million pieces as the combined forces of our bodies slammed into it. For a moment, I felt a sense of weightlessness until gravity took hold of us. In midair, I jerked my body, clamping Saera to my chest, my back directed at the ground so I would hit the pavement first. Hopefully, my suit, which should protect me, would also protect Saera.

I hit the ground hard, feeling the painful reverberations through my bones. On the other hand, feeling them at all meant I was still alive. Saera grunted as I held her to my chest. Glancing at her, I noticed that her eyes were open, and my screen told me she was undamaged. We had landed in a side alley adjacent to the main entrance of the old justice house.

My eyes shot up to the second floor, where smoke billowed out through the broken window. Movement at the gaping hole fueled the urgency to get out of there.

"Did we make it?" Saera groaned. I shoved her off my chest, and she grunted some more.

"Come on. We've got to move," I said. She shook her head and clambered to her feet, pulling me up with her. We held each other in balance for a moment, but then I heard the familiar click of a magnetic weapon. I shoved her away from me and against the wall as I caught another round of energy in my back. The integrity of my suit started to fail, increasing the pain as the energy struck and I fell to my knee. I pointed the weapon still in my hand up and fired until the figures hovering out of the hole disappeared.

"Run!" I shouted at Saera as I reached for my upper arm and slid two disks from a holster. Saera hesitated, glancing up at the shattered facade of the building as she stood with her back pinned to the wall. "Go," I said as I caught her gaze.

As she started to run down the alley toward the back of the old justice house, I flung one disk at a side entrance to the building where it stuck on a metal door. The other one I threw in the opposite direction of Saera running, where it would be likely for enforcers to come bursting through the front door. The magnetic disk clamped onto a ventilation valve near the entrance of the alley. The motion-activated explosives would pack quite a punch, taking out anyone who ran past, even an enforcer. I just hoped there weren't any innocent bystanders around at the moment of the blast.

With that, I started to run after Saera. The alley intersected a busy street, and even in these early hours, it was already bustling with people. Just as I stepped around the corner, a loud explosion sounded at the other end of the alley. Someone shouted, and people crowded around the entrance to the alley to see what was going on.

The fire evaporated quickly, but the black smoke billowed up until it would eventually hit the dome. A woman holding a young child covered her mouth with a hand as if something horrific had happened, and it probably had for the enforcers or officers that had gotten themselves caught in the blast, but there wasn't anything to see from this distance.

A middle-aged man glared at me as if I had just kicked him, but I understood what he wanted. I made a show of scanning the alley and gave him and the others my assessment of the situation.

"The disruption is a faulty valve. Please remain calm and continue your business," I said in my most official-sounding voice. Before I had met Saera and the others, I would have probably stayed and controlled the scene, but times had changed. I turned to see if I could spot Saera, and I saw her short blond hair bounce as she ran against a current of people. Without further explaining myself to the crowd, I ran after her.

As I followed it wasn't hard to determine that Saera was still focused on the thing that had gotten us into trouble in the first place. She seemed hell bent on either finding Harand Sulos, lord and master of ArtRep Enterprises, or this team of hers. Not even jumping out of a second-story window had changed her mind.

As I caught up with her, the city skyscrapers that could almost touch the dome shield loomed over us. The buildings that held the city's richest gleamed in the light penetrating the grimy dome. It wasn't as impressive as the colorful rainbows that decorated the buildings at night, but this felt less artificial and more real. Perhaps that was why no one ever bothered to rinse the dome from all the dirt and grim it had gathered over the decades. It reminded us of the reality that this planet had only a limited lifespan left.

As I jogged behind Saera, the crowd on the street diminished, and she became easier to track. Not that it was hard following her with a high-tech scanner strapped to my head, but I spotted her more easily. It was early in the day, and this area seemed to be still at rest.

These folks didn't need to get up at ungodly hours. They didn't have to stand in line for hours at a time to wait at the food distribution centers to get their rations for the week. They didn't have to work a dirty job that included scraping all kinds of gunk off the spirals of the Hymag lines. It seemed strange that within a society that promised equality for everyone, some always found a way to get ahead of the rest.

The streets were quiet enough that I felt I could intervene, and I quickened my pace. Saera must have heard me, because she glanced over her shoulder and saw me. She didn't increase her speed, though. When I was running next to her, she gave me a lopsided grin that felt fabricated. She knew she had screwed up and now felt the shame of it.

We passed an alley, and I performed a quick scan. As the data returned clear, I grabbed Saera at the waist and lifted her off the ground. She yelped and kicked out her legs, but I didn't stop until I had us tucked into a recess in the wall of the alley.

"What?" she said, disgruntled as she realized she had no place to go except to talk to me. I opened my mouth to speak but then heard Harp inside my head. From Saera's rolling eyes, I could tell she heard him too.

"What the hell were you two thinking," Harp said, not sounding at his most charming best. In fact, his voice would have sounded downright intimidating if it wasn't for the fact that he was miles away. "Saera, you compromised the mission and you..." He paused as if the right words had slipped his mind.

"We needed that intel," he continued. "This could be crucial to the survival of the people on this planet."

"Wait, what?" I said as his words sunk in. *How did we get from saving a few thousand Subterrans to the survival of everyone on this planet?* Not wanting to sound dismissive toward Subterran lives, I rephrased my thoughts and asked, "What do you mean, the people of this planet?" From what I had seen of the information scrolling down the screen, nothing had indicated anything like that.

"That is not the point," Harp said defensively, and from the tone of his voice, I sensed he was hiding something. I glanced back at Saera to gauge her response to what Harp had said, but it seemed her mind was elsewhere.

From the moment Harp had started talking, Saera's cheeks had flared bright red, and her eyes looked wild in her head. I had a feeling she could jump out of her skin at any time.

"You ignored a direct order," Harp continued to

say.

"We can talk about this later," I said, my voice hard.

Harp either ignored me or didn't care and said, "Return to the rendezvous point now!"

"You don't get to bark orders at us," Saera said, finally snapping. "I'm not your little soldier, and neither is Maecy—not anymore." Tears sprang from her eyes, and I felt my chest tighten. The word *soldier* echoed inside my head. Saera had told me that ArtRep had me working as an enforcer for almost two years. The image mirrored back inside that office at the hospital looked relatively young. How old was I, twenty-two, maybe twenty-three, but more importantly, how old had I been two years ago? *At what age had I decided to become a soldier and in what war?* Saera had been reluctant to tell me about my past, but I needed to know. I was missing too much backstory here, and Saera needed to fill me in.

"Harp, get off the line," I said.

"You listen to me—" he started to say, but I cut him off.

"Kyran, I know you're listening," I said, and I could almost taste the venom that exuded from my voice. "You cut this feed."

"I...huh..." Kyran stammered, and I was sure he faced Harp's cold stare.

"Screw this," I said under my breath. I was getting tired of this, and I ran a check with my heads-up to see if anyone might be listening in or become a threat, but as far as the device was concerned, there was no one around. No one stood to peer out a window of the two tall buildings rising to create this alley, and no one hid behind a dumpster or the pile of discarded energy cylinders further down the alley. The empty containers that were used to fuel all kinds of devices could be picked up for replacement at any time, but for now, we were alone. With a verbal command, I powered the device down and pulled it from my head.

Sweat covered my brows, and I wiped a hand over my face, and then I listened. The voices in my head remained silent, and I glanced at Saera with my own eyes. She grinned and nodded.

"They're gone," she said.

"Talk to me," I said.

"We don't have time for this," she said. "We-"

I shot her a look that basically said: "Dare to contradict me." It seemed to work. Saera leaned against the wall. Her gaze softened as she raked an uncertain hand through her messy blond strands.

"This is a bad idea," she said. This time it was my turn to snap.

"You could have killed us both back there," I said, pointing a finger at where we had come from. "Now, I think you owe me some kind of explanation or else I'm gonna kick your butt."

"I'd like to see you try," Saera said, snorting a laugh.

"All right, that's it." I threw up my hands in defeat. "I'm leaving." I turned to step out of the recess, but then I felt Saera's hand on my arm.

"Okay, okay. I'm sorry," she said as she tugged on

my arm. Her shoulders slumped as she relented to my demand. Then her knees buckled, and with her back against the wall, she slid down to sit on the ground inside the narrow recess.

I mimicked her move, sinking down the wall. Our knees touched as I took up a seat across from her and placed the heads-up on the ground by my side. She wrapped her arms around her waist as if she wanted to protect herself. Staring at the ground, she said, "You know, I said that to you once."

"What?"

"That you were going to get us both killed." With that, she looked up, and I could see the guilt appear in her eyes. "Harp had you under his spell of doing the right thing, and you ate it all up." As she spoke, her voice was soft without a hint of accusation, but filled with remorse. "He didn't know you as I did—how reckless you could be. He just saw the potential and pulled you into his merry band of rebels."

From the information stuck in what I used to call my database, I knew the rebels primarily helped workers escape the dreadful situations inside the power plants occupied by the Combined Districts of Tenebrae. I wondered if I had been involved in those kinds of operations. I resisted the urge to ask due to a greater need to hear what Saera had to say.

"It wasn't all Harp's fault. I should have warned him, but I didn't," she continued. "I was so mad at you—our last words were spoken in anger, and then you were gone." She tilted her head back and leaned it against the rough granite wall.

I wanted to say something but heard a rumble in

the distance before I felt a slight tremor in the ground. My gaze lifted upward as a shadow started to fall over us, blocking out the orange-red glow casting off the buildings. The rumble grew louder, and I felt an urge to cover my ears. Over our heads, the massive hull of an intergalactic freighter soared by, high above the city and its protective dome. It took few minutes for the large spacecraft to pass over us and about half that long for the engine noise to fade.

I couldn't remember the last time I had seen one of these ships, which didn't come as a surprise, but somehow my brain held the knowledge that it could be months between the arrival of these transports. Rumor had it that the crews on these ships were still looking for viable planets that could substitute for a new home, but people had been saying that for so many years that it seemed unlikely. Only those highest in rank would know the real purpose of these ships.

My eyes followed the vessel as it slowly disappeared in the distance, heading for the outer-rim landing platform far outside the city. The ship's interruption gave me some time to work through the information Saera had given me. It was hard to relate to her story, because even though it included me, I couldn't remember it. I could tell she was upset, and obviously, I had hurt her, but how could I apologize for something I couldn't remember? *And what would that apology have meant?*

"So," I started to say as I turned back to Saera. Her head twitched before she faced me as if I had pulled her out of some distant world. "If you hated the rebel thing, whatever they do, how come you joined it?" Her face lifted into a half-smile.

"Because I want to stop those bastards from tearing apart our families," she said, and her half-smile shifted into a malevolent grin, "and for plain old revenge."

I raised an eyebrow at the coldness in her voice, and her eyes reflected hard and cold as ice. I imagined not many people would be able to hold her stare, but somehow, I managed. A million stories seemed to exist behind those eyes, and I had played a part in most of them. I wanted to know those stories, but would it make a difference in my decisions?

"I trust you," I said, aware of the lack of logic as the words exited my mouth. "I don't know why, but deep down in my gut I know I do." I hesitated, wanting to choose my words carefully, but Saera pushed.

"So…" she said sounding impatient.

"You have to admit that this is totally insane, right!" Saera grinned and then shrugged as if I were exaggerating. "Last night, I was still carrying out verdicts to uphold the law, and now you have me breaking those laws. You can't expect me to follow you blindly." The look on her face told me she had expected just that, and she was probably right.

I let out a breath in exasperation and buried my face in my hands. As I rubbed my temples, Saera shifted, and I felt her hand on my knee. I barely detected the touch through the thick layers of my suit, but it made me glance up at her. The hardness in her eyes softened as concern replaced it.

"I know it has to be hard getting into all this without knowing why or how, and I firmly believe that you need to find those memories on your own, but since these aren't yours..." she said and then hesitated. Saera closed her eyes for a moment as she searched for what to say. The gesture made my heart sink and for some reason I dreaded her words to come. "I am going to this, with or without you, because when you first disappeared and then later they told me you were dead..."

I tried to hold her gaze as she took another pause, but it became harder to do so as her eyes started to fill with tears. "For me that was a hard thing to digest, considering we had spent most of our lives inseparable."

The pain that had been so evident in Saera's eyes the night before returned, and my heart sank even further. "And now you're sitting across from me, and we have a chance to get you back...I'm not going to sit around until someone flips a switch, able to kill you from a distance. I won't let that happen—not again. And I won't let Harp use the others for this game he is obviously playing, not without me being with—"

Saera stopped herself from finishing her sentence and took in a sharp breath as if she had just caught herself from saying something stupid. I narrowed my eyes, watching her carefully as she seemed to compose herself, and I took the time to pounder the two things she had let slip. I didn't know who she had meant by "the others," but it seemed we've been having same inkling about Harp. His words about saving the people of this planet had suggested that he knew more than he was letting on.

"Help me save the people whose lives have been stolen by ArtRep. Help me stop that bastard and save you," Saera added. "I can't answer your questions, so I need you to trust me…please." She sat back and let her head fall back against the wall.

It seemed odd that she was asking me to save myself by walking straight into the face of danger, but the pleading in her voice took me aback, and she had a point. It was better than waiting for Sulos to flip the switch. As soon as anyone found out that I had gone off the grid and that they might have a rogue enforcer on their hands, someone might decide to get rid of me.

Unfortunately, with her actions Saera had probably expedited that decision. I didn't think killing Sulos was our best option, but as time passed, the odds of him killing me grew.

Once the incident at TED was analyzed, they would know for sure that they were dealing with a faulty AR, and that wasn't something ArtRep could allow to continue. Besides, this was bigger than me. All those Subterrans living under ArtRep's thumb deserved a chance to reclaim their lives. The thought of them sent a shiver down my spine.

"What about Harp?" I asked.

"What about him?" she simply replied.

"I don't know," I said and hesitated. There was obviously a connection between these two, and I didn't know how deep it went. I didn't want to say something that might piss her off. "Something doesn't add up."

Without hesitation, Saera shrugged and said, "This is what he does best. I know he doesn't tell us everything and the occasional slip of the tongue isn't even that. He tells us exactly what we need to know to get the job done."

It seemed Saera hadn't missed a beat and was well aware that Harp wasn't telling us everything.

"And you still trust him even if he doesn't tell you everything?" I asked.

A smile formed on Saera's face as she said, "Of course." As if she read the doubt on my face she added, "and you will too—again."

I let out a long breath that caused Saera to eye me thoughtfully. All of this was a lot to take in, and it seemed more than my brain could handle now, but what was it I had to lose? My sanity might have been at risk, but I guessed that was overrated anyway. I grinned at the thought that I had probably lost it already and looked Saera in the eyes.

"All right," I said as I nodded my head, and that brought a faint smile on Saera's face.

"Yeah," she said under her breath.

"Yeah," I replied, mimicking her whispered voice. Saera seemed relieved and exhilarated at the same time, as if she couldn't wait to get moving.

"The others?" I asked as an afterthought, hoping to catch her at an unguarded moment. I cocked my head and scrutinized her.

"Crap," Saera muttered under her breath. "I thought I had explained about the questions."

I shot her a look that more or less said, *I can't help myself*, and shrugged. She narrowed her eyes at me and bit her lower lip. As she shook her head in mock disbelief, something I couldn't quite read flashed across her eyes, but it brightened her face, and so I didn't think it to be a bad thing.

Then she said, "That's for you to find out."

I groaned and this time I shook my head in disbelief; this was starting to get annoying.

The sound of a vehicle passing the alley at high speed pulled me away from her gaze. The noise made me aware of the city waking up around us. Of course, TED would be on full alert after our little visit, and I could imagine them informing ArtRep of an incident involving one of their so-called ARs. But would ArtRep prepare for a visit from us, or would they have every enforcer in the city looking for two criminals? Perhaps our little mishap at the old justice house might work to our advantage.

A plan started to form inside my head as I glanced around the buildings and saw an old, rusted ladder leading up to a walkway. Similar constructions led up all the way to the top of the building. The structure looked old, but it would do. With a smile on my face, I turned to Saera. She watched me with a thoughtful expression.

I grabbed the heads-up lying next to me on the ground and pursed my mouth to blow away some of the dust that had gathered on the darkened glass. Ignoring Saera's gaze, I got to my feet and patted dirt from my suit. Then I held a hand out to her.

"Wouldn't they keep more information on an ArtRep computer than they would on a TED computer?" I asked. Saera's eyes widened as she looked up at me. Her gaze shifted to my outstretched hand before she took it with her own.

"Probably," she said as I helped her get up.

Chapter fifteen

Reece

The tension in the room was palpable after Maece had interrupted the feed and left us staring at a blank screen. Her defiance brought a smile to my face, and I couldn't stop grinning, not even as Harp shot me a disapproving glare.

"That's my girl," I said elatedly.

"You won't be grinning like such an idiot after they get themselves killed," Harp said sharply. He was right of course, but it didn't wipe the smile completely off my face. I knew Maece and Saera had a knack for beating the odds. They had done it all their lives—surviving through the harshest conditions, taking care of not only themselves, but also the small band of misfits they had gathered around them over the years.

My eyes left Harp's hard glare and fell on Riffy before they shifted to Kelle. We almost had our gang back together, and we wouldn't let anyone come between that.

Kelle caught my gaze, and her dark eyes were telling, even with the lack of expression on her face.

We had been at this long enough to know each other's thoughts. I grinned and even showed some teeth as I noticed the tiniest of twitches of Kelle's mouth.

"Riffy, my man," I said, slapping him on the shoulder, "get our gear ready." Seemingly without thinking about it, Riffy grabbed one of our bags off the floor when he caught Harp glaring at him. Riffy froze instantly. It wasn't hard to see Harp could still get to him.

Kelle on the other hand crossed her arms over her chest, scrutinizing the scene and shooting Riffy a hard glare of her own. That didn't go unnoticed either and it pulled Riffy out of Harp's grip. He shrugged as he continued picking up our stuff and found his way to one of the empty tables standing of to a side of the platform.

"What the hell do you think you're doing?" Harp asked. I pushed out my lower lip in an exaggerated display of disbelief.

"Oh, c'mon, you didn't have us make this trip to watch the show on the screens," I replied. Behind Harp, I could see the shock on Kyran's face as he fumbled for his HDA and stuck it between his teeth. Harp glanced over his shoulder, but Kyran had already busied himself by tapping his virtual keyboard. Seemingly satisfied that his subordinate wasn't paying any attention, Harp took a step closer until his face was inches from mine.

"Suggesting bringing you in has created this mess in the first place," he said in his calm voice. "It's bad enough Saera makes her decisions based on emotions. I can't have an entire team out there unable to act rationally."

He turned his head and his gaze shifted to Kelle. It was a subtle hint, but I caught it. He felt we were too emotionally involved and he was right—we were. But then, so was he. His gaze shifted back to me, and I had known him long enough to recognize his *this-is-for-the-greater-good* speech was about to kick in, so I decided to intervene.

I stepped closer. If it had been anyone else, I would have grabbed his elbow and pulled him out of earshot, but that would never work with a man like Harp. As expected, he didn't even flinch as I invaded his personal space and spoke close to his ears.

"Don't forget I know you, Harp, and I know your objectives," I said in a whisper and hoped Kelle or Riffy wouldn't hear. "You never needed the information gathered at TED. You already knew all about those Subterrans, so you probably went in there for Kyran to find some code or door key that will get you into ArtRep. Am I getting close to the truth, Harp?" I waited a moment to see if he wanted to add something to what I had said, but then I continued. "This is exactly how you wanted it to turn out, so don't give me that emotionally involved crap. Don't pretend I don't know why the council is pressuring you to get inside the ArtRep buildings."

I backed off and wanted to step away from him, but in a quick move Harp grabbed my jacket and pulled me close again.

He let out a slow breath that tickled my ear before he said, "You and Maece knew when you signed up for this that Sulos was using Subterrans and that it's probably part of a bigger plan. We needed to find out what Sulos was up to. Maece becoming an enforcer was the only way to get our hands on the technology that could make that happen. I'm not going to apologize for that."

Harp released his grip on my jacket, but before I stepped back, I said, "Except Maece doesn't remember, and Saera doesn't know any of that. Still, you had no problem sending them in blind, and now you want to pretend that you don't want us to go after them."

I lifted my chin as I held Harp's stone-cold gaze. My attempt to stare him down failed as I caught Kelle eyeing the exchange with a frown on her face. I wasn't sure she hadn't heard anything, but I had a feeling she would have spoken up if she had. Kelle tended to be protective of the ones she loved, especially Saera, and would lash out at anyone who threatened their safety in any way—even Harp. Those specific character traits that I would usually connect with Maece had rubbed off on Kelle over the years.

"I need someone in there I can trust not to make this about anything else, but the information we need to appease the council so that they will take actions against ArtRep to save our people," Harp said as if our little exchange hadn't happened. I noted that his words were carefully chosen and weren't far from the truth.

The council was aware of the abuse of our people in the plants and how ArtRep used them as enforcers, but helping them wasn't their primary agenda. They wanted to know what Sulos was up to, and I had a feeling that they wanted in on whatever he had planned. With the right intel, the council might even be able to force his hand.

"I know the stakes," I said as I forced myself to keep to the script that Maece and I had agreed to years ago. "We all do—we've read the files and seen the images downloaded from TED." I might not agree with everything Harp does, but that didn't mean I'd betray the trust he held in us.

Harp raised his chin, but his eyes didn't lose the suspicion in them, and he was right for it. Not telling my friends about Harp's, but mostly the council's, hidden agenda had been one of the hardest things I ever had to do—that and saying goodbye to Maece before ArtRep turned her into an enforcer.

"Then you understand."

"I understand," I replied, "and I know you understand that we work as a team and that whatever Saera has decided as to what we should or shouldn't do—she knows we'll be there to back her up."

I straightened my shoulders to underline my resolve. "They have a kill switch that could kill many of our own, including Maece, and if Saera and she set their minds on fixing this problem, then we are going to back them up. So I suggest you start coordinating."

Harp frowned before he started shaking his head.

"Don't be an ass," Kelle said, watching the exchange. "You know you won't be able to stop them or us. Besides, you were the one who involved us in the first place."

Harp turned to face her, surely with the intent to give a death ray glare, but as soon as his eyes caught hers, his expression softened.

Harp had always had a soft spot for the young woman. She had been the youngest back when he'd brought her to us, and as unimaginable as that might seem now, Kelle had always yearned for his affection.

We never were the typical loving family, but Harp had given us a roof over our heads and, with his limited abilities toward affection, tried to be a father figure. To his credit, he hadn't started training any of us until we'd reached the age of fourteen.

Harp held Kelle's gaze for a long moment before his eyes turned up toward the dome-shaped ceiling. He shook his head, and a hint of a smile graced his face. Then he turned to me and said, "Gear up. Then we'll talk."

With that, Harp turned and walked away from us. I flashed a wide grin at Kelle, who had molded her face back into her brooding glare. She might not have known she was arguing for something Harp had planned for us to do anyhow, but I appreciated her effort. I just wished I didn't have to keep my friends in the dark, but at this point, it couldn't be helped.

"Seeeee," I said elongating the word, "I always knew you were his favorite." Kelle's mouth twitched, but feeling gracious with a hint of gratitude, I wanted to spare her the discomfort of having to forfeit a smile. So I wrapped an arm around her and pulled her into a hug. I bent to kiss the top of her head, and then without giving it a second thought, I released her and made my way to Riffy. Imagining her cheeks going bright red put a smile on my face, but I refused the urge to look back.

Chapter sixteen

Maece

With Saera in tow, progress was a bit slower than it would have been on my own. Without an exoskeleton suit, she couldn't jump from rooftop to rooftop—at least not the bigger gaps—and once we neared ArtRep Enterprises, the height of the buildings would have been nauseating to most people. Saera hadn't seemed bothered by heights, though, which was a good thing.

I turned to look behind me and saw her glancing over the edge of the glass structure. She wobbled and threw out her arms to steady her balance.

"Hasn't anyone ever told you not to look down while you're walking on a glass overpass between two skyscrapers?" I yelled at her. Her arms still waving like one of those flying animals that used to live on this planet, she glanced up to face me.

"No," she said exasperated, "but then I've never done this before."

I glanced down and scanned the street below. The people walking the streets looked no bigger than a pinprick. As I zoomed in with the heads-up, the picture cleared, and I started to recognize certain figures. Figures like the enforcers roaming the streets.

Instead of their usual pairings, I noticed they moved in groups of four and even six. Fortunately, we hadn't encountered any of them up on the rooftops. We were pretty high up, and perhaps enforcers didn't think it possible for us to travel along the roofs of the tall structures. It could also be that they had never considered it. I wouldn't put it past Kyran to have placed the suggestion in my head. Either way, I was glad to see most of the enforcers heading for the outskirts of the city. It made me feel hopeful that there wouldn't be many of them guarding the ArtRep building.

"Maybe we can use the front door next time," Saera said as she drew closer, "instead of this insane excursion that is probably going to get me killed."

The structure used as a bridge connecting two of what were three towers was wide enough to walk over comfortably, except someone had decided to use see-through glass in the construction of the overpass.

This had been a complaint of many of the people either living or working in the towers. One needed a strong stomach to walk over the glass to reach the other side. If you looked down to see where to place your feet, you would glance down a five-hundred-foot drop. Walking across the overpass's roof didn't prove to be a cakewalk either.

"You okay?" I asked and held out a hand for her to take. She ignored my question but took my hand greedily, and I guided her across the last few feet of the bridge.

"Although," she said climbing over the railing to get to solid ground, "I do prefer this to swinging from a rooftop."

The memory of Saera dangling off that rope brought a smile to my face.

"I thought you did rather well," I said, managing to contain myself from blurting out into full-blown laughter.

"Oh, shut up," she replied and started walking across the roof.

"Hey, you were the one that wanted to do this," I shouted after her. Ignoring me, she pointed at the third building with a similar bridge connecting the two structures.

"That's it, right?" I said. I already knew the answer, because the name and location of the building were something TED had decided I needed to know, but it seemed the question formed on its own accord, and it felt like a familiar thing to do.

"That's it," she said as I stopped by her side. "Actually, this is one big ArtRep building, but that is the one where Sulos's office is located."

We stood there staring at it for a while, and I wondered which one of us would be the one to bring it up first. It was one thing to break into a building, but something else to break into the files of a highly secured system. We needed Kyran, whether we liked it or not. I didn't want to be the one who suggested that we needed to contact Harp, so I hoped Saera would come to her senses. As I waited for that to happen, I let my head fall back and stared up at the sky.

Somewhere buried inside my head sat memories of blue skies with white clouds. As part of the Tenebrae Enforcer Department, we were required to know the history of our planet, and those blue skies were part of that. These days we didn't get blue skies anymore. These days we didn't get to see any of the sky most of the time, except for that massive bright-and-orange disk hovering over us. It was as if peering into the flame of a candle so close that everything around it faded into nothingness.

"Do you think we should call Kyran?" Saera said. Her voice pulled me away from the sun, and I lowered my head to face her.

"That's what you were waiting for me to say, right," she said as she leaned against the fence that was meant to protect us from a five-hundred-foot drop.

"I was thinking about it," I replied, "but now that you mention it…"

Saera narrowed her eyes.

"Well, I guess we both were thinking the same thing," she said. I shrugged.

"We could use the help getting in there."

"Do it," she said.

I used the heads-up to reestablish a connection before I said,

"Harp? Kyran? Anyone out there?"

"Hello."

Surprised at the sound of the tiny voice, I glanced at Saera.

"Tyrel, is that you?" Saera replied.

"Hi, Miss Lux," Tyrel said. The image of the shy

young woman with the multicolored hair flashed into the forefront of my mind, and I wondered what she was doing on the line.

"Where are Harp and Kyran?" I asked.

"Oh…hi, eh…Miss Lux," she said in her timid voice. "Shall I get them for you?"

"Yes, you do that," I said, sounding more condescending than I had planned. Saera gave me a hard look and shook her head disapprovingly. "I mean, please, if you would," I added quickly. "Thank you, Tyrel." As soon as the connection ended, I said to Saera, "Better."

"She's a good kid, but insecure," she said. "She just needs a little guidance."

"I'd be insecure with that hair," I said. Saera sighed and turned her head to face the building across from us. It stood at least three stories taller than this one, which meant the glass overpass didn't connect with the roof.

"Saera, Maece, you there," Harp's voice spoke over the coms. Before he could say anything else, Saera spoke up.

"Colrin, if you start moping again, we'll cut you off." There wasn't much threat in her voice, but it seemed to work.

"Are the both of you okay?" Harp asked, sounding concerned.

"Fine," I replied for both of us.

"You're at the ArtRep Tribes Center," Kyran exclaimed. The line fell silent for a moment, and I imagined the look Harp must have given Kyran to clamp his mouth shut.

"Plan?" Harp asked.

"We figured we might get you that information after all," Saera said.

"Does this mean you have changed your mind about Sulos?" Harp said sharply. Saera cleared her throat before pulling a face that made me wonder if what she was about to say would be sincere.

"Maecy and I had a talk, and she convinced me of the bigger picture," she said. "We need that intel and, with it, to find a way to disable the bombs stuck in our people's heads."

Because with the heads-up she wouldn't be able to read the shock on my face, I poked a finger into her chest and lifted my hands and shoulders in a *what-the-hell* gesture. I didn't even know most of the bigger picture, so how was I supposed to convince her of it?

Saera shook her head dismissively and pressed a finger to her lips. I dropped my arms in dismay and waited for Harp's reply. It took a while as if he needed to think it over, but then he said, "On what tower are they exactly?"

Saera perked up and grin formed on her face. Then she planted a fist against my shoulder. The gesture was meant to be playful, but as soon as her fist connected with my suit, she pulled her hand back, waving it in pain, and held it to her chest.

"What the hell is that thing made of," she said in a whisper as if the guys on the other side wouldn't hear us.

"We're on the one in the middle," I said in answer to Harp's question.

"All right," Harp's harsh voice said as he came back over the coms. "We need to develop a plan, and it might take a while. In the meantime, you wait there."

"So, what…you think this is a good idea now?" I asked, ignoring Saera as she glared at me wide-eyed.

"Tyrel will explain," Harp said before he fell silent.

"Great," Saera muttered and sank to the ground with her back against the fence.

"Eh…Ms. Lux?" Tyrel's voice chimed in my head.

"Yeah," Saera and I replied in synchronized voices.

"Oh…eh…I mean—" Tyrel started to say until Saera cut her off.

"Why don't you start calling us by our first names like you've always done. Might be less confusing," she said. "I think Maecy can handle it."

"Okay," Tyrel replied hesitantly. "Ms.…I mean Maece, could you run a scan of the main building?"

"Sure," I said and pointed my heads-up in the direction of the building as I moved to stand next to Saera where she sat on the ground. With all the light bouncing off the windows, the building looked almost white by the green overlaying my vision.

"What's your first name?" I asked Tyrel as letters scrolled across my screen.

"Just Tyrel," she said, "or Ty."

"Okay, Ty. Is that your first or last name?" I asked. The words had barely left my mouth when I felt a tap on my leg. As I glanced down to face Saera, she wore this wan expression and slightly shook her head.

"Maece. The scan," Tyrel said.

"Right, sorry."

As my gaze shifted back to the building, the line fell silent. I figured there to be a story behind Tyrel's one name and apparently a personal one, although Saera seemed to know the details.

I had almost finished my pass of the building and listened to Tyrel's fingers tap on the smooth surface of her workstation as the young woman's hesitant voice came over the coms.

"I don't remember it," she said. "We, uh...fled from one of the Tenebrae power plants when I was six, and my mom didn't survive the trip. I was raised inside the Subterran foster system, but never stuck around long enough to share a name with anyone, so..."

I sighed heavily, not sure what to say when she added, "There, I'm done."

"I'm sorry," I said, but it came out as a sort of afterthought that didn't do her past justice. "I mean..." My voice faded, but it seemed Tyrel wasn't looking for sympathy.

She said, "That was a long time ago, and I made it. Others haven't been that lucky and are still stuck at those plants."

From the expression on Saera's face, I could tell she had also recognized the determination in Tyrel's voice.

"Was that what the intel was about?" Saera asked.

Tyrel confirmed the question and then said, "The plants are producing a lot more power than is necessary to sustain the cities. They are running at a hundred and twenty percent constantly, and they have been for years. Those plants were never built for that kind of production schedule, and the effort needed by the people is horrendous—they are dying down there." Her voice broke on the last sentence.

"What!" Saera exclaimed as she sat up straighter. "That isn't possible. We would have known if that were happening. The Subterra government would have intervened."

"It's true," I said as I turned to sit next to Saera. I had seen some of the intel before I broke the connection and had run after Saera. The images of men, women, and children forced to hard labor had remained fresh in my memories.

"How did this happen without us knowing about it?" she asked. Saera shook her head in dismay as if what Tyrel had said couldn't be possible. Shock and disbelief radiated from her face, and I placed a hand on her shoulder as a moment of silence fell over us.

I had some previous knowledge of the power plants. There were four of them within the Combined Districts of Tenebrae. All four were remnants of what we had lost, conquered by Tenebrae during the war. After the war ended, both sides had come to an agreement to leave the four plants under the management of Tenebrae. This so-called peace agreement had forced Subterra to relinquish these major underground power suppliers along with all its workers.

Subterra already controlled the main food resources, and the districts wanted something substantial to even the odds. A deal was made that had left thousands of Subterrans stranded within the new Tenebrae borders. The way the information sat configured in my mind, I would have assumed that those power plants were run and worked by the same people as the cities above. Although not perfect, the people living aboveground were treated with at least some form of dignity. As an enforcer, I never had any reason or memories to doubt that this would be different for the people living underground.

"What are they doing with the power?" I asked.

Saera's head perked up, and her mouth opened, but she waited for Tyrel's answer.

"We don't know," she replied. "That's why Harp has decided to go with your plan and break into ArtRep to find out."

"Oh," I said.

A crack sounded over the line as if the transmission was interrupted, but Tyrel's voice came back a second later.

"Kyran's calling," she said. "I'm breaking the connection. Contact you later."

The line disconnected, but it didn't silence the noise in my head. There were too many unanswered questions. Answers to questions that felt as if they were on the edges of my memories, trying to bleed through, but unable to penetrate my thoughts. Frustrated, I removed the heads-up and let my head fall back against the fence. I dropped the device in my lap and pinched the bridge of my nose.

"You okay?" Saera asked.

I nodded without turning to her. "Too much information to process," I added.

Saera snorted a laugh. "You should have plenty of space up there," she said. Somehow, I recognized the attempt at a joke in her words, but it didn't resonate. From the corners of my eye, I squinted at her.

"Too much?" she asked, sounding innocent.

I just tilted my head back and groaned.

Harp had left us hanging for several hours now, and meanwhile, the planet had started to turn its back on the sun. A blood-red sky bled from the horizon up into the semidarkness. The city had taken on its usual colorful facade of brightly lit buildings, and I had to admit that it made the city easy on the eyes. It didn't stop the thoughts from running wild inside my head.

"Whose teddy bear did Kyran stick in my head?" I asked. The image of that grimy bear, with its squashed nose and beady eyes, kept popping up in my mind. Boredom had left me with nothing else to do except sifting through the few memories I did have. Saera didn't reply, and I glanced at her, wondering if she had fallen asleep, but her eyes were open.

I had a feeling that I might snap at her if she intended to shut me down again with her little speech about why it was important to her not to share my background, even though I had promised to refrain from asking too many questions. To my surprise, she said, "Mine."

I drew out the silence after her admission, hoping

it would prompt her to explain. "Then yours after you coerced me into giving it to you."

Chuckling, I pulled a leg up to my chest to prod an arm up on it and shifted to face her.

"I doubt I'd be able to coerce you into anything."

"Well, you did back then," she said with a tiny smirk, "exactly four hours and six minutes after you came to live with us."

"Us…," I said hesitantly. "With you and Harp, you mean."

Saera grunted as if I had said something preposterous, but then gave me long sideways glance as if thinking whether to continue. It seemed obvious that her refusing to share was a form of protection, but I wondered if it was herself or me she wanted to protect. She finally blinked and snapped out of it. Then she shifted on her butt to face me, crossed her legs, and sighed with exaggeration.

"We kinda stuck together after our parents died," she said, "and no, not our…ours, but first yours and later mine—we lived in the same building."

"How'd they die?" I asked.

"Same as mine—work mishap in one of the power plants."

Frowning, I stared at her.

"Surprise," she said with an insincere, broad smile, "we're Tenebrae power plant brats." It dawned on me that Saera and I had a similar background to Tyrel's. Like her, we also must have fled the power plants located in Tenebrae occupied territory.

Saera opened her mouth to say something else as a green light on my heads-up started to blink. I picked up the device but hesitated to put it on. I locked eyes with Saera and regretted the interruption. Even if there might still be a way to reverse this amnesia thing by removing the device in the back of my head, I felt a need to know things now.

"Finally," Saera said as I placed the device on my head. A moment later Harp's voice came over the coms.

"We've determined your entry point, and where to go from there," Harp said. "Your little stunt has most of the enforcers roaming the city in search for two female saboteurs, and most of the building's security guards are guarding the lower levels of the building."

A bunch of data scrolled down my screen, including a scheme of the building itself. I glanced at Saera, who looked anxious as she listened intently to what Harp had to say. "You'll need to get into Sulos's office which is on the top floor. From there Kyran and Tyrel will guide you through the process of getting the intel," he added.

"Jeez, Harp," I said trying to relieve some of the tension, "that was at least three sentences."

Saera's lips straightened into a thin line, but I noticed the tiniest of twitches, which could have been mistaken for a smile. "Come on," I said after Harp's lack to reply. I got to my feet and then held a hand out to Saera. "Let's get this over with."

Chapter seventeen

Maece

Slowly, we walked across the glass overpass that bridged between the second and third building. The sight of Saera's face going even paler than I would have thought possible made me decide to stick close to her. I felt the slightest tug on my belt as she held on to it while I guided us across the glass panels.

"You didn't seem to have this much trouble with heights before," I said, trying to keep a conversation going, although it occurred to me this probably wasn't the best topic to keep her mind off the five-hundred-foot drop below our boots.

"This is not fear of heights," she replied. "This is fear of insanity, and I don't want to talk about it."

"Then what do you want to talk about?"

"Nothing," she said adamantly. Silence followed as we neared the building, and I looked up. This building was taller than the one we had left behind us, with three added stories on top of it. This didn't enable us to climb the fence as we had with the other building.

"Almost there," I said, hoping to sound

reassuring. Saera clung to my belt as I sensed her stopping. I turned to face her, which forced her to release my belt.

"Whaah," she yelped and grabbed my arms.

"Hey, hey…look at me," I said as I placed my hands on her shoulders. Her eyes turned to face me, but she didn't seem to find the comfort she needed from staring at the reflection of her own fear. I lifted the heads-up up on my head and tried again. "We're gonna do this together, okay."

She cleared her throat and nodded. Keeping my movement to a minimum, I unhooked a clasp from my belt and uncoiled about seven feet of cable. I looped the cable around Saera's waist, fastened it, and then hooked it onto my belt, all the while keeping my eyes on her.

When we first started our trek across the city, using the buildings to keep us from being spotted by the enforcers, Saera didn't seem that troubled by heights. It must have happened when she was forced to jump from the entertainment-center building.

I had jumped the gap with the aid of my suit, but Saera wasn't able to make the distance. After her jump, I was supposed to steady her rope, but I fumbled it, and she fell several feet before I regained my grip. Fortunately, none of the visitors enjoying an afternoon of virtual reality features had heard her screams. The incident had her pretty shaken up, though, and it seemed to last.

Her glance followed mine as I scanned the smooth surface of the building. At least the surface appeared to be smooth, but I was glad to see the shield brokers jutting out. The square shaped metal blocks were evenly positioned all over the sides of the building and acted as fuses for when the building's individual shields went up.

The dome protecting the city was old, and many of the privileged folks living around here had lost their faith in its reliability—so they made sure that the buildings they lived in had shield backups. If indeed the shield failed, an underground Hymag line would be able to bring the residents to safety deep underground. The government provided certain individuals or groups with these kinds of redundant systems. Most of them lived around these parts—near the ArtRep building and government facilities. Fortunately for us, along with the ventilation grids, these shield brokers would work as a foothold.

"Chester," Saera suddenly said.

I turned to her and asked, "Who?"

"The bear," she added as her wild-eyed gaze caught mine. "That's the bear's name."

I grinned and tugged on the rope. The force of my pull made her take a step forward.

"Come on. You can do this," I said and stepped up to the wall to find my first handhold.

As I climbed, I kept glancing down and held a diligent eye on Saera, who seemed to have turned to talking to keep her nerves in check. She took her time, placing each foot with care on one of the fuses and calculating every step. As she did, she talked.

"Chester was this kid that lived on our block," she said, "just a few floors down."

"I named a bear after a kid I knew?" I asked.

"No," Saera said exasperated, "it was my bear, remember."

"Oh yeah, and I coerced him from you," I said. "Tell me—how did I do that as I was what four…five years old?" Looking up, I saw we had almost reached the top. After that, we needed to climb the fence, but then we'd be safe—well…safer.

I found another foothold and steadied myself as I felt a sudden hand grab my calf. I froze, afraid to move until Saera found something else to grip. With my heads-up, I noticed her elevated heart rate and heavy breathing.

"How did you know that?" she asked.

"Know what?"

"That you were four or five."

I glanced down at her, not sure how to answer, and decided on, "You told me."

Saera shook her head, and with my heads-up, I could clearly see her eyes had gone wide, but her fear pheromones had decreased. *She had told me, hadn't she?*

"So how did I do it?" I asked, ignoring her reaction. I hoped to keep up the distraction.

"You were staying with me and my mom one night when your parents and my dad were at work at the plant," she said. "There…there was an explosion, and they never came home."

I blew out a breath as I released the last fuse and grabbed hold of the first bar that would lead us up and over the fence. This wasn't the story I had hoped for, and it didn't make for a good distraction. Finding out both of my parents had died on the same day as

Saera's dad probably should have hit me harder than it did, but then I didn't remember my parents.

Saera, on the other hand, did, and it must have been hard for her to revisit those memories. I hated to be the one to bring that pain to the surface, and I considered changing the subject but didn't know how, and for some reason, the fragmented memory of that bear seemed important. It was the only thing I had that represented something of the person I used to be. Besides, I had finally managed to get Saera to talk, and I wasn't about to shut her down.

"That must have been hard on you and your mom," I said.

Saera grunted something after reaching for another fuse, and she stuck her foot into the next ventilation hole.

"It wasn't easy," she added between her labored breaths. "Mom was suddenly on her own with three mouths to fill."

"I stayed with you after that?"

"Yep," she said, sounding a bit more upbeat. "I suggested to Mom to kick you out, but she wouldn't part with the doll-eyed, frizzy-haired you, and I learned to live with it."

"That's very gracious of you," I replied as I reached for the next bar and pulled myself up.

"That's me, gracious and—" she started to say, but the sound of a boot sole squeaking on the smooth surface cut her off.

"Oh shit," she muttered. I tried to brace myself, but Saera's sudden weight jerking on my middle pulled me off balance, and I lost my footing.

Fortunately, my fingers were locked around the bar as my body slammed into the building.

A thud followed, accompanied by a yelp. My heart skipped a beat at the thought that the cable I had used to secure Saera with might have snapped, but then I registered her weight tugging at my waist.

"Hold on!" I yelled without anything else sensible to say.

"Hold on to what!" she shouted.

Glancing down, I saw her arms flail and thrash against the smooth surface of the building, trying to find one of the fuses for a hold. Her boots thumbed and squeaked in a frantic matter against the slick surface, and her body swung from left to right.

It occurred to me that anyone inside the building seeing her would immediately alert the guards, but that wouldn't matter if Saera were to fall or if we were both to fall.

"Stop thrashing," I said in a loud voice, hoping she would register. Instead, Saera cried out in fear, and her feet bashed even harder against the panels. I only had one choice, and that was to pull us both up and over the fence before the cable snapped. Using the added strength that came from the built-in exoskeleton of my suit, I started to climb. I grunted as I found my footing and grabbed the next bar.

"Don't you dare let me fall!" Saera yelled. The fear in her voice was evident, but focusing on my task, I failed to answer. Jamming my foot into a slit, I forced myself to stand straight and wrapped an arm around one of the bars. I turned sideways and reached for the cable. As I caught it, Saera looked up, eyes wide. Trying to steady the cable, I wished I wasn't wearing that damn heads-up so I could look her in the eyes. I wanted to calm her, but my voice would have to do.

"Easy," I said, "just calm down—"

"Calm down?" she exclaimed before I could finish my sentence.

"Look up to your left," I said, ignoring her. "There is a fuse right above you."

She managed to grab it, and the back-and-forth movement of the cable lessened.

"Now raise your right foot a few inches," I said. "There is a vent right there."

Saera lowered her head, attempting to see what I was talking about.

"Don't look down," I commanded.

She froze and then looked up.

"Trust me: it's there," I said.

Easing her foot up, she found the hole and relieved the stress on the cable. I huffed out a breath as the strain of her weight lifted off my waist.

We both took a second to catch our breath and find our bearings before I managed to guide her with my voice, telling her where her hands and feet should go next. Slowly she clambered up the last few feet until she could raise herself by my side, and I wrapped an arm around her. She glanced up, eyes wild from the adrenaline pumping through her veins.

Those blue eyes bored into me, finding mine through the visor as if the tinted glass wasn't even there. Beyond those wide pupils, I found something else—gratitude maybe—something that triggered a series of images bleeding through the blockage. Saera and me, sitting on a narrow bed in a tiny room. Bleak walls surrounded us while sobbing could be heard from the connecting room. Saera's arms were wrapped around me, and my tiny chubby fingers were clamped around that grimy-looking bear.

Chapter eighteen

Reece

My heart raced inside my chest, and I noticed Kelle's tight grip on my upper arm as I peered through the long-range image enhancer. For a second, relief that Kelle wasn't holding me with the prosthetic arm dulled the panic raging inside my chest. If she had used her robot arm, I'd probably be squealing in pain from her tight grip.

"Oh, my god, I can't watch," Riffy said as he covered his eyes to shield them from seeing Saera dangle off a five-hundred-foot-high building. I held my breath, having my own trouble watching the scene unfold. Fortunately, Maece kept it together, helping Saera to find her footing and climb the rest of the building. At my side, Kelle sighed in relief, and I closed my eyes as I remembered to breathe again.

Seeing her for the first time in so long—actually seeing her—reminded me of how much I had missed Maece. The thought of losing either of them wasn't something my mind could deal with, so I lingered as I watched her remove her heads-up to talk to Saera.

I had to stifle a gasp, not to draw Kelle's or

Riffy's attention, but the woman standing on the rooftop of that building took my breath away, which I would have called a cliché if it hadn't just happened. Her dark skin reflected bronze, almost golden, in the sun's gleam, adding to her statuesque appearance. Shorter, less frizzy hair from what I remembered, had become a mess from wearing the heads-up, but zooming in on her face, I could tell that her eyes held the same intensity that they had always held.

The second building of the ArtRep towers gave us an excellent view of the two women who had bridged the glass walkway and had climbed to the top of the third structure. That building held all the information needed to save our people and remove ArtRep's final hold on Maece. She'd be free of them after we removed the device from her head.

The prospect was a good one, but I couldn't help wondering what else we were going to uncover. What secrets did those mainframes inside that building hold, and what was the council or the Subterran government going to do with that information?

I had a feeling Harp had the same suspicions as I had that there had to be more going on. In fact, it wasn't just a feeling—I knew he did. Knowing Harp, he'd probably have several contingency plans ready just in case he learned something he didn't like. Harp might act like the loyal soldier doing the council's and the government's bidding, but his loyalty was to the Subterran people and, if I'd be honest, to us. He might not act like it all the time, but over the years, he had proven to all of us that he cared.

The so-called terrorist attack on TED had set the

law enforcement department on a frenzy. Large groups of enforcers searched the city to find the aggressors, leaving the ArtRep buildings only guarded by their in-house security. No one had ever attempted to gain access to the highly secured buildings, but then we never had anyone with enforcer skills at our disposal.

Harp still feared Maece's mind was too fragile. Kyran had done everything within his power to make sure that her brain was ready to trust Saera and distrust her former employers, but that didn't mean it would keep. Her mind could relapse—doubting her decisions—and this worried Harp.

I had known about the memory loss even before Saera had spotted Maece in that broadcast. We all knew Maece had volunteered to infiltrate Tenebrae and gather information. What only Harp and I knew was that she had volunteered to get herself caught and become an enforcer.

She had confided in me, making me swear not to tell anyone. That had been the hardest thing I ever had to do, lying to the others and eventually letting her go. I hadn't agreed with Maece's decision, and I had even tried to talk her out of it, but that lady had always been of the stubborn kind.

If I hadn't known better, I would have sworn that she and Harp were related. She thought her cause to be just, and nothing would have kept her from trying to help the people stuck at TED forced to work as mindless drones for the Combined Districts of Tenebrae. She knew there might be some alternative motives behind the council's actions, but she firmly believed that getting our hands on enforcer gear would give us the edge we needed. That it would gain us access to intel that would help us free our people.

We probably all felt like that, growing up under the tight rule of the sun-lover cities and all. If Harp hadn't pulled us out, we would probably already have died working in one of those power plants. Although I'm not sure if any of the others would have taken the risks Maece had.

It suddenly occurred to me that I didn't know if Saera had found out about me knowing of Maece volunteering, and that veered my thoughts into a different direction. Saera would kill me if she found out. She was so devastated after Maece had left, thinking she'd died.

None of us could console her, except maybe Kelle. I glanced down at the tiny woman, noticing she had released her grip on my arm and now held onto the railing surrounding the edge of the roof with an absent smile on her face. She should make a habit of that, because it lit up her face.

For a second, I wondered if she would have told me if Saera had found out about me knowing of Maece's volunteering. Saera would have surely confided in Kelle, and I then decided Kelle would have given me the heads-up. I blew out a breath, figuring I was safe for a little while longer.

"Is it okay to look?" Riffy asked in a high-pitched squeak. His eyes were clamped shut and his face contorted into a grimace. I smacked him in the head.

"Come on, you big idiot. Let's get ready," I said, picking up my backpack.

Maece and Saera had reached the top of the tall building across from us and would surely be working with Kyran to override security. I stopped at the door leading back inside and waited for Kelle and Riffy to catch up.

Like me, they wore a similar getup to the enforcer's suit. It was more of a Subterran knockoff without a lot of the high-tech bells and whistles, but it added some muscle strength because of the similar exoskeleton. Unfortunately, it didn't do much to protect you if you got shot by a magnetic blast.

Despite the similar clothes, the pair approaching me resembled nothing of the bred-for-killing, broad-shouldered enforcers. Kelle almost looked like a child playing dress up, and Riffy barely fit into his suit. But there wasn't anyone I would rather have by my side than the tiny sourpuss and the oversized dingbat— although I wouldn't have minded adding Maece and Saera to the lineup.

Tyrel's voice piped up in my head as I opened the door to gain access inside.

"Reece, can you hear me?" she asked in her usual tentative voice.

"Loud and clear," I replied. Kelle tapped her ear with a nod, and Riffy gave me a thumbs-up. "As do the others."

"Good," Tyrel said, "you are cleared to move down one level and start across the walkway, but it might take a little longer to gain you access on the other side."

"What's the holdup?" I asked, not liking these kinds of surprises. It had taken Kyran quite a while to get his programming in place before he managed to guide us past the security measures and guards. He hadn't said it in so many words, but I knew for sure he had been only able to do that because of the data that had been gathered at TED.

I didn't have to be a genius to figure out that he'd been hacking at some new code—his cursing and questioning remarks had done that for me. Kyran had assured me that he would get us inside once he had gained access to the system with the help of Maece's head-up, but it had taken a long time.

Because Harp was reluctant to trust Maece's state of mind, he hadn't told them about us tagging along, but I knew it shouldn't come as a surprise to Saera. I just hoped Maece wouldn't shoot us since she didn't know us anymore. There was also the fact that Saera had clearly protested our involvement. That was something that didn't surprise me as my eyes fell on Kelle. It wasn't that she doubted our abilities, but over the years, we had developed a certain way of doing things, and that involved all of us working together.

"Kyran has some trouble working the other building's systems."

"I don't like the sound of that," Riffy chimed in as he trotted down the stairs leading us one floor down.

"He's working on it," Tyrel said, her voice sounding shrill. Kelle, who stood waiting for us at the staircase exit, shook her head and then sighed, saying, "Why doesn't this surprise me."

Chapter nineteen

Maece

My heart raced even though my feet were planted firmly on the solid surface of the roof. The numbers scrolling down my screen indicated a heart rate that could have matched Saera's, although I didn't think mine came from dangling five hundred feet in the air. Somehow the memory of that grimy bear had made it past the barriers erected by the device planted in the back of my head, and it screwed with my body's physical reactions. Even my hands were shaking.

I had the good sense to scan the rooftop for any company, but then I ripped the device from my head. The thing made me feel trapped and made it hard to breathe. Saera stood by the fence, holding it with one hand and bending over to catch her breath.

"I stayed in your room that night," I said with the intention of asking a question, but the words came out forming a statement. Saera glanced up with evident shock in her eyes. "We sat on a bed inside your room surrounded by gray walls. There weren't even any windows, and you kept the few clothes you owned in a pile on the floor."

Saera drew in a breath as she stood up straight, but kept quiet as if she wanted me to figure it out on my own, and so I continued. "That's when you gave me Chester."

Her chin rose, and her eyes softened, lifting some of the coldness from them as her mouth curved into a smile. She took a step closer and then wrapped her arms around me in a hug.

"Told you," she whispered near my ear. It took a moment to let the words sink in, but then I wrapped my arms around her. If any doubt had remained inside my head about why I was doing this, then this little piece of memory had solidified my belief in Saera. This time I didn't just see the image, but I felt the strange combination of joy and sadness, along with the comfort given by her. The sensation brought me a feeling of being safe—back then and now.

"Guess I needed some help," I said in a low voice. She chuckled and pulled back but left the palm of her hand to cup my cheek. Her hand felt warm against my skin, and even though this form of contact still felt alien to me, I felt its warmth seep into my chest, where it filled my heart.

"Come on. Let's go do what we came here for, and then maybe I'll tell you how you got stuck in a defecation receptacle, and I had to come rescue you," she said. With that, she turned away from me and made her way to the roof exit. I glared at her for a moment before I placed the heads-up over my eyes and said, "I'm not sure I want to know about that one."

The words had barely left my mouth when a

different voice echoed inside my head.

"I don't know, sounds like an interesting tale to me," Kyran said.

I had all but forgotten about the people listening in, and the thought of Harp, Kyran, and Tyrel hearing our conversation about a teddy bear set my cheeks on fire.

"Why don't you keep from eavesdropping on private conversations and work on a way to get us inside," Saera said, standing by the door that would get us off this roof. Shaking my head in defeat, I crossed the roof to where Saera stood waiting.

The roof's surface had a similar smooth plating to the sides of the building. From a distance, the paneling seemed to have a reflective quality, but from up close, they appeared see-through. What I hadn't noticed before was that there were thin wires running from left to right through the panel itself that then connected with its neighboring panel.

I glanced up, peering over the rooftop and beyond. This was the highest building in this city, and it gave me a clear view of the barren wasteland that lay beyond our protective dome. A slice of orange-red light emanated from the sun from where it couldn't hide behind the horizon. A slight buzz came from the panels catching the light, and it dawned on me that they were using this building and probably every tall building in this city as accumulators to collect energy.

More energy—everything seemed to be coming back to that every time. I shook the thought from my mind as Kyran retorted on the coms.

"You would have been inside already if you

hadn't decided on hanging around."

"Well, I would like to see you climb up a—" Saera started to say, but I cut her off.

"A little focus here," I said, wondering why Harp hadn't already intervened. Saera gave me a frown but then relented. "Kyran, why don't you give us an update," I asked. Acting on information was still one of my primary habits, and it seemed the smart thing to do in this situation. Kyran cleared his throat.

"Tyrel and I have been working on breaching the system ever since you've managed to get at a close enough range," he said. "We haven't enabled full access, but we did tap into the smaller security systems, including roof access."

It seemed ArtRep didn't fear anyone entering from the rooftop. The building was high and barely accessible if you weren't an enforcer, and they had all of those under their command—at least that's what they had thought. Kyran continued by giving us an update on what they had found out about what was happening inside the building.

Apparently, an emergency meeting had been called, and a bunch of scientists had gathered on the twenty-third floor to discuss the problem with the enforcer designated 959. It wasn't a surprise to hear that, but what I did find surprising was that the entire board of the company, including its CEO Harand Sulos, were waiting for an update two floors up from the scientists. These two floors, along with the ground floor seemed to have attracted most of the security forces.

"They're afraid," Kyran said.

"Of what," I asked.

"Of you," Tyrel said, "who else." She sounded a little stunned that I had to ask the question. "Their system has been infallible for many years and if a person with the capabilities of an enforcer might learn how to think for itself…or herself, that person might come looking for revenge."

At the mention of her last word, I glanced at Saera. With a smirk on her face, she guided her hand to her back and pulled a weapon from under her black jacket.

"I'd wonder who would ever come up with that idea," she said. I shook my head and mouthed, *"No."* She shrugged, but in the back of my head, I knew this might become a problem. Turning toward the door, she asked, "Can we go now?"

With information scrolling down my screen and Kyran's voice in my head, Saera and I moved through a maze of hallways. Unlike the insides of other buildings that I had seen, this one had a soothing environment. The walls were a pallet of soft greens and blues as if they were painted in a time before the wormhole mishap changed our lives. Actual wooden side tables stood in different places to decorate the hallways and paintings in all shapes and sizes hung on the walls. An eerie silence drifted around us as we crossed the thickly carpeted floor.

"The second door on the left should be Sulos's office," Kyran said.

"Is that wise?" I asked.

"Just go," Kyran replied.

A glance at Saera told me she had absolutely no problem with entering Sulos's office. Fortunately, the hallway to the office stood empty, and we had no problem entering.

"Wow," I said under my breath as I entered the room. "I know there isn't that much in my head to compare it to, but this is unreal."

I stopped to let Saera enter before closing the door behind me and glanced around as Saera took a couple of steps inside.

Thick, plush carpet covered the floor with a comfortable-looking seating area on one side of the room. On the other side of the room, the carpet edged over into what looked like a hardboard wooden floor, indicating a workplace. A massive desk stood in the middle of that area. Statues carved out of wood or stone decorated the interior along with paintings, and curtains were drawn to block out the view of the expanded sun hovering over us. Saera walked over to the work area and knelt to knock on the floor.

"This is actually wood," she said, sounding amazed. I had no interest in the wooden floors or any of the other lavish items. My eyes went up to the light source hanging in the middle of the room. Tubes emitting light extended from the center, curving into a flowery shape. A black marble sat in the middle of the piece, slowly turning on its axis.

"Already got that one," Tyrel said, anticipating my question. The marble was placed too obviously into the piece to be decorative, and the turning indicated a monitoring device. I kept my eyes on the device a little longer and hoped Kyran and Tyrel were as good at defusing the security systems as they claimed to be.

"Over here," Saera said, standing behind the desk. I hadn't seen her go over to it, but by the time I got there, she had already found Sulos's access terminal. She tapped her fingers on the smooth surface of the desk to turn the thing on as I lifted the head-up to set it on my forehead.

"Just sit back and relax," Kyran said. "Oh, and Maece, please stay close this time."

"Me?" I replied, appalled, and I raised my eyebrows at Saera.

"Don't look at me like that. I didn't ask you to follow me," she said.

"If I hadn't, you would have ended up in a bioprinter," I said. "Or worse, I could have scrapped you off a wall."

Waving a dismissive hand at me, Saera decided to take Kyran's advice and plopped down in Sulos's desk chair. She raised her legs onto the desk and stared at a screen hanging on the wall opposite from us. Within seconds, the colorful images of stars and solar systems switched to black pop-up screens filled with green letters.

The tapping of fingers echoing inside my head made it impossible for me to relax.

"Tyrel," I said, "are you monitoring the rest of the building?"

"Me and three others," she replied. "We've got you covered." This didn't reassure me, but it felt nice to have them try.

Kyran's fingers moved as if possessed, and the

movement translated into red letters blinking across the screen.

"Come on already," Saera said under her breath. She wasn't as relaxed as she wanted to appear.

An Access Denied screen flashed several times, but the line on the other end of the coms stayed silent. Either Kyran didn't wish to explain or was too focused on his task to do so.

"Maece," Tyrel said, "you might be interested to know that you've been recalled for evaluation."

"What is that supposed to mean?" Saera said before I could.

"It means that the scientists want to pick you apart," she said. "A do-not-incinerate order has just been issued to your fellow enforcers."

"Great," I said. I rubbed the back of my neck and moved around the desk, so I could sit on it while I waited for whatever Kyran was doing. With the heads-up resting on the top of my head, I pinched the brim of my nose. The device felt more and more like a burden strapped to my face, but I didn't dare remove it. If anyone found us inside this room, I would need it.

"You okay," Saera asked. I tilted my head to one side to stretch the muscles in my neck and then glanced over my shoulder to face her.

"My head feels…I don't know…heavy," I replied.

"That's called a headache," she said.

"Right," I said just as the screen flashed Access Granted.

"Yes!" Kyran's excited voice boomed over the

coms. Although the string of words and images quickly shifted into a stomach-churning affair.

Chapter twenty

Maece

My eyes were glued to the screen, taking in the information as it scrolled by. Kyran had filtered out the everyday company dealings and narrowed the data down to specific search subjects. They ranged from the self-destruct capabilities of the device stuck in the back of my head, ways to get the device out of my head, and the increase of power generation. However, the peril threatening my head seemed to have taken a backseat. Most of the images dealt with the current and past conditions within the power plants. But then judging by those images, the urgency was imminent.

Over the past twenty years, the ArtRep company with its CEO Harand Sulos had increased the power plants' output without any regard to its employees or the people living in and around those plants. The power plants were much like cities of their own, buried deep underneath the ground where they would use the inner core's heat to generate power. Routed back up to the Combined Districts of Tenebrae, the power would be used to support the dome shield, the oxygen plants, and the general population.

The pictures of gaunt faces and bodies that were no more than skin over bone spoke of the desperate situation of the people living at those plants. ArtRep had an extensive security presence stationed in and around the plants to keep the population in check, and from the looks of it, the stationed enforcers used force to maintain it. The sight of the men, women, and even children working the heavy machinery was heartbreaking.

"It has gotten worse," Saera said, her voice a mere whisper. From the corner of my eye, I saw her wipe a tear from her cheek. "Why are they doing this?" Sorrow was evident in her voice.

"All the power they are generating would be enough to overload the dome and every other system hooked up to it," Kyran said.

"If it's too much, what are they doing with it," I asked.

The screen shifted, and a map of the known surrounding area appeared. With some nifty keystrokes, Kyran followed the power lines leading out of the city.

"That is near the outer-rim landing platforms," I said as Kyran zoomed in on the map.

"They are packaging and shipping it," Kyran said. The sight of those discarded energy cylinders down that alley where Saera and I had stopped to talk came to mind. The vessels used to store power came in all sorts of shapes and sizes. Smaller models were used inside the speeders that crowded the streets, while bigger ones were used to power Hymag lines.

"But where?" Saera chimed in.

"Here," Kyran replied, exasperated.

The grid zoomed out until Tenebrae became only a mere dot on the screen and even further. Blackness surrounded the earth where the sun couldn't reach the emptiness of space. Kyran zoomed out until even the sun became a speck of dust among a galaxy of stars. Then he started to zoom back in.

Avoiding our solar system, he homed in on a nearby system that on the map only seemed to be a short hop from ours, but was probably trillions or hundreds of trillions of miles away. The screen focused on a planet surrounded by two moons and something else.

"What is that?" I asked. My eyes lingered on what looked to be a man-made structure that in size came nowhere near the size of the smallest moon, but must still have been enormous as it drifted in orbit of the planet.

"Those are the beginnings of a new world," a voice replied.

At the sound of the unfamiliar voice, I whirled around and with a twitch of my head dropped the heads-up back over my eyes. In the same swift motion, I drew my weapon and pointed it an elderly gentleman.

Saera nearly fell from her seat at the sound of the man's voice but recovered quickly.

"Who are you?" I asked as my weapon pointed at the man's head. Creases lined the short man's face, and his gray eyes blended nicely with his white hair. His tailored suit was made from a lightweight fabric, but unlike the usual sandy colors worn by Umbras citizens, his was a near-black color of blue.

"I should be offended," he replied in a calm voice. Too calm considering he had a weapon pointed at his head. He lifted his arms and indicated the room. "You are in my office after all."

My heads-up started working in overdrive, trying to determine where the man had come from and if he had any company. The device didn't detect any other visitors, but it did find a hidden door just as a panel in the wall slid back into place.

"I thought I would introduce myself," he said. "Although I am disappointed that Colrin hasn't shown up himself."

Without turning my head, my eyes shifted to see Saera. She had drawn her own weapon, but she held it at her side. Her adrenaline levels spiked even higher than after she had dangled from the roof, but her exterior looked calm and collected. The man, who I probably should have recognized from his pictures to be Harand Sulos, stood seemingly unnerved as he watched us with his hands slightly raised at his sides. *Was he waiting for a reply from us?* As we stood there, I silently hoped Harp would present himself over the coms and tell us what to do, but it stayed eerily silent on the other end.

"Well, I'm sure he's listening in," Sulos said, looking smug. "I want to congratulate you for finally achieving your goals." He said the words in a loud voice, addressing Harp who wasn't even inside the room. Saera's grip on the gun handle tightened, but this only seemed to amuse Sulos.

"I'd always had my doubts when your protégé showed up at our doorstep," he said, turning his gaze on me. "It just felt too convenient to have captured this prominent member of the Subterran resistance and turn her into one of our pets."

My heart slammed into overdrive, and I focused on my breathing to at least keep the rest of my body steady. The way he was looking at me with that smirk on his face made my stomach churn.

"No one believed me when I told them it was a trick. No one believed someone belonging to people so technologically inferior would ever be able to crack our code and set an enforcer free," he said as he slowly lifted his hands. I tilted my head slightly, my weapon aimed at the space between his eyes. On the other side of the desk, Saera's hand twitched, but he would be long dead before she would even be able to raise her weapon.

To my surprise, the man started to applaud. Loud claps filled the room as he said, "It might have taken you two years, but you have successfully infiltrated my company to expose our plans, and now I have a proposition for you."

It remained silent on the other side of the coms, and I figured one of us would have to say something. It seemed he hadn't informed security, or at least they hadn't kicked down the door shooting their weapons. I wanted to keep it that way.

"We're listening," I said, keeping my answer short. If Sulos knew Harp, then I could assume he knew the man wasn't a talker. Saera's head whipped sideways to give me a hard look. Like me, Sulos ignored her, and he gestured toward the seating area.

"I'm an old man, Ms. Lux," he said, taking a step in the direction of the couch. "If you don't mind."

Without lowering my weapon, I took a step back to let him pass. Sulos didn't seem at the least impressed by the weapons as he sauntered across the room to the seating area. Saera moved around the desk, and I waited for her to join me. Standing next to me, she whispered, "What are you doing?"

"How should I know?" I whispered back. Sulos was out of earshot, but I didn't want to take any chance. "Where's Harp?"

When no one replied, my blood started to boil. I couldn't believe they would just keep us hanging here.

"Did we lose the connection?" Saera asked. I checked my screen and shook my head. She drew in a deep breath and glanced around the room.

"Well, we're not dead yet, so maybe you should go talk to him," she said.

"What, why me?"

"Because he didn't address me before, so I'm guessing he doesn't wanna talk to me," she replied. "Besides, you're the protégé."

I could almost taste the bitterness in her voice at the last words, but she had a point. Saera lingered behind me as I cautiously moved toward the seating area. My screen informed me our immediate surroundings were clear, but then I had thought that before Sulos showed up. He watched me as I approached with a gleeful expressing on his face.

"Please sit," he said, indicating a chair.

"I'll stand," I said, my weapon pointed at his head.

"Suit yourself. Then I'll talk," he said. "By now, your leadership will have seen a copy of the intel you have recovered from my workstation—correct?"

"Agreed," I replied with no idea if that were the case.

"Then they know of our little resort in another part of this galaxy."

I gave him a quick nod to satisfy his questioning look, and he continued, "It has taken many resources over many years, and we are not done yet. We need to continue our efforts to build a new home, and we need the resources of this world to do it."

"And you're willing to abuse the people of Subterra for your comfort," I said in a bitter tone.

Sulos raised his old body to sit up straighter and punched his fist on the armrest of the chair. Apparently, I had hit a nerve.

"This is not about our comfort," he said, raising his voice. "This is about saving our civilization. This planet is dying and the only way—"

Getting tired of his rant, I cut him off.

"These cities and this civilization will be able to survive for several hundred more years. Your goals could have been accomplished without enslaving the people of Subterra, so don't tell me you're not doing this for yourself."

"Besides, we're not interested in your reasoning," Saera said as she moved to stand by my side. "Just tell us what your proposition is."

Sulos crossed his legs, straightened his jacket, and relaxed into his seat.

"Do nothing," he said.

My eyes narrowed as they met his to determine if his intentions were sincere, even though the software running a check on his facial expressions told me he was.

"Leave everything the way it is, and we'll make sure there is room for your leadership along with enough people to help us build a new world."

At my side, Saera looked as stunned as I felt before she snorted a laugh.

"Yeah, right," she said sounding amused, "I don't think that's going to work for us." The words had barely left her mouth as her expression changed, and her eyes grew cold. "You think we're willing to sacrifice thousands so a few can have a life of comfort."

Sulos had no trouble matching her expression, except that, along with the coldness, something evil hid inside his eyes. He shook his head in a slow, deliberate motion and lifted a finger to wiggle in a similar manner.

"No," he said, "if you do not comply, we will use our technology to open up another wormhole and drain the remaining energy from the sun and leave this planet for dead within a year."

As he spoke, my eyes took in the green letters scrolling down my visor, and I took in the information downloaded from Sulos's workstation.

"What you call the beginning of a new world is

nowhere near finished, and I doubt you have even started on the planet itself," I said. From what I had gathered, that space station or whatever it was supposed to be was only the first step. For whatever reason, the planet that had the station orbiting around it wasn't ready to sustain human life. It would probably need terraforming, and that could take decades. "You won't risk this planet until you can be sure you'll have a place to escape to."

Sulos chuckled before clearing his throat. "My dear," he said, "it is true that we would prefer to continue as we have. The resources this planet provides us with will certainly expedite the process, but make no mistake about it: if need be, we'll be ready within a year to leave you all behind to die on this miserable planet."

Sulos narrowed his eyes as he looked straight at me, and I wondered if he wanted my heads-up to confirm that he spoke the truth. He added, "Make no mistake: we are both willing and able to flip the switch that will bring on the destruction of this planet, but we are not fools and are also willing to seize opportunities where they lie—the question is, is your government ready to make the right choice?"

For the first time since Sulos had entered the room, Saera lifted her weapon to point it at him.

"You're not going to get away with this," she said.

"My dear, I'm afraid you won't have a choice in the matter," Sulos said. "The choice lies with the Subterran leadership. We've had many dealings with them over the years, and I'm sure they'll know what's best."

"Subterran leadership isn't here right now," Saera replied.

"Killing me won't stop this," Sulos said.

"Won't stop me from trying." Saera's voice sounded strained, and my heads-up noticed the slightest tremor in her hand holding the weapon. Her vitals were rapidly rising from angry to furious, and I didn't think it would take much for her to pull the trigger.

Considering what Sulos had told us and the way he had dismissed the horrible treatment of the Subterran people stuck in those power plants, I wouldn't have minded killing the bastard myself, but I doubted it would bring us anything.

"Besides," Sulos said, "you are forgetting the fact I could kill your"—he paused and then glanced at me —"sister and any other Subterrans in our employment in an instance." Then he waved a dismissive hand at us and then gestured toward the exit. "I suggest you leave or I'm forced to inform security."

Within seconds, a word scrolled across my screen. It was a message sent by Kyran. Both he and Tyrel had been silent, and I had wondered if they had experienced technical problems. My mind shocked into overdrive as I read the one-word message: *Incomming.*

Automatically my eyes shifted to the door at the same time it started to open, and an enforcer came rushing in. Saera noticed the unannounced visitor as well and pointed her weapon in the enforcer's direction.

The man, who would have appeared massive enough on his own, looked ominous in his exoskeleton suit. His weapon had been drawn before he'd entered the room, and it told me he must have been waiting for us outside the door. Sulos, who must have assumed that his message had been delivered, had signaled him somehow. We were nothing more than a nuisance that had forced him to make a statement to the Subterran government about his interrupted plans, and now he was done with us. A click sounded as the enforcer pulled the trigger on his weapon.

I reached out to grab Saera, positioning my body in front of hers to intercept the energy weapon's burst of power. Instinctively, Saera responded by making herself small and ducking to the ground. The energy blast hit me in the back, and I hissed as the pain spread along my neck and shoulders.

Not waiting for the pain to fade, I turned to aim my weapon and fired twice, hitting the enforcer in his chest. My weapon was set to standard ammo, and besides making the man stumble back a few steps, it didn't do much else. As he stumbled, the enforcer reached for his belt. From the numerous times that I had seen that move, I knew he was preparing his weapon for the kind of firepower my suit couldn't save me from.

Still sitting in his chair, Sulos cursed. He knew as well as I did that an explosive round from the enforcer's special brand of ammunition would be enough to kill him too. Perhaps even hoped to beat the enforcer to it when he said, "Extermination order, disable E95—" The energy blast that struck him in the middle of his forehead stopped him from finishing his sentence.

For a moment silence fell over us, and we all froze. Even the enforcer faltered and lowered his weapon. Still crunched at my side, Saera's arm was stretched out, weapon in hand, and pointing at Sulos. She just stared at his body with vacant eyes as if the blood trailing down his forehead and nose was the most interesting thing she had ever seen.

Then everything slammed back into fast-forward motion. An alarm started to blare, probably attracting every enforcer and security officer to the top floor of this building. Behind me, the enforcer already in the room must have received orders on his screen, because he raised his weapon. Remembering him changing the ammo, I pulled Saera up and forced her in the direction of the desk. It wouldn't serve much as cover, but it was close to the hidden door that Sulos had used coming in and probably our only way out.

Halfway across the room, I glanced over my shoulder and realized we would never make it to the door. Within thousandths of a second, my screen informed me of the pull on the trigger and the estimated time of firing. It also informed me of another enforcer entering the room, but that wouldn't matter if I didn't time this correctly.

Focusing on the screen, I kept moving. Fortunately, Saera had composed herself and was also moving now. Digits rapidly counted down, and I dropped to the ground, taking Saera along with me. The enforcer's weapon fired in the same instance.

It only took a second to realize I had miscalculated. Pain ripped through me as if a hot knife sliced into my skin, but feeling the pain also meant I was still alive. A direct hit would have ended my life in an instant, and so the primary detonation was still to come. Unable to stifle a scream, I landed on top of Saera, who hit the ground hard, and I used my arms to protect her head.

The explosion that followed drowned out the alarm as I felt the heat of residual flames burn my hands and singe my hair. I clamped my teeth together to keep myself from screaming in agony.

Around us emergency fire extinguishers activated, forcing a white substance into the room to kill the flames, but it also made it harder to breathe. Seconds later the ventilation system kicked in, and the white substance along with the lingering black smoke from the explosion was sucked from of the room.

I wanted to turn and point my weapon at the enforcer, who was surely waiting to finish us off, but I couldn't move. Instead, Saera wrestled her arm free and aimed her weapon at our assailant. She kept firing, but the low voltage rounds that her weapon used wouldn't make a dent in an enforcer suit. I was barely able to keep my eyes open, but I caught Saera's, even though she wouldn't be able to see mine with the heads-up still strapped to my head. It wasn't hard to read the fear in those eyes. Then there was a thud behind us, and her head shifted to face the enforcer while her body relaxed.

"Hey, sis...sss," a voice that sounded strangely familiar said. "How do you say sis plural?" The question wasn't met with an answer. Instead, I heard a smack followed by another, but this time with a disgruntled "Hey!"

"Focus, Riffy," another voice said. This one sounded female. Raising my head turned out to be more painful than I'd thought.

"Easy," Saera said as she maneuvered from under me. The light hurt my eyes as someone removed the heads-up. Squinting, I gazed up into blue eyes and an infectious smile.

"Hey, beautiful." The voice triggered something other than just recognition, and a tingle ran through my body, giving me goose bumps on the parts of my skin that hadn't been scorched.

Trying to get the room and the people in it into focus, I blinked. A dead enforcer lay at three pairs of feet with what I thought to be a knife sticking from the back of his neck. As I blinked again, it became harder to keep my eyes open. The thought of the dead man's blood staining this nice carpet lingered in my head before it all faded to black.

Chapter twenty-one

Maece

I opened my eyes to fingers snapping in front of them. The repetitive sound droned inside my head and didn't help with the headache festering there. A voice joined in with the snapping.

"That's it. Focus on me."

Eyes blinking, I tried to do just that, but focus wouldn't come. Agitation from the constant finger snapping did come, and I lashed out. My fist hit something harder than expected, and it was followed by a groan.

"Ouch," that same voice asking me to focus said, but this time it came with an elongated whining.

"There you are," Saera said, and I assumed it was her hand holding mine. I blinked a couple of times and then found her. The presence of three others shocked me into an upright position. I hissed as a sharp pain ran up my arm, into my shoulder, and down my back. Ignoring it, I pressed against the wall as I tried to gain a defensive position. Saera gripped me by the arm that wasn't hurting and spoke in a soothing voice.

"It's okay. You're safe for now," she said.

"Whatever that means," the voice from before said. Ignoring him, I glanced around the narrow hallway, and after determining we were alone, I turned to the faces hovering around me.

Those blue eyes from before were sitting at my left side, and they came with a cheeky grin on a rugged-looking face. It occurred to me that he was quite handsome despite the shaggy, sand-colored hair and the stubble on his jaw. This strange, familiar tingle ran through me again. His smile widened as our eyes met, and before I could drown myself in them, I glanced away, facing the others. A kind face with a set of gray eyes and chubby cheeks greeted me next. They stared at me while the young man's mouth hung open in a half-smile.

At my right I found Saera sitting as she watched me with an expectancy I couldn't place. Close at her side sat a young woman who seemed to have barely left childhood, but her eyes held something that made her appear much older.

"Who are you?" I asked. My throat felt raw, and I cleared it. Around me, disappointment became evident as eyes shifted to the ground. I gauged Saera who had a similar disappointing gaze.

"They're…" she said hesitantly, "your past." I instantly knew what that meant, and I felt a hint of annoyance stir inside me. Saera wasn't going to explain.

"We're your family," a bright voice coming from Chubby Cheeks exclaimed. Two hands rose simultaneously, and from his left and right side,

Chubby Cheeks was smacked in the head. The girl huffed, and the guy sitting next to me said, "What did I tell you about being focused?"

"How else is she going to know if we don't tell who we are," Chubby Cheeks said, swatting away the hands. He acted annoyed at his companion's antics, but they seemed amiable enough.

"I guess names won't hurt," Saera said, pointing out Reece, Riffy, and Kelle. I nodded as Saera introduced us and then stuck a hand up to wave hi. A wide smile created a dimple in Riffy's chubby cheeks, and his eyes brightened as I acknowledged him. The young woman named Kelle seemed a bit more reserved, and I couldn't read the meaning behind her intense gaze.

The pain that rushed up my arm wasn't nearly as bad as the pain in my head when Saera had introduced herself, but I couldn't contain a hiss.

"Here, let me," Reece said. He gestured at Riffy, who fiddled inside a bag before he gave him something that looked like a gun with a giant needle sticking out. I flinched, inching back, but Saera held me in place.

"I've already given you one of these. They help with the pain and healing," Riffy said. "I promise it won't hurt." As if reconsidering his words, Riffy shot Reece a look. "At least if lover boy here doesn't screw it up."

Reece lifted his hand as if he were trying to smack Riffy in the head again, but the young man with the chubby cheeks raised his chin defiantly. Reece scrunched up his face at Riffy and then held up the device. He wiggled it playfully while he raised an eyebrow as if that would make me more willing. I glanced at Saera who gave me an encouraging nod and then turned back to Reece.

"If you hurt me, I'll punch you," I said, only half meaning the words. Reece grinned.

"I believe you," he said, pointing a finger below his eye where a bruise had started to form. "You did that already." My eyes narrowed in on the bruise, realizing his face had been what my hand had hit when I startled awake. Before I knew it, I felt a blush creep up my cheeks and the need to apologize as he said, "Now, look into my pretty eyes." It became apparent he had to fight to keep a grin off his face.

"Why would I wanna do that?" I replied.

"Because, I'm afraid you'll hit me again after, and drowning in my gaze will distract you enough so you won't feel the shot," he said and then leaned close to my ear. "I know you want it too." That blush I had felt creeping up before returned with a vengeance. That brought a wide grin to his face, and I turned away from him only to stare into the faces of the others, who were all looking at me sheepishly. It gave me the feeling that they all knew a secret that I wasn't allowed to know.

Without me noticing, Reece had slipped the needle in just above my collarbone and had already pulled it out. He grinned, raising a hand to protect his face as if I was going to hit him. My composure had returned enough that I managed to grant him a faint smile, but I figured we didn't have time for antics.

"What did I miss?" I asked.

Saera started to explain how we had come to hide inside Sulos's secret escape route, while I felt the drug Reece had given me take effect. The burning sensation that ran up my arm and down my shoulder all but disappeared. My head started to feel as if it was cradled on a soft cushion. It felt kind of nice. Without the headache, it was a lot easier to take in the ramble of words thrown back and forth inside this tiny hallway.

The four of them seemed so in tune, as if they had known each other forever. In turns, one of them would shoot me a glance, give me a smile or a grin, and then turn back to the conversation. It was quite a show to watch.

Even though the conversation was intended for my benefit, I had trouble holding my attention. While the effects of the drug started to fade, my strategic mind started to take over. *Why the hell were we still in this hallway?* Lights in a soft tone lined a tiled path cradled by two walls and stopped at a door to my left. To my right, the hallway seemed to be a dead end.

"Why are we still sitting here?" I asked, returning my gaze to Saera. It was Reece on my other side who reacted. His mouth fell open, and as if appalled, he covered it with a hand.

"You haven't been paying attention," he said and gasped. "It's as if you don't even care about what we have to say anymore."

I frowned at his reaction and then turned to the others with raised eyebrows.

"Is he always like this?" I asked. The two women's faces stayed placid, but Riffy nodded his head vigorously. His eyes held an odd sense of pride in them.

"Reece, you might want to give her some time to acclimatize to your charming personality," Saera said before she started on her tale again. To her credit, the recap didn't sound as if she were repeating herself.

It turned out Sulos hadn't just created this hallway to sneak up on uninvited visitors; he had also kept it a secret from probably everyone. Kyran hadn't even been able to find it inside the system and had only learned of it because of the scan I had made with my heads-up.

That was why the others were taking their time. It wouldn't be likely for us to be found in here with Sulos dead, and it seemed I had needed the time recover. The blast had barely skimmed my back, but the integrity of the suit had been diminished by the previous weapons fire. It had still protected me but hadn't been able to stop the liquid flames from burning my flesh.

Fortunately, in this day and age, if something didn't kill you in an instant, then there would probably be some substance to remedy physical complaints or near-mortal injury. So they had stuck me with a needle and waited for me to wake up.

In the time that had passed, Kyran had alerted them that pretty much the entire enforcer team had descended on the three ArtRep buildings.

"So, now what?" I asked as I flexed my shoulder and sat up straighter.

"That is the million-dollar question," Reece said.

"What's a dollar?" Riffy asked.

"That, my friend, is one of the mysteries of life," Reece added, giving Riffy a friendly pat on the back.

"Could you just be serious for once," Saera said, raising her voice.

"Nope," Reece said, sounding smug.

"Why then don't you just shove—" Saera started to say, but cut herself of. Her eyes glanced down, and as I followed her gaze, I noticed Kelle had placed a hand on her arm. They shared a look, and I narrowed my eyes, unsure of what to make of it.

"Why don't we just leave?" Riffy asked, "I mean, didn't Kyran say this hallway would gain us access to a secret elevator or something so we could get out?" My eyes shot to him in surprise. No one had seemed to be bothered to tell me about that.

"No," Saera said. "I mean yes, but we have to do something. We can't just leave with ArtRep still having a firm hold on the people they have recruited to be enforcers, and we can't just let them continue to enslave our people in the plants. We need to be the ones to stop them."

"Why?" Riffy asked. I couldn't help the sympathetic look I gave him. His expression reminded me of a confused little kid. A confused little kid who looked a lot like Riffy but younger. I forced the memory from my mind and returned my attention to Saera. She gave me a knowing look, and I had the feeling I knew what she was going to say.

"We can't trust our own government to do the right thing."

"I say we blow the place up," Reece said.

"Wait, what?" Riffy asked.

"What good would do that for us?" I asked.

"Well, for one it would make me feel better," Reece said as he counted the fingers on his hand. He paused at the second finger.

"And two?" Saera asked.

Reece stuck out his lower lip and shrugged.

"Fun."

Saera shook her head, but her next words told me she was entertaining the idea.

"These buildings hold their main production lines for making enforcers."

To me, that seemed like a good enough reason to blow the place up. I was lucky enough to have most of my enforcer memories wiped from my mind, but the images of that young boy back in that alley before and after I had pulled the trigger still haunted me. ArtRep had made us do things that in a normal life we wouldn't even have considered dreaming about. It was the stuff of nightmares, and I wouldn't want to submit that to anyone, but an added thought crossed my mind.

"What about the people inside the buildings?" I said. The words had come out softer than I'd intended them to, but it caught the others' attentions.

"We could create a distraction or force them out," Reece said.

"That still doesn't answer Maecy's question," Saera said. I looked at her, not sure which question she meant. "What good would it do us?"

A long silence settled around us. Riffy scratched

his head while Reece stretched his legs. I blew out a breath as a reply came from an unexpected mouth.

"What if we expose their secret?" Kelle said.

Instantly all our gazes shot in her direction. It took a moment for her words to settle, but as they did, I started to understand what she meant. If we exposed the fact that ArtRep was building a new world by using the much-needed resources of this planet, causing its own people to suffer while the selected few could indulge in what this new world had to offer, it would ensure riots of a scale these districts had never known. We just needed to empathize that they were willing to leave most behind—not just the people of Subterra, but also the majority of the people living in the cities. Kelle hadn't said much up until now, but that hadn't stop her from thinking it through.

"Okay, you lost me," Riffy said. Saera shook her head, patted Riffy's knee and offered a gentle smile.

"ArtRep has kept this new world they are building a secret for a reason. They want it for themselves and do not wish to share with people they decree unworthy, and that includes most of the Tenebrae population."

"But they need those people to build it," I added, "and need them to provide the resources needed for the build at least for one more year."

"This could interrupt their travel plans," Reece said. "It would not only bring every Subterran on our side but probably most of Tenebrae."

"It took you long enough."

We all reacted a little shocked at Harp's voice

sounding in our heads. He must have been listening to our banter the whole time.

"So you agree?" I asked. Silence fell around us as we waited with anticipation for the voice to return on the coms.

"It's not hard to agree to something I had on my mind myself," Harp said.

Reece snorted a laugh. "This is exactly why you are his favorite," he said, pointing a finger at Kelle. She kept her face stoic until Saera wrapped an arm around her, and I noticed a blush creeping up Kelle's neck. The sight lifted my lips into a smile, but it faded as I thought of the impending consequences.

"There could be riots," I said. "People could get hurt, and what about Sulos's threat to open another wormhole near the sun's core? It might go supernova and leave the world for dead within a year."

"A lot can change in a year," Reece said.

"I agree," Harp said.

Chapter twenty-two

Reece

I didn't know whether Harp had waited as long as he had because he only pretended to have figured out this plan on his own or if he wanted us to figure out on our own what he had planned all along. When it came to Harp, I would probably bet on the latter. That man never did anything without a solid reason behind it, but I figured he wasn't about to explain that.

The others didn't seem to mind that Harp hadn't explained his reasoning; they had made up their own reasons for broadcasting the information. I guessed that Harp hadn't liked what he had learned and feared the council might be tempted to make some wrong decisions concerning Sulos's plan to escape the planet. He had worked with these people for so long that he practically knew how their minds worked.

After all, the members of the council and the government were human, and the promise of a free ticket to a place advertised as "the new world" could act as a hell of a bribe. The only way to keep the council or the government from doing something stupid was to get that information out there for anyone on this planet to see.

Harp's plan was simple enough that Riffy or even me could have come up with it. Following Maece and Saera had let us right where we needed to be. We had already extracted the information, now all we needed to do was broadcast it, and wasn't it a coincidence that we found ourselves in one of the biggest communication hubs in the city?

The feeds leading out of this building wouldn't only allow us to broadcast in Tenebrae territory, but it would also allow us to reach every power and oxygen plant, remote outposts, and Subterra. The information would become available to every tablet, terminal, or whatever kind of data-streaming device with access to a relay station—even my own wrist device would have access. If we did this right, we could reach about every person alive on this planet, at least, that we knew of, and all of them would know what Sulos had planned for this world. Everyone would know how he was willing to abuse the people and resources of this world to benefit those who already had everything.

I glanced at Maece, who seemed relieved that we didn't have to blow up the building. If I was honest with myself, then I could do without that too. I got to my feet and held out a hand to her. She eyed it with suspicion for a moment but then decided to take it. Halfway up she groaned. That shoulder must still be bothering her. I grabbed her under her good shoulder to pull her up the rest of the way.

"Thanks," she said under her breath.

"Not a problem." I couldn't help but relish in the contact. Grinning like an idiot, I held on a bit too long and she raised an eyebrow at me.

"Sorry," I said as I released her. I pretended to cough and looked everywhere except at her. This was too damn hard. I didn't know how to act around her. This woman that I grew up with of whom I knew every detail of her life and then some. I chanced a peek at her and confirmed to myself that she was a woman.

Not that I doubted it, but in a few years, a lot could change growing up, and she had definitely changed. She had changed so much that it was hard for me to keep my hands off her. I closed my eyes to force myself not to look at her tight curves or her ass or her—God help me.

"Not a problem," she said. Instead of facing her, I nodded and grabbed my pack off the floor. Riffy leaned against the wall, waiting for what was to come. Sweat coated his forehead as he tapped a nervous foot on the ground. Saera stood with Kelle talking a bit further down the hall. They had their fingers laced together, and an actual smile graced Kelle's face. A big one.

I could understand them wanting a little privacy away from us. They hadn't seen each other in weeks, and I had some idea of how that felt. I found Maece at my side staring at the two.

"She hasn't told you," I asked.

"She hasn't told me anything," Maece replied. She smiled, and it was a beautiful smile, but I could tell a hint of regret hid inside it. "I have to admit that

I am a bit envious." Her voice held a sadness that was hard for my stomach to bear.

"Of Saera and Kelle?" I asked with a sheepish grin plastered on my face. It wasn't hard to guess what she had hinted at, but I felt it as my duty to defuse heartfelt situations with some comic relief. Fortunately, it seemed to work because she grinned and then said, "Perhaps."

I glared at her and hoped my mouth hadn't fallen open. Looking thoughtful again, she added, "You're all so close. You can add to each other's thoughts without uttering the words, and I feel like I'm just tagging along for the ride."

Regaining my composure, I cleared my thoughts. "Well," I said, "even if you don't get all your memories back…" I hesitated, and I hoped that didn't deter from the statement I was about to make, because I believed it with all my heart, but I couldn't help feeling the pain of all those lost memories. "Trust me when I say that you will feel that connection again. Think of us as new friends whose trust you don't have to earn anymore."

She absently nodded, her eyes on the loving pair who I imagined had as much trouble at keeping their hands off each other as I had with keeping them off Maece.

Forcefully pulling my eyes away from Maece, I opened my pack and took out an extra suit.

"Okay, lovebirds," I called out, heading in their direction, "it's time to gear up."

Maece seemed entranced as she watched Saera shed

her clothes to change into the Subterran version of an exoskeleton suit. Her eyes were glued to Saera's bare back and the elaborate tattoo that decorated her skin.

"You should see yours," I said as I came to stand at her side. Maece cocked her head, but her eyes didn't dwell from the detailed drawing of the mystical bird that seemed to be born out of fire.

"I don't have a…" she started to say but stopped herself. Her eyes shifted to her suit as if she just realized that she probably wouldn't remember if she did have a tattoo. "You've seen it?"

I felt heat creep up my neck and figured it must have shown, because Maece stared at me wide-eyed. Clearing my throat, I returned my gaze to Saera's back. Although I considered Saera to be more of a sister than anything else, I could still appreciate the toned physique. That was until Kelle shot me a knowing look that roughly translated into *back the fuck off.*

I scratched the back of my neck, and my gaze returned to Maece, who looked at me expectantly, and I realized I hadn't answered her question.

"We all have them," I quickly said. "Not the same, but similar enough. They kind of match our personalities."

Maece's gaze returned to Saera, who finished pulling the suit over her shoulders and effectively hid the artwork that edged from her back onto her shoulder and along her arms.

I couldn't decipher the look in her eyes as Maece turned without another word and started to walk down the narrow hallway. As she pulled a hand through her hair, I realized that I couldn't even begin to understand how lost she must feel, and I wished I could somehow help her.

Trying to shift my focus, I joined the others in our wait for Harp. Knowing Harp, he would be going over the details of the plan with Kyran. They had to create a file that held the right amount of information to trigger enough of a fallout aimed at setting right the wrongs of this world. Kyran would need a program to upload that file and get it ready to broadcast. ArtRep's systems were massive and infinitely complex. Things like that would take time to prepare, but I had a feeling Harp probably had a scenario ready for moments just like these. He might not understand the technical stuff, but the man knew his strategies.

As time ticked by, the hallway around me had fallen silent. Riffy lay on his back, arms supporting his head, and his breathing came in a slow, steady rhythm. That kid had always been able to sleep anywhere. Saera had sat down across from me, with Kelle huddled by her side. Their fingers sat laced on Saera's lap, and Kelle's head rested on her shoulder, but Saera's gaze held concern as she kept an eye on Maece, who stood leaning with her back against the wall at the far end of the hallway.

I had a feeling that I understood why Maece tried to pull herself away from our group. She had told me as much—she didn't feel she'd fit in. Maybe she thought of herself as an intruder if she sat too close. Glancing at Saera, I suspected she didn't understand.

"She's okay," I said in a whisper so Maece wouldn't hear me. Her heads-up lay on the ground where we had left it, so she couldn't have the device to decipher our words either. Saera glanced up as if surprised at my words. Then her eyes shot back to the end of the hall.

"I know…I just worry that…" she said before hesitating. Our eyes locked and she finished her sentence, "we might not get all of her back."

I shook my head, not willing to think like that. We had gone through too much, all of us. I couldn't just bury those memories. Besides, she had me jumping through too many hoops to get her where I wanted her—where I needed her—well, at least until she shot me down. Saera threw me an apologetic look as if she could read my thoughts.

"I'm sorry," Saera said. "I can't even imagine what I would do if…" She glanced down at Kelle and smiled at her lovingly, before gazing back up at me. "How are you doing with all this?"

I raised an eyebrow and took in a breath before I said, "You know, keeping my pants up where they belong." Saera scowled at me, and I grinned.

"I'm hopeful Spiro will be able to fix her," I added. I wasn't just trying to put Saera's worries at ease. I really did think that the man in a child's body would be able to help Maece.

Spiro had been one of the first kids Harp had taken in, and although his appearance fooled most, he was the oldest of all of us. As a baby, Spiro had a similar neuro-device as Maece had now implanted in his head. A jolt of electricity from one of the Hymag lines had left him near death, but somehow, he had survived. The incident had also rendered the device in the back of his head useless, although something had changed inside him. His body had stopped growing, leaving him stuck in a child's body with the mind of…I don't know…a god.

I always wondered if it been a freak accident or if Spiro had touched the spirals on purpose at the same moment a Hymag happened to rush by. He never spoke of it, and if he had, I probably wouldn't have understood. Spiro had a way with words that made it hard for my brain to translate. Still, I've loved him like a brother from the day we'd met.

He had been the one to convince Maece to go on this mission in the first place, and he had promised us that he could help her after. Of course, Saera didn't know this yet.

"We'll get her back," I said confidently and confirmed it with a nod.

Saera's smile was unconvinced as her gaze shifted back to Maece.

As if she sensed Saera's reluctance, Kelle shifted her head on Saera's shoulder and said, "For once I think he might be right, Saera."

Kelle's confirmation made me believe my own words, and I smiled at her. Then she cocked an eyebrow as if wondering where all this kindness had come from. I stuck my tongue out at her.

It wasn't long after that the device in my ear beeped, and Harp came on. Riffy woke with a start after I stuck a finger in his ear.

"C'mon, sleepyhead," I said and reached out a hand to help him up. Maece noticed and I gestured for her to join us. Not before long we all stood in a small circle more or less ready for action. As before every mission, I made eye contact with every one of them and found a healthy amount of tension and focus edged with a little fear. Fear was good; it would keep us on our toes.

Lastly, my eyes caught Maece's absent gaze. I couldn't be happier to have her back, but that look left a tinge of doubt stirring in my gut. Watching the feeds of her and Saera escaping TED had confirmed what I already knew. Maece could handle herself in a tight situation—she was an enforcer after all—but a lot had happened the past thirty-six hours.

"Okay, Harp, give us the details," I said. His low, scratchy voice reached us through the com devices stuck in our ears. This almost felt like coming home in some disturbed kind of way now that Maece was back.

"Three teams," Harp said, coming straight to the point, "package delivery, doormen, and extraction. I wasn't—"

"What's our exit?" I asked, cutting Harp off. He paused, and I think I might have heard something like teeth grinding.

"The elevator at the end of the hall leads to an unregistered Hymag line that should get you out of the city."

"Sweet," I replied, dismissing the annoyance in Harp's voice. "I like those kinds of surprises."

A lone sigh filled my ears, and around me, the

others shot me disapproving glares. I just shrugged but decided to keep my mouth shut while Harp spoke.

"Saera, Kelle, you will secure the Hymag. Riffy, Reece, you keep our exit clear and, if needed, backup Maece," Harp said. "Maece, Kyran will use your heads-up to link up—" Harp hadn't finished his sentence, but this time it wasn't me who interrupted him.

"This is not how we work," Saera said in a sharp tone that made me raise my eyebrows. If she wanted our attention, then she had it. Even Harp was silent on the line. "Maece isn't going in alone—she's with me, that is how it always worked."

"This situation is different," Harp said.

"How!" Saera said even more sharply than before. I almost never doubted Harp's choices. He was good at this, and I had a feeling I knew why he wanted to change our routine.

"This building is filled with enforcers, and Maece wears the only suit that can withstand multiple rounds without it affecting her."

"Bullshit," Saera chimed in. "Her suit is compromised and won't be any more effective than ours. I'm going with her."

"Saera," Harp said, trying to reason with her, "I need you to prepare the Hymag."

"But that's usually Reece's job," Riffy said, sounding surprised.

"Exactly," Saera said. "He's faster at it and a better pilot." That brought a smile to my face because although I had known that, it was nice to hear Saera finally admit it.

The only reasons I could think of that might have caused Harp to change our usual approach were that he either didn't trust Maece or Saera. Come to think of it, it might be the combination of them. They had created quite a mess running around town, but that had been a common thing back in the day.

Kelle shot a couple of indecisive glances between Maece and Saera. It seemed my young friend wasn't completely sure about our old friend either. Certainly, not when Saera's life might be at stake. Her eyes settled on Saera's as if silently asking a question. Saera lay her palm on Kelle's cheek and gave her the slightest nod. Then Saera raised her chin and said, "We do not deviate from the routine. This is how we work best." As I thought about it, Saera's argument seemed to make sense. Maybe something like muscle memory would help Maece through the motions; it seemed to have worked at TED.

"Fine," Harp said exasperatedly after a moment of silence. "Reece, Kelle—Hymag; Riffy—door; Maece, Saera—delivery." Another moment of silence seemed to cut the tension, and as if in an afterthought, Harp added, "Don't forget the heads-up."

The com line fell silent again after that. I straightened my shoulders and clapped my hands together.

"With the entertainment out of the way," I said, "what do you say we get to work."

Chapter twenty-three

Maece

"Here," Riffy said in a gentle tone. He held out the heads-up. My gaze was still locked on Saera's flushed face. Though grateful for her efforts to keep things as they were as if I had never left, I sensed something other than that seemed to be on her mind. I didn't yet understand her relationship with Harp because she hadn't told me, but something inside told me it hadn't been this way before. A sense of guilt filled my chest as if I were the one responsible.

Riffy nudged my arm, pulling me from my thoughts, and I turned to him. I nodded. "Thanks, Riff," I said as I took the device from him. His eyes lit up, and he almost beamed with excitement. He shifted his feet, his boots squeaking on the tiles. Seeming nervous, he glanced to his left where Reece hugged Saera. They said their good-lucks and be-safes before Reece trotted our way.

As Saera embraced Kelle, I understood Riffy's hesitation, but that didn't mean that I knew what to do. I shifted as uncomfortably as he did. He watched me with big eyes, and his face scrunched up as if deep in thought. The way he stood there, a flash of his young self penetrated my mind. I decided to go with it and pulled him into a quick hug.

"I'll see you soon, Riff," I said and released him. His eyes grew even bigger along with his smile.

Reece reached us and patted Riffy on the shoulder.

"Hey, buddy," he said, "why don't you go call up the magnetic lift for us."

Riffy nodded and stomped down the hall with a purpose. Reece stared at me with his head cocked to a side and a lopsided grin.

"What?" I asked.

"You just made him and me happy people," Reece said. Narrowing my eyes, I watched him with suspicion, wondering what weirdness would exit his mouth next.

"You are the only one that has ever called him Riff," he said. The twinkle in his eye lacked any sign of mischief, but only conveyed joy. Without any warning, his arms wrapped around me, and he pulled me into a hug.

"Be safe," he whispered near my ear. Heat spilled over into my body, where his cheek caressed mine. My skin started to tingle from where it spread down my neckline. Had I been wearing my heads-up, I probably would have been tempted to analyze the strange sensation, but at that point, I was glad I was just able to experience it.

"You too," I said as he released me from his grip. Flashing one of his by now famous grins, he trotted off to join Riffy at the elevator.

I turned and slowly made my way to Saera, who was still holding Kelle in a tight hug. I stopped as that hug turned into a passionate kiss and lingered for what seemed like an eternity with me having no idea where to turn my eyes in this narrow space.

"Breathe," Reece shouted from the end of the hall.

Both women pulled back and smiled before I heard Saera's whisper, "Be safe."

A reluctant Kelle nodded, and releasing Saera's hand, she walked over to me. Her dark eyes were hard as steel as she sought my gaze. She stopped in front of me, and our eyes locked. Amazed at the intensity in those eyes, I had trouble holding her stare. After a long moment, those same eyes softened as if something had shifted, and she placed a hand on my upper arm.

"Keep each other safe, okay," she said in a soft voice that barely reached a whisper. I dipped my head in understanding. With that, she released my arm and headed for the others.

Saera stood biting her lower lip when I looked up.

"That's my girl," she said as I stepped closer.

"I've noticed," I replied, glancing over my shoulder. We walked to the door that would lead back into Sulos's office, and all the while Saera kept looking at me expectantly.

"What?" I asked.

She bit her lip again and said, "Well?"

"Well, what?"

"Well, what do you think?" she asked.

I glared at her, not sure how to interpret this, unless...

"You two weren't together before I left," I said. She shook her head like a little kid.

"And because it's a new thing, we're allowed to talk about it."

"Well, yeah," she replied.

"Well, since there is no way for me to know that, you might want to say that next time," I said.

Saera pulled a hand through her messy blond hair and scrunched up her face as if she hadn't thought of that.

"Sorry," she said and paused. "Well?"

I raised my shoulders, chancing another glance at Kelle.

"She seems young," I said.

Saera playfully shoved me in the shoulder. "She's turning twenty-one next month."

Shrugging again I said, "Maybe if I knew your age that would mean something."

Sadness crept into Saera's eyes. It wasn't as painful as I had seen it before, but it still made my heart sink.

"I'm sorry," she said, "it's just...I wanted to share this with you for over a year, you know and I..."

"I get it," I said, stopping her struggle to finish her sentence. "It's confusing, and to answer your question, I've met her about what five minutes ago, and she doesn't say a whole lot."

Saera smiled widely as I continued.

"But it's obvious she cares about you, and clearly you about her, so that's good, right."

We both blew out a breath at the same time.

"Patience," Saera said.

"Patience," I echoed as I turned to the door.

I edged the panel hiding Sulos's escape route open and let my heads-up scan the room beyond. As it signaled clear, I gave Reece and the others a thumbs-up. Reece returned the gesture, and I eased the panel further open so Saera and I could fit through the opening. Holding my weapon at the ready, I moved ahead of her. My suit might have been shredded at the back, but the front would still do perfectly fine when it came to holding off an energy blast.

It took about two steps inside the room to see our plan wouldn't exactly go as planned. The place sat empty and dark. At first glance, it appeared just as it had the first time we had stepped inside. Sulos's body and that of the enforcer had been removed, leaving only a few dark stains of blood. The problem was that the area where Sulos's desk stood had suffered a direct hit from the blast. Charred remnants of the shattered desk were left behind along with the almost unidentifiable remains of his access terminal.

"This is going to be a problem," Kyran said.

Stunned, I glanced over the room and then at Saera. She shrugged, and I shook my head. If we wanted to access the feeds to broadcast our data packet, then we needed a terminal to create an uplink. Sulos's access terminal in combination with my heads-up would have provided Kyran the tools he needed. Now that Sulos's terminal had been destroyed, we had lost our means to connect with the feed.

"Reece," I said into the coms, keeping my voice low, "this might take longer than we thought."

"What's the problem?" he asked. I threw an exasperated hand in the air, indicating the room, and gave Saera a look, ordering her to explain.

She scowled as she said, "How is this my fault?"

"It's hardly mine, considering the fact I was the unconscious one."

Footfalls sounded inside the narrow corridor, and a second later Reece's head popped up in the door opening.

"Oh shit," he said, "that had slipped my mind."

"Slipped your mind," Harp said, startling the three of us.

"Well, it's not like you couldn't have known," Reece said in defense. "I thought Kyran had covered the HUD data?"

"I did, but it never showed the area where the desk stood," Kyran piped in, sounding offended.

The bickering over the coms took on a life of its own, and I wondered if those previous missions—which, at this point, I felt glad that I couldn't remember them—had been this crazy. Harp tried to silence the chatter, and it worked on Kyran, but from Reece's expression, I could tell he enjoyed this too much. He kept at it with Saera, who said, "I can't believe you let us go out on this meager intel." Addressing Harp, she was pouring fuel onto the fire. Even Riffy added his opinion over the coms.

"I don't think you can lay this all on us," he said.

"Guys, can't we just agree that you all screwed

up," I said in a raised whisper.

Reece glared at me as if he couldn't believe what I had just said.

"Oh, what? And leave you off the hook?" he said, appalled.

"Unconscious," I offered again.

"No," he said, "that doesn't count." Despondent, I raised my arms, finding this entire conversation unreal. Reece grinned and shot Saera a mischievous smirk. No one seemed to care that we were standing inside the highly secured office of a man we'd just killed and that everyone inside this building was probably looking for us.

"I've found a secondary workstation from where we can access the system and upload the files." Tyrel's timid voice sounded foreign to me as it entered my ear. Reece's face turned serious as he asked, "Do we need any additional changes to the plan?"

"No, we're good," Tyrel said. "It is going to take longer, though. The terminal is located in Sulos's private lab a few floors down."

"Great. Thanks, Ty," Reece said, and the others followed suit. I just stood there, glaring like an idiot.

"Tyrel works best in a loud environment," Saera said.

"And we live to serve," Reece added.

"So, Saera and I need to go down a couple of floors, find the terminal that Kyran can use to broadcast the intel, and then get back up here," I said, but I had a feeling it wasn't going to be as easy as it sounded.

"Ty," Saera said and continued after the young

woman replied, "can you see if you can find another way down to the Hymag platform in case we need it."

"Already on it," Tyrel said as I heard her fingers tapping in a rapid pace.

"It looks like we have everything under control," Reece said. "Now get out of here; me and the kids have a Hymag platform to clear." Reece threw us one of his half-assed smiles and then disappeared into the narrow hallway, sliding the door shut behind him.

The information concerning the location of the secondary workstation slid across my screen.

"You guys are crazy," I said as Saera walked past me and headed for the door.

"No more than you," she replied.

I paused at the door, taking in the information that seemed to be coming from Kyran again. While Tyrel had searched for the secondary workstation, Kyran had breached security and determined that this floor had been abandoned after the explosion. Enforcers were sweeping the tower floor by floor going down, and they had now reached number twenty-five. This was the floor where Sulos had held up while he had waited for information from the technicians staffing the lab.

Two floors down from us, Sulos's private lab was located, and that was where we needed to go. So, in theory, Tyrel should be right. If the remaining enforcers had joined the search, then the two floors below us should be clear for us to move around.

"What was that all about?" I asked, walking at Saera's side as we moved through the by now familiar hallways with their pallets of soft greens and blues.

The thick carpet under our feet muffled the thread of our boots, and we moved almost soundlessly.

"Tension killer," she said. I raised an eyebrow, turning to her, but then realized she wouldn't be able to see with the heads-up over my face.

"Tension what?" I asked.

"Reece gets into nervous, usually inappropriate, humor, while Kelle goes silent. Riffy is, well, Riffy, and Tyrel likes noise while she needs to work under pressure."

"I see," I replied and pondered over it for a second before I asked the question. "So what is your thing?"

Saera barely shifted her head to glance at me, but her smile was evident.

"I talk," she said, "about anything and everything."

"Like you did climbing the building?"

"Yep."

We turned another corner and found the stairwell we needed in order to take the final floors down. At the door, I paused, wondering if I should ask the question on my mind, because Saera hadn't been the most forthcoming about answering my questions—well, at least not about the things I really wanted to know. I knew she wanted me to find out things on my own, but that could take ages.

"What was my thing?" I asked.

Saera shook her head in disbelief, and I reached for the door handles, assuming she wasn't going to answer when she said, "Isn't it obvious."

I turned to her, only able to guess at what she

meant.

"You ask the questions." When I didn't reply, she added, "Your nerves calm from hearing me talk, and to keep me talking you ask the questions."

On a weird level, that made sense. It added to the explanation of why the group was so fierce against changing who was going with whom. There was so much I still needed to learn.

"I probably lack the experience due to memory lapses, but doesn't this seem too easy to you?" I suggested in a hushed voice. The wary look in Saera's eyes told me I wasn't far off.

"Systems indicate all is clear," Kyran said over the coms. I eased the door open onto a hallway that had more in common with what I had seen in the hospital than the ones a few floors up, with their cozy carpet and decorations adorning the spaces.

"That's what you said the last time," Saera reminded him.

"That was different," he countered. "Sulos's hideout didn't register on any of the systems."

"Neither did the enforcer waiting for us outside the office," I added as I took a cautious step into the hallway. The white floors and walls were spotless. My heads-up didn't register a single fiber, hair, or any other DNA-related material. It was as if no one had ever set foot in the place.

I took another step and paused, half expecting an alarm to go off, even though our trek through the bowels of this building had gone without incident so far. A couple of staircases and hallways had led us to the other side of the tall tower. The fact that we hadn't encountered any enforcers or regular officers hadn't eased my mind. In fact, it made the knot that had formed in my stomach tighten further.

"This doesn't look like a lab," Saera said as she stepped out from behind me and glanced around. "It's just an empty hallway."

"This should be it," Kyran said. His voice sounded thoughtful, which felt a bit unsettling.

"I don't like the sound of that," I muttered.

With less caution than I would have liked, Saera strode forward.

A red light blinked on my heads-up, and I opened my mouth to warn her, "Watch it, there are —"

She yelped as one of the white walls shifted, and its smooth surface shimmered. It might have been a trick of the eye, but it looked like a ripple on a body of water after a stone had been tossed into it. As the wave-like motion ceased, it revealed a six-foot-wide window protected by an energy barrier. Saera dropped to her knees at the sight of the transparent surface. She glared at me as I ignored her and stepped closer to see inside the room behind the newly formed window.

"You were saying," Saera said as she got to her feet.

"I wanted to warn you that the walls were energy barriers," I replied.

"And!"

"And that they are one way."

"Right," Saera muttered.

Through the window, we could see a small room of about ten square feet in size. It seemed the hallway connected to a bunch of smaller labs. Someone, or perhaps more accurate something that used to be a human being, lay in the middle of the otherwise empty room. Saera gasped, and I had to swallow hard.

With the heads-up, I could see every detail of the mutilated body. Skin bulged in places where it shouldn't, as if broken bones were trying to break free from the flesh. But these bones weren't broken. Joints seemed to have been reinforced and looked like... well...mine. The curves of the man's body resembled mine as I wore the exoskeleton suit, except he wore his suit on the inside.

"They must have used a bioprinter to create..." Saera started to say, but she was unable to finish her sentence. For a moment, I wondered if I should finish the sentence for her, but by saying what? I had no idea what ArtRep was trying to do here. Maybe they wanted better enforcers, or they needed advanced people at their new-world facility. *Who knew?* All I knew was that this man had suffered and would probably continue to suffer for whatever it was they wanted him to become.

"Ladies," Kyran said in a whisper. He could see the man as well as us through the feed from my heads-up but had chosen not to comment on it. Instead, he had sent the information indicating where that secondary workstation was from where we could upload our broadcast. My heads-up signaled a warning, indicating a door at the end of the hall. It flashed bright green on my visor's screen, and I nudged Saera.

Windows popped up along the wall every seven or eight feet and seemed to be triggered by our movement. I scanned the room for bionic or heat sensors but came up empty. Something was causing these barriers to reveal themselves.

"No alarm bells have gone off," Kyran said.

"That doesn't mean they haven't detected us," I replied. The feeling of unease that came with the fear of being detected simmered in the back of my mind as we moved further down the hall.

Each room displayed a different disturbing scene. In one we saw a teen, maybe twelve or thirteen years old. I couldn't tell if it was a boy or girl. They had him or her hooked up to a computer bank, and wires ran in and out of that young person's body. I stared into lifeless eyes that made me hopeful that this child wasn't aware of what was happening.

A cold shiver ran down my spine, and I felt like tearing through the wall, but I wouldn't be able to help these people like that. We needed to finish our mission. Ahead of me, Saera had willed her gaze to the floor with more success than I had. I couldn't stop myself from glancing through every window that opened, but I managed to keep walking.

A tinge of relief settled inside me as we reached the door flashing green. One more window to go. I took in a breath and shifted my eyes in its direction. What I saw in there stopped me cold. A man lay inside a cylindrical contraption with his ankles and wrists bound. His mouth mimicked what I could only describe as a scream, and instead of hearing him, I could feel his pain. His eyes were open wide, and tears slid down his temple while robotic arms moved over his body adding layer upon layer of muscle and skin tissues.

Something blinked on my screen, and I assumed it tried to warn me of my elevated heart rate, but I didn't need the heads-up to remind me of that. I could feel it rage inside my chest like a wild beast trapped in a cage as the memories of a similar tube flashed across my mind. It wasn't this man's pain that I could feel; it had been my own.

Robotic arms hovering in front of my eyes before they started to tear at my flesh sent a sense of dread through my body that resulted in my hands shaking uncontrollably. I clutched them into fists, taking a sharp breath as I tried to flush the memories from my mind.

A hand on my shoulder startled me, and shocked, I turned to face Saera.

"I've been calling you," she said. Her voice was soft and filled with concern. In a distant corner of my mind, I heard Kyran's voice echo that we needed to move.

"Are you all right?" Saera asked.

My eyes returned to the man inside the room, and Saera's gaze followed mine.

"Bad memories," I said. Unable to face Saera, I turned and walked toward the door.

Chapter twenty-four

Reece

"Come on, Riffy," I said, keeping my voice low. "You're using up all the space here." Riffy grabbed a metal rod for balance and shifted his position. It had taken us a while to override the lift's security features, and we had even been forced to enlist Tyrel's help, but in the end, we had managed just before Kyran had informed us that Maece and Saera had located the workstation. Even though it had taken us longer than we would have hoped to get this lift going, it seemed we were still good on time.

Lucky for us the magnetic lift had a more classical design and looked like a box with actual wooden panels decorating the walls. It didn't seem wise to just take the magnetic lift and ride it down to the Hymag platform without knowing what to expect. The lift was part of Sulos's secret escape route, but that didn't mean nobody else used the Hymag platform in the lower levels of this building. So, after Maece and Saera left for their part of the mission, we decided to descend into the belly of the beast on the roof of the small box.

I maneuvered over the hatch that we had used to climb up from inside the lift onto its roof and placed my feet on either side of the opening.

"Ready?" I asked. Kelle was sitting in position beside the hole as she looked up and nodded. The lift's velocity reduced, but not enough to take me off balance. Just in case, I grabbed hold of Riffy's shoulder and used my free hand to grab Kelle's belt. Confirming that my grip was solid, I said, "Ready when you are."

Silent as ever, Kelle lowered herself headfirst down the hole. The box slowed even more and then stopped. Kelle eased forward, hoping to get a look of what was awaiting us for when the doors opened. She signaled for me to lower her some more. Her belt and my hold on that belt were now the only two things that kept her from falling nose first.

"Clear," she said.

"You sure," I whispered. Kelle glanced up and cocked an eyebrow. She was sure. I lowered her further, and when her feet pointed to the ground, I released her. She landed in a crouched position and stayed there, watching whatever it was she was watching.

"I'll go first," I said, turning to Riffy, "in case you get stuck." That earned me his middle finger, a gesture that had been around for who knew how long. I grinned and took a step to drop into the hole.

My hands shot up, and I grabbed the edge of the opening before my legs hit the ground. I dangled for a moment, catching my own impression of what awaited us on the outside of this box. I groaned as I saw the short hallway with three doors, and then I dropped to the floor. Blowing out a breath, I passed Kelle and stepped into the hall. Damp-looking walls and three doors. I half turned, glancing over my shoulder to see Kelle still sitting in her crouched position.

"What was it you were looking for?" I asked.

She stood as if she attempted to shoot me with her glare and stepped out of the box. Her eyes never left the doors as she said, "Doors can open."

Behind us, a loud thud sounded as Riffy landed inside the box. To keep myself from any snide remarks, I didn't turn to see how he had landed, but I could imagine it. I tapped the coms device lodged in my ear.

"Hey, Ty, I need a little help," I said. "Door number one, two, or three?" I heard Tyrel's fingers tapping ferociously on her virtual keypad. Unfortunately, we didn't have one of those nifty heads-up displays like Maece had. Those things made for way better access. In Tyrel's hands, I'd bet she'd be able to perform magic tricks with it beyond words.

Another misfortune for Tyrel was that Harp always favored Kyran, and although the boy wonder was good, he couldn't come close to our little girl magnificent. For Tyrel, this meant she got stuck with the minor assignments, and usually that meant getting stuck with us. We had nothing to complain about, though. Tyrel hadn't grown up as part of our crew; she wasn't one of Harp's kids, but she could have fooled me.

Harp wasn't the only one to rescue kids from the

plants, although he was one of only a few that didn't do it entirely for selfish reasons. Sure, wanting us to join his organization was selfish, but to his credit, he had given us the choice. Other kids weren't that lucky and were often used as cheap labor. Tyrel had been one of the lucky kids if you don't count losing both parents by the time she turned six.

Tyrel let out an exasperated sigh before she said, "This might take a while."

Patience wasn't one of my strong suits, and after bothering Riffy for a while and pacing the narrow space until I feared I might have worn out a path on the floor, I stretched my muscles. Kelle gave me an annoyed look as the popping sounds that I made with my mouth started to go on her nerves.

"Okay, found it," Tyrel said, sounding as excited as a shy girl could ever be, "just give me one more minute."

To give my mind something else to do, I switched channels. This wasn't exactly protocol. We were supposed to focus on our part of the job, and Tyrel or Kyran would monitor each other's feeds. They would inform us if there was something we needed to know, and if necessary, we could switch to the main channel. Still, I felt curious.

As soon as I switched, voices battered my hearing, frantic chatter going from Kyran to Harp and then back to Saera.

"She needs help," Saera all but yelled.

"Stay with that HUD," Harp said.

"I don't understand how this happened," Kyran said, underlining the conversation. Panic was evident in their voices. In the background the clear sounds of weapons fire combined with a struggle were evident.

"Goddammit, Saera," Harp said, raising his voice and apparently losing his cool. "If someone takes a shot at that thing, then everything will have been for nothing." Knowing Saera, what Harp's plea fell on deaf ears. I had heard enough.

"Ty, doors, now!" I said. Kelle and Riffy looked at me in surprise. They hadn't heard what I had.

"I know," Tyrel said in her timid voice. She had been listening. I stepped up to the door, glancing at them one at a time. She must have known what I was thinking, because Tyrel shot me a warning, "If you choose the wrong one it will trigger an alarm."

"The alarm has already been triggered," I said. That bit of news also triggered Kelle and Riffy. Both drew their weapons and stepped in line behind me.

"Do you want them to know your escape route?" Tyrel added. She was right, of course.

"Reece," Kelle said. She spoke my name as if it was a question. I glanced over my shoulder, and I knew she could read the reply on my face.

"They're in trouble," I said. "I want this platform cleared in three minutes." Before I could add anything, else Tyrel said, "Second door on the left."

I glanced at the doors and said, "So it's the middle door."

"The screen reads, second door on the left," Tyrel replied. I opened my mouth to speak, but then felt Kelle's fist in my back.

"Focus," she hissed.

"Right," I said and pressed the panel that was

supposed to open the door in the middle.

Relieved at the sight of two officers and not enforcers, we slipped into the large open space and hid behind a column. The space resembled Harp's little hideout and looked like a cave, but on a much smaller scale. Something the two places didn't have in common was the massive pillars that seemed to carry the roof of this place. Two rows of columns carved a path from the door we had just come from to the platform where a single Hymag stood parked. The pillars provided some much-appreciated cover from the men patrolling that platform.

With a hand, I gestured at Kelle and Riffy, and they both nodded before they fanned out on either side of me. I started counting, and by the time I reached thirty, I moved out from behind the column. As if I belonged, I walked down the path between the rows of pillars and headed in the direction of the two men. The rest of room was large and empty, except for a platform that led up to the Hymag and some box-sized spaces that looked suspiciously like the magnetic lift we had just used. It seemed Sulos had built more than one way to sneak out of the building. With my firm stride, my boots were loud inside the hollow space, and both men turned at the same time to see me approach.

They paused as if unsure of what to make of me. In my suit, I looked like an enforcer but without the headgear. It took them a little longer than I expected to come to the right conclusion. Their eyes widened as they realized that, in fact, I wasn't an enforcer. A grin formed on my face at their clumsy attempts to draw their weapons. I spread my arms wide in a welcoming gesture as I kept my pace.

"Hey, guys, what's up," I said cheerfully. "I heard there was a party here."

"Stop right there!" one of them shouted before he even had his weapon pointed at me. Wearing heavy-looking assault gear, they might have looked impressive if it weren't for their baby faces and the evident shock in their eyes of not knowing what to do.

"Stop!" the kid on the left shouted again.

"Oh, come on," I replied. "Don't tell me you're not willing to share."

With both of them pointing their weapons at me, I stopped and added, "Pretty boys like you wouldn't mind some company, right."

"Identify yourself," the one on the right said. The shock had lifted from his face, and his jaw clenched. This kid might mean business after all.

"Haven't you heard," I said. "I'm the new babysitter, and I'm here to tuck you in."

"Funny," the one on the right said. "Chase, secure him, and I'll call it in." Chase swallowed hard and took a step toward me. The other guy had barely reached for his com device when two energy blasts hit them from the sides. Their bodies crumpled to the ground.

"Took you long enough," I said aloud as Kelle and Riffy emerged from the shadows.

Kelle raised an eyebrow with a hint of a smile on her face. Then her eyes shot past me, and she simultaneously shoved her artificial elbow into my side. The sudden force exerted by the tiny woman took me off balance and sent me reeling sideways. The strength Kelle could wield with her mechanical arm didn't surprise me anymore, but feeling the pain, it brought to my ribs even while wearing a protective suit knocked the breath from my lungs.

It happened so fast that I barely had the chance to register the jerky motion Kelle's body made before she fell. My head snapped to the side, catching sight of the officer holding his weapon outstretched. He stood on the platform next to the Hymag, and I figured he must have emerged from its cabin.

"Riffy!" I shouted as I reached for my weapon and veered sideways, hoping the movement would catch the officer's attention. From my peripheral vision, I saw Riffy grab hold of Kelle's limp body as he started to drag her behind one of the pillars. He knew what to do, and I forced myself to focus on the young man holding the weapon.

"Hey," I shouted, desperately trying to draw the man's attention, but he seemed blind to me as he fired his weapon at my friends. I fired my weapon. Usually, I tended to be a pretty good shot, but the magnetic blast missed its target. At least I had caught the officer's attention.

Heart pounding, I raced toward the platform. I couldn't let myself dwell on how Kelle and Riffy were doing. Kelle was a tough kid, and Riffy knew what to do, even though he didn't always act the part. Instead of letting the dread consume me, I morphed it into hate and stormed right at the man.

The officer shifted his aim toward me. That kind

of took me off guard because I hadn't thought any further than drawing his attention. The weapon fired, and the energy blast looked like a white bolt of fire hurling straight at me.

I threw my body to the ground, rolling twice before I stopped in a crouch and fired. The man ducked, and my charge missed. He cursed as he turned, heading back toward the Hymag. I couldn't let him get inside. If he hadn't already alerted security, then he certainly could from inside there, and if he locked the door, we would have lost our only way to get out of here.

Getting back to my feet, I fired, taking the man off balance as he stumbled while ducking to avoid my barrage of magnetic blasts. I jumped up onto the platform, and using my momentum, I slammed into the man's torso. He grunted as my shoulder ripped the air from his lungs. We both hit the ground with a thump.

The man looked like he didn't know what hit him. His eyes shifted frantically inside his head, and his hands searched for the weapon that had fallen from his grip. As he struggled underneath me, I had no interest in seeing the fear in his eyes. The fact that this officer was a kid barely out of training didn't interest me either. All I could think of was the look on Kelle's face as her body jerked before she fell to the ground. An afterthought came in the form of what Saera would do to me if anything happened to Kelle.

Weapon still in hand, I brought it down on the young man's face. The impact made his nose crack, and I hit him again after which the blood started running freely. His body went limp, and instead of checking on Kelle and Riffy, I did what I should have done in the first place.

Maybe Maece's reappearance had affected me more than I had anticipated. Nerves had plagued me all day, but I hadn't expected it to make me act sloppy. This shouldn't have happened. Silently cursing myself, I stood, weapon raised, and made my way to the Hymag to search its interior and to clear the area.

"The area is clear," I said as I knelt next to Riffy. Kelle sat propped up against one of the columns, her face the echo of a ghost. Her jaw flexed as Riffy pressed another gauze on her upper arm. Kelle hissed in pain.

"It burns," she said through clenched teeth. Her suit had taken most of the blast, but with our inferior technology, it provided only minimal protection. The fabric diverted most of the heat but couldn't protect the skin as the energy penetrated like molten lava.

I glanced at the scorched flesh that ran along the length of Kelle's arm to where her prosthetic began at the elbow. Smoke billowed up where bits of metal from her robotic arm had become red-hot and singed the flesh. It looked terrible and incredibly painful. With some effort, I tried to keep the heart-wrenching feeling in my gut from showing on my face.

"That little scratch," I said.

Kelle saw past my fake grin and said, "That bad, huh?"

At a loss for words, I placed my hand on her

head.

"We need to get her someplace where we can keep her stationary for a while, so I can shoot her up," Riffy said. His hands moved efficiently as he filled a cylindrical vial with fluids from several bottles before placing it in a dispenser and injecting the needle into Kelle's arm. "These are just against the pain," he said. "I need to be sure that you'll be able to lay still for at least twenty minutes before I can inject you with something that'll help the healing process."

Riffy glanced up from what he was doing, catching my eye and then nodding in the direction of the Hymag.

"Copy that," I said. From Kelle's drooping eyelids, I could tell the drug Riffy had given her had started to work. Not waiting for Riffy, who was putting the medical supplies back into his pack, I eased my arms under Kelle. "Let's go for a ride, princess," I said in a whisper. Kelle groaned as I lifted her off the ground, but didn't comment on my princess remark. That had me a little worried as I rushed her inside the transport, until I placed her on one of the benches inside the Hymag and her foot kicked out to catch me in the knee.

"That's my girl," I whispered. Bending over her, I kissed the top of her head.

Riffy entered the Hymag at the same time Tyrel announced herself over the coms.

"Ty, where have you been?" I asked. The distraction from before had kept me from wondering, but hearing her voice suddenly made me realize she'd been absent the entire exchange.

"Sorry," she said.

"Tyrel, we have secured the Hymag," I said. "Kelle got hurt. Are Maece and Saera on their way down?" Saera and Maece were skilled at getting in and out of trouble, but from what I had heard over the coms, their situation sounded intense. In this instance, I crossed my fingers and hoped they had been able to get out of their tight spot. We needed to get Kelle out of here, but I feared the worst.

"They're pinned down on the east corner of the building," Tyrel answered in strained voice. She didn't say it, because it wasn't her call, but I could tell Maece and Saera were in big trouble.

"We have to get them down here," I said.

"How about those magnetic lifts?" Riffy said. I glanced at him and then out the Hymag door and into the open space with its stone pillars. Riffy had noticed the additional magnetic lifts as I had, and his idea might just work if we managed to figure out which one we would need to use.

"Ty, get those fingers tapping, I need to know which one of those magnetic lifts will get us closest to Maece and Saera."

Chapter twenty-five

Maece

I didn't know whether it was the concrete or my body that I heard breaking. My back sat pinned against the wall while that enormous monstrosity of a man that we had seen lying on the floor inside that cell held an iron grip on my throat. My hands clawed at his, trying to pry his fingers from my neck to get some precious air inside my lungs. The tips of my boots barely touched the ground as I heard the gears and hydraulic hinges grinding underneath the man's skin. He raised his arm, and I could already picture his fist plowing into my side again. I didn't have to imagine the pain. I already felt it.

An enforcer watched us from a distance, weapon raised. He waited patiently, and I wondered if he was supposed to drag my unconscious body or my corpse down this hallway. About half a dozen officers struggled to pick themselves off the floor where I had left them. I had taken down five and was about to challenge the enforcer when someone had released this thing from its cage.

I had no idea what had gone wrong after we'd

entered the room at the end of this hall. All seemed fine as we waited for Kyran to make his connection to the system through my heads-up. Without a warning from Kyran or any other of Harp's people monitoring the operation, the officers swarmed the hallway as if they had known that we would be there.

In a split second, I had tipped the heads-up from my head and had shoved it into Saera's hand. All I had thought to do was to buy us some time to finish the upload. That's why I had decided to confront our uninvited guests heads-on and stop them inside the hallway before they could reach Saera. Everything after that had been a blur of motions. My fists had connected, and I had fired my weapon with precision even without the heads-up. I should have been able to have taken them out without a hitch, even that enforcer—if someone hadn't had the brilliant idea of setting this freak on the loose.

As darkness invaded my vision, I registered a door opening somewhere inside the hall. It wasn't hard to recognize Saera as she shouted her equivalent of a battle cry. I wanted to warn her, to tell her to get out, but I felt the strength fade from my body and my consciousness waver. The freak's body jerked, and his hold on me lessened. He turned to face Saera, who'd fired her weapon, alternating her aim between the freak and the enforcer.

The hand on my throat was pulled away, and I sank to the ground, gasping for air. I still felt the darkness pull at me as the com piece in my ear crackled.

Tyrel's voice kept me from falling over the edge

of unconsciousness, and I tried to focus on what she was saying. This wasn't an easy thing to do among weapons-fire and an oxygen-deprived brain.

"Maece, we have eyes on you. Help is on the way," she said. "The file on that thing reads it is still human—it can be killed."

Taking deep breaths, I lifted my head to get a grip on the scene unfolding around me. The freak and the enforcer were driving Saera into a corner near the door of the office we had used to upload the files. The freak bled from several penetration wounds but kept moving. The small-caliber rounds from Saera's weapon weren't a match for him. The enforcer merely held an arm up to shield the unprotected parts of his face from the projectiles exiting Saera's weapon. The rounds just bounced off his suit. He hadn't fired his weapon, so I figured they wanted us alive—at least for the moment.

I looked for my weapon, but it had found its way across the hall and lay too far out of reach. Silently cursing, I got to my feet. My body ached, especially in the shoulder where the protectiveness of my suit had worn off.

Soundlessly, I moved behind the enforcer. If I wanted any fighting chance against that freak, then I needed to take him out first. Saera caught sight of me as I slipped a blade from the sheath strapped to my belt. The moment she saw me, I knew I had to act fast because the enforcer's heads-up would register the eye movement.

Surely enough, the enforcer turned, lowering the hand he held up to shield his face. The other hand lifted to point his gun at me, but it was too late. In one swift motion, my blade had found its way between his defenses and slid along the length of his throat. Blood splattered the ground, and the shields embedded inside the wall fluctuated as the dark-red fluid hit the energy field. I reminded myself to not look inside the room beyond the shield. Another look at that torturous bioprinter wasn't something I thought I could handle right now.

"Go," I shouted as I whipped the hand wielding the knife around and slammed the blade into the freak's back. To my shock, it didn't fully enter as it hit something hard. The freak flung out his arms with a loud growl. I ducked as his giant fist tried to find my face. Saera did the same, and the freak's other fist rammed the wall just above her head.

"You need the heads-up," Tyrel shouted over the coms, "if you want any chance to make a dent in that thing. Also, the upload should be done by now."

"Got it," Saera called out as our eyes met, and I nodded. She bolted in the direction of the door.

Drawing the freak's attention away from Saera, I drew a smaller knife from a sheath strapped to my upper arm, dropped down on one knee, and cut him. I had hoped to sever the muscles in his calf, but instead of slicing through the skin with ease, I felt the blade grind on metal. Tyrel was right, if I wanted to hurt this thing, I needed the heads-up to tell where to strike.

The freak growled, spinning at high speed, and lashed out with his claw-like foot. He caught me by surprise and kicked me hard in the side. The force of the blow sent me skidding several feet across the ground. I groaned as I pulled my cheek from the sleek floor. I shook my head as the freak came barreling down at me. With a quick glance at the door, I rolled away from the advancing monstrosity—*where was Saera?*

The freak's foot stomped down where my head had been just a moment ago. The thing was fast, and I needed the heads-up to calculate and predict its moves.

"Saera," I shouted as I tried to get to my feet and ducked away from the raging figure. I moved too slowly, and he caught my arm. My knife clattered to the ground, and I screamed in pain. It felt as if my arm was about to be wrenched from my body. Instead, he flung me backward, and I hit the shielded wall. The displayed window wavered, and a rippled water effect ran up the energy barrier as my body sunk down to the ground.

I gripped my arm; it felt as if it had been pulled from its socket, although I didn't think that was possible as long as I wore the suit. The copper taste of blood filled my mouth, and I spit it out before I pushed myself into a sitting position.

The freak had no intention of stopping his onslaught as I scrambled across the floor to create some distance. My boots lost their grip on the slick floor as I pushed off, and the soles squeaked.

A quick glance down the hallway told me my knife was out of reach, but the freak's effort had thrown me close enough to my weapon that I could almost reach it. Ignoring the pain in my arm and the rest of my body, I scrambled across the floor on hands and feet.

"Saera," I shouted again as I pushed off in a final effort to throw myself at the weapon. Something stopped me short of a few inches. That same something jerked my leg, and I felt my body leave the ground.

The only things running through my mind were pretty much obscene curse words that I didn't even remember knowing as my body was hurled through the air. This thing was obsessed with throwing stuff. Within a fraction of a second, I registered Saera appearing at the door before I slammed into her. We both crashed to the floor in a heap.

"Jeez, Maece," Saera said, sounding breathless, "I was on my way."

I looked up at her equally breathless and opened my mouth with the intention of asking what had taken her so long, but I froze at the animalistic scream that came from the hallway. Another scream followed the sound, but from someone with more human qualities, and this one was born out of fear.

Perching ourselves up in the door opening, I watched the freak drag an officer by the leg. I hadn't even thought about the half dozen men that I had managed to incapacitate before someone had released the freak. That's what getting your ass kicked by an enhanced mutilated creature apparently did.

One or two of the remaining five officers had crowded the magnetic lift and relentlessly hit the panel to summon the transport for a swift escape. The others were trying to make their way to the staircase. I guessed the freak had other ideas.

He dragged one of the officers by the leg, kicking and screaming. At the door of the lift, one of the other men stood and watched restlessly, as if debating whether he should intervene, but then he turned to join his comrades.

At my side, Saera's eyes grew wide as the freak stopped and grabbed the screaming man by his uniform.

"Get back," I said. Having experienced it myself, I had a pretty good idea of what was about to happen.

With no time to get to our feet, I grabbed Saera around the waist and pulled her back—dragging her inside the room.

Fortunately, she had the sense to cooperate. As we pulled our feet across the threshold, I reached up and slammed the controls to close the door.

The door started to slide into its locked position as something, or rather someone, crashed against it and stopped it from closing completely. The officer's broken body lay crumpled inside the door's opening. His head had cracked open, exposing a gray, bloody mash. The freak had thrown the officer's body to stop us from locking ourselves in. Apparently, that thing was smarter than it looked.

"We've gotta move," I said, staggering to my feet and pulling Saera up along with me.

"Yeah, but where to?"

I glanced around the room. It was a dead end. Feeling the unsteadiness in my legs, I grabbed hold of a table to keep myself from keeling over. My breathing was labored, and along with the tinge of panic that started to surface, it took some effort to stop myself from hyperventilating. As if sensing my discomfort, Saera wrapped an arm around my waist to help steady me. She had a worried look on her face as she studied me.

"Are you okay?" she asked in a strained voice.

I nodded, unsure if my voice could hide the emotions I felt. Unwilling to disclose my feelings and the fact that my throat hurt from where that freak had gripped me, I kept my mouth shut—it even hurt to breathe.

Saera's eyes were wide, and her breathing was heavy, but without my heads-up, I couldn't be sure what she was feeling or how she was doing. The sight of her led me to believe she was scared as I recognized that feeling inside myself. That sensation of fear that once had felt so alien to me spiked as a hand gripped around the edge of the door.

I glanced at Saera, who swallowed hard. Then she lifted her hand and handed me the heads-up she'd been holding.

"Kyran's finished with it," she said. For a split second, I wondered if he had succeeded in getting the data out into the world, but that would have to wait. We had bigger problems.

The officer's body wedged between the door twitched. Quickly, I placed the heads-up over my eyes and took in the room. A second later, the body was yanked away from the door opening. A soft thud announced the landing of it somewhere inside the hallway.

With a loud growl, the freak wrenched the door open and stepped inside.

"Oh shit," Saera muttered. I took a breath to gain my composure and forced myself to stand on my own as I shifted to maneuver in front of Saera.

"Eh, Maecy...what's the plan?" she whispered near my ear as if that thing hearing her would make a difference. A scan with my heads-up registered only the lowest of brain functions and indicated a device lodged at the back of the freak's neck.

The freak took another step forward. Its broad shoulders had barely fit through the opening of the door. Eyes that rolled inside oversized eye sockets homed in on us. The freak's entire face looked as if it had been sculpted around a helmet.

Cheekbones had doubled in size, and its forehead looked as if it had come from a prehistoric creature. My heads-up took it all in, and I felt the panic I had felt before had loosened its grip on me. The device strapped to my head had already depicted the weak spots that I would need to hit if I wanted to survive this next encounter, and although it didn't make the fear go away, I did feel I could breathe again. My confidence slowly returned.

"I'm gonna distract it," I said in answer to Saera's question, "then you're gonna bolt." Saera took hold of my arm, and I sensed she was about to speak. "Saera, don't argue. I'm just gonna be long enough for you to get past the door. Then I'm right behind you."

"Sure," she replied, drawing out the word.

Instinctively we both took a couple of steps back as the freak moved forward.

"God, that thing is ugly," she said as she hung on to my shoulders. "And naked, very naked."

"Get ready," I said, ignoring her.

"Are you sure about this?" she asked, "I mean, look at that thing."

"Saera!" I said. Saera yelped, but it wasn't from the sound of my harsh voice. The thing had grabbed a chair standing by the table and lifted it over his head. In a reflex gesture, I shoved Saera and then ducked down, heading in the opposite direction. The chair slammed into the wall and broke on impact. Pieces clattered to the ground as the freak screamed.

From my peripheral vision, I could see Saera hunkered down against the wall, protecting her ears with the palms of her hands. I wondered if the bioprinter had altered this thing's vocal cords. The sound it produced must have been one of the most awful things that I had ever heard.

The thing glanced across the room as if it were assessing it. Its eyes fell on Saera. I stood, wanting to draw its attention, but then shots were fired inside the hallway. The freak only hesitated for a moment at the sound before it set its sights on Saera again. I had already seized the moment as I pushed off with all the strength my suit had to offer and slammed my shoulder into the creature. Catching it off balance, it staggered back into the hallway. Within seconds of entering the now less-than-sterile hallway, I used the heads-up to give me the lowdown of what those shots I had heard meant.

The doors to the lift where I had last seen the remainder of officers trying to find a way out stood open. The bodies of those same men now lay on the floor in pools of blood. Riffy stood at the lift's door, holding it open while, from the corner of my eye, I caught Reece standing over the body of the enforcer.

"Saera!" I shouted as I pushed at the freak's body. Its back collided with the energy field, and the window's integrity fluctuated.

It didn't take the freak long to overpower my hold on him. My strength was no match for his, and he overturned our position, slamming me into the shield and made the barrier shimmer again. At least I had its attention.

As if on cue, Saera stepped into the door opening as I shouted her name again, but it was Reece who claimed her immediate attention.

"Lift...now!"

At that point, the freak decided to lift me off my feet. For a moment, I wondered if he were about to throw me after Saera, but then Reece's magnetic blast slamming into its side made the giant falter, and he released his grip on me. My legs buckled from underneath me, and I crashed to the floor. The freak threw his hands in the air and growled like an animal.

The tiny bit of respite felt welcome and allowed me to catch my breath. My heads-up registered the sound of a gun sliding across the floor before I heard it myself. As if on autopilot, my hand reached out to receive the weapon tossed by Reece across the floor.

"Now, don't start spraying those," he shouted, "or we'll all get a tan." I lifted my head in time to see his hand make a gesture that hinted at an explosion. The hint was enough to tell me he had loaded the enforcer's weapon with the special ammo. I would have to create some distance between me and the freak if I wanted to survive the blast.

Reece grimaced as the mechanically altered body turned to face him.

"Wow, there," he said as he raised a hand to shield himself from laying eyes on the deformed giant, "ever heard of pants?"

Reece fired another couple of rounds at the creature as he muttered, "That is just wrong." Then he turned on his heels and bolted in the direction of the magnetic lift.

"Whenever you're ready, babe," he yelled over his shoulder. Without wasting any time, I kicked out my leg and connected as hard as I could with the freak's knee. Except for some metal grinding inside the leg and a reflective step forward by the freak, the kick hadn't done much, but then I didn't need much. Just enough to escape from the grasp of the freak who had found a renewed interest in me after he had stopped growling.

On hands and feet, I scooted across the floor. My boots squeaked on the slick tiles as I managed to get to my feet. Ahead, Saera gave me an anxious look as she stood inside the box that would hopefully take us down to the Hymag while Riffy and Reece seemed to be fiddling with the doors.

"Go," I shouted, and as if he had read my mind, Reece slammed a fist into one of the buttons that set the lift in motion.

As I got halfway down the hallway, I probably should have felt my nerves jump into overdrive as I watched the heads of Saera, Reece, and Riffy disappear while the box lowered itself. But somehow there wasn't an inch of doubt in my mind that they'd never leave me behind.

As the three of them disappeared, I raised the weapon in my hand and swung it to point behind me. The freak hadn't wasted any time to make his pursuit and sat right on my heels—too close.

At the lack of choices, I pulled the trigger, and as I felt the kickback of the weapon reverberate through my arm, I forced my legs to move faster. From the information fed to me by the heads-up, I immediately knew something was off. There had been too much of a time delay, and just as I glanced over my shoulder, I witnessed the explosion at the other end of the hall. I had missed the freak. The damned thing was too fast, and I had miscalculated my trajectory.

Getting too close to the lift and our only escape route, I couldn't risk the damn thing following us. Without another thought, I fired the weapon again and again. I kept firing until it clicked empty.

This time I didn't have to wait for the heads-up to inform me of the situation because I could already feel the heat at the back of my neck before a shockwave took hold of my body and flung me forward. With a bone-crushing sensation, I felt my body slam into the back wall where the lift used to be. A quick thank-you raced across my thoughts as I figured that Reece and Riffy must have been tinkering with the door to keep it open.

As gravity took hold of me, I could only hope that my suit had enough integrity to protect me from the fall, because that lift had gone down a lot faster than I would have liked.

Chapter twenty-six

Reece

The massive explosion overhead wasn't hard to miss. Neither was the loud thud as something landed hard on the roof of the box. For a second, I allowed myself to wonder, or hope, that the thud we'd heard wasn't what we all probably knew it to be. I couldn't even register the faces riding down with me on this lift as the box started to shake and groan before I felt a moment of weightlessness. A loud hum followed by a whooshing sound suggested that the magnetic field used to put the lift into motion had failed.

I did register the oh-shit looks going around and Riffy's yelp as the box we occupied plummeted to the ground. Fortunately, we had covered most of the distance down, and even our lesser versions of the enforcer suits managed to withstand the force that our bodies had to endure as the box crashed. Without feeling the need to check if the others were okay, I shouted, "Riffy, door!"

The landing had unhinged the door, and Riffy needed to pry it open. Knowing he would get it done, I reached up and unlatched the trapdoor to get access to the roof of the box. It took a few tries, but with some brute force, I managed to get it open. All the while Saera kept an anxious eye on me.

Looking up, I couldn't see Maece or detect any movement. Straightening my back and bending my knees, I nodded at Saera. Without hesitation, she planted her foot on my thigh and pushed herself up to reach the opening.

As she climbed through, I stole a glance at Riffy, who had the door open a crack. On the watch for more bad guys, he slowly eased it open. The thought that Kelle was still out there, camped out inside that Hymag crossed my mind, but then loud cursing caught my attention, and I looked up.

The sound of footsteps reverberated down as my eyes found Saera moving over the opening. Soft words I couldn't decipher had me worried. The heads-up flew down at me, which nearly hit me in the head, only fueled the bad feeling that stirred in my gut.

"Riffy," I said as I grabbed the heads-up. He had barely turned my way before I tossed it at him. With a clumsy move, he managed to clutch the device to his chest and threw me a questioning look. "Take that and go check on Kelle."

"She should be fine," Riffy said. "I've dose—" I cut him off with a kill gesture while simultaneously Saera spoke up.

"Reece," she said as she looked to be pulling a heavy load.

"Nothing," I replied as if it had been programmed inside my head.

"What?" she asked as she poked her head over

the opening. Her face looked even paler than usual, and the wild look in her eyes sobered me up quickly.

"Can you ease her down?" I asked, not even bothering to ask how Maece was doing. The look on Saera's face told me enough.

As Maece appeared hands-first through the opening, I shot Riffy an urgent look.

"Go see to Kelle," I said in a loud whisper. Riffy turned and climbed out of the crashed lift box.

"Riffy," I called after him as I reached up to catch Maece.

"Yeah?"

"Use the heads-up," I said. I didn't watch him place the device on his head. By then Saera had eased Maece down, and I held her in my arms. She looked like hell. The sturdy suit still covered her body, and I could only imagine the damage underneath but hoped the remaining integrity had been enough to protect her.

Unlike her body, her face showed the mess she was in. Blood seeped from a cut on her head down her face and matted her hair. Beside massive bruising, it also seemed as if her jaw was broken.

I shifted her in my arms to get a better hold of her and felt a need to utter soothing words, but I feared my voice would break and let loose a whole bunch of emotions I wouldn't be able to contain. I still needed to focus; we weren't out of trouble yet, and I needed to keep it together.

As I climbed out of the box, Saera landed behind me with a thud. Glancing around the large space, I didn't notice any movement. Riffy stood on the Hymag platform, surveying our surroundings with the heads-up sitting on his head. With Saera on my heels, I started to make my way to him.

"Why haven't you started it up?" I shouted. Riffy threw up a hand in exasperation as we neared the entryway to the Hymag.

"Because it won't start."

"What do you mean it won't start?" Saera said. Crossing the empty space between the lift and the Hymag platform, she had stayed close by my side, keeping a careful eye on Maece, but at Riffy's declaration, she pushed past him into the transport.

I followed her closely, but I was stopped in my tracks and nearly bumped into her with Maece still in my arms. Instead of heading straight to the pilot's cabin, she rushed to the bench, where she found Kelle lying motionless with her eyes closed.

"She's okay," Riffy quickly piped, in what sounded like damage control. We both knew this Hymag wouldn't be big enough for us to hide if there was anything more than a scratch on Kelle. I just hoped Riffy's drugs had done their part and had healed most of that crater of a wound that had been left behind on Kelle's arm.

Maece groaned as I placed her on the bench across from Kelle.

From what I could tell, Saera took a quick inventory of Kelle's condition—checking her pulse and pupil reflexes. She moved fast, and Maece's head had barely touched the seat before she shoved me aside.

"Get this thing running," she said without sparing me a glance. My eyes lingered on Maece's bruised face for another fraction of a moment before I turned and made my way to the pilot's cabin. If we didn't get out of here. it wouldn't matter what shape Maece was in because we'd all die if they caught us out here.

"Riffy," Saera called out just before I reached the cabin, "Maece needs you—switch."

I heard their footfalls behind me while Saera took Riffy's spot guarding the exit and I slipped into the pilot's seat. It didn't take me long to figure out something was wrong. Everything seemed frozen in place—not even a single light blinked as my hands came down on the buttons. Finally, I rammed my fist into the console.

"Son of a…" I started to say but stopped myself and glanced around the cabin. I drew in a breath in the hope of a calming effect. Letting frustration take over wasn't going to help us get out of here.

Looking over my shoulder, I saw Riffy hunched over Maece's unmoving form. "Dammit," I muttered and slipped out of the seat.

"What's wrong?" Saera asked, standing at the Hymag's exit. Sparing a glance at Riffy as his hands worked on Maece, I noticed Kelle had awoken and eyed me wearily.

"Hey, you," I said and reached to touch her leg. She looked groggy, but gave me a half-smile, and coming from Kelle that said a lot. It told me she'd be okay.

"I can't get the damn thing to start," I said and

recognized the frustration in my own voice. I moved to the back of the Hymag where Saera stood at the door. Her brows furrowed while her eyes remained fixed on something outside the transport. Before I could ask what was wrong, she raised her weapon and dropped to a knee.

"You better think of something fast, because we've got company," she said in a loud voice so it would reach over the sound of her weapon as it discharged. In a reflex, I hunched down, although I knew the Hymag to be impervious to the standard rounds of any weapons fire. It wouldn't stand long against those special rounds that enforcers carried, but then I didn't think that whoever had assembled outside would be that desperate yet. Besides, I figured they'd want us alive at first.

I glanced outside and saw several figures clad in black and gray taking cover behind the large pillars. Saera was a good shot, and she'd be able to keep them at bay for some time, but it seemed as if the word had spread around about us, because more officers carrying heavy armory filed into the room.

"Son of a..." I muttered as I turned to give the controls one last try. In my gut, I already knew the chances of me getting this thing moving were zero to none, but I had to try something. Handing ourselves over wasn't something anyone in this group would consider, and the only alternative would be dying inside a metal cylinder that refused to do what it was made for. I didn't consider that an option either.

"Riffy," I said as I passed, "we've got trouble. Prepare to help out Saera."

He glanced over his shoulder in Saera's direction as he asked, "Why aren't we moving?"

"If I knew that we'd be doing it already," I said. I couldn't help the agitation in my voice. I flinched at the impact of a high-powered projectile weapon against the hull of the Hymag, but it was Maece's voice that stopped me in my tracks.

"Reece," she said in a hoarse voice, "I can help." One of my hands had balled into a fist and hovered in the air midstrike, with the intention of striking an unsuspecting wall panel. I withdrew my fist, turned back, and rushed to where Riffy was still kneeling at Maece's side. Kelle had shifted into a sitting position and watched Maece with the same wide eyes that I'd caught in Riffy's gaze.

"Reece."

This was the second time in a short period that I'd heard my name called out with a sense of urgency, but this time it was Saera. She ducked behind a door panel, and weapons fire ripped through seats at the back of the craft. I tapped Riffy's shoulder and pointed a finger at Saera.

"Go," I added. Without hesitation, Riffy got up, drawing his weapon, and as he headed to the back to help Saera, I took his spot at Maece's side.

To see her like that would have taken me aback anytime, but it was Maece who refused to let me linger on her bruised and blood-covered face. She grabbed my arm and started to pull herself up.

"Baby, wait," I said. The words were out before I could even think about it, and if there had been more time I might have scolded myself, but it didn't seem

Maece had heard. Besides, screw the idea of letting her figure things out by herself. If I were about to die here in this tin box, I wanted her to know how I felt about her.

Maece pushed herself up on the bench and grabbed one of my shoulders for support. She squinted against the light, and I realized she wasn't wearing her heads-up. I found it on the floor where Riffy must have left it. Picking it up, I showed it to Maece and she nodded.

"Help me," she said, her voice sounding groggy. It was obvious it was hard for her to form the words with a jaw that couldn't be anything but broken.

"To do what," I asked, sounding as surprised as the look I noticed on Kelle's face.

"Get me…up front," she said before a grown escaped her mouth. Leaning heavily on me, she got to her feet. Her head shifted to take in the action at the back of the vehicle before her eyes landed on Kelle. The tiny woman's eyes nearly jumped out of her sockets as Maece pulled a hand over Kelle's cropped hair. The gesture, as familiar to me as it would have been to Kelle, raised several questions that I knew had to wait.

Maybe Maece remembered some enforcer way to unlock this Hymag so we could get the hell out of here. As fast as her body allowed me, I moved her down the aisle until we reached the pilot's cabin.

By the time I had her seated, sweat covered her brows. Her dark skin had acquired a ghostly white sheen as her eyes shot across the controls. Behind me, I heard Saera shout something incomprehensible.

The fact that I saw Kelle slide off the bench and struggle to find her footing while holding a big gun in her hand that still functioned didn't seem like a positive sign. The state she was in, Kelle probably shouldn't have been moving, but apparently, the enemy forces were more than the others could handle.

"Eh…do you even know what you're looking for?" I asked as I helped Maece with the heads-up.

Maece's hand reached out to one of the screens, and she started typing. Numbers flew across the screen as she said, "I need…to access the main system…to grant…permission for transport." Her words came all broken up as if they needed to be put together like some sort of puzzle. She grimaced, and it looked as if it cost her quite a bit of effort to be doing whatever it was what she was doing.

"That is not possible," a hesitant voice reached my ear.

"Nice of you to join us, Kyran." I had nearly forgotten the people that had supposed to be our eyes and ears on this mission, and I couldn't remember the last time I'd heard them.

"We've been working on the problem on our end, but there is just no way to reach the Hymag system—it is not connected to the grid," he said as lights started to blink on the console. Maece's fingers still typed away on the different keypads, and my eyes widened as I saw the main screen light up with the command codes I'd been looking for.

"You did it," I said and glanced over my shoulder. It wasn't too late yet. The Hymag hadn't been breached, and Saera, Riffy, and Kelle held their ground. Just as I turned back, Maece's head lolled forward, and I caught her in my arms as her body slumped. Trying to support her head, I removed the heads-up and felt something solid and cold on her neck just under the base of her skull. My hand came back soaked in blood as I eased her back into the seat.

I forced myself not to think about the piece of metal that seemed to sit lodged inside Maece's head. At this point, I had no way of telling whether something had struck her or whether the fall down the lift shaft had dislodged the device implanted in her head.

The fact that she had known how to activate the Hymag made me lean toward the latter, but there was no way to be sure, and now wasn't the time.

"Leaving," I shouted over my shoulder as I set the controls from the copilot seat. It took some effort because I wasn't used to handling the controls from the right side of the cabin, but I managed.

Behind me, I heard loud sighs as the exit door slid closed.

"It's about time," Saera muttered. "Where the hell is Maece?" I didn't wait for her to get up to the cabin or for any of the others to take their seats. The explosions of magnetic rounds increased against the hull, and it wouldn't be long before someone might decide to pull out the big guns. I throttled the engine and punched it. The Hymag launched itself into the tunnel, and within seconds the sound of explosive rounds impacting on the hull faded as we picked up speed.

Chapter twenty-seven

Maece

Frantic voices pulled me out of the darkness, and I wondered what was going on. It was hard to open my eyelids that felt as if they were glued together. I forced them open, but as the light hit my pupils, I squeezed them shut. Someone had removed my heads-up, making everything seem brighter than it should.

I sensed that my body was in motion, as if someone were carrying me on a stretcher. My curiosity stronger than the light annoying my eyes, I opened my eyelids again. Peering through half-open slits, I saw the backs of two men. Above me, I recognized the domed roof of the cavern where Saera had first brought me to meet Harp.

A jolt sent a sharp pain through my body, and I expected to hear a scream rising from my throat, but no more than a groan exited.

"Watch it, you idiot." The words were clearly spoken by Saera, and I searched for her. I tried to say her name, but the effort made me cough, and I tasted blood in my mouth. A face blocked my vision, but instead of Saera, the balding doctor came into focus.

The doctor who had removed my memory pain eyed me with a grim expression on his face.

"Stop," he said in a loud voice, "she's awake." The moving sensation halted. I opened my mouth to speak, but the doctor planted his hands over my face and then shined a bright light into my eyes. I closed my eyelids and wanted to swat the light from his fingers, but I couldn't move my hands. I tried to lift my head to see if my hands were tied down, but I couldn't manage that either. I wanted to fight against the restraints, but my body hurt too much. My voice didn't work either, but it didn't stop me from trying to find out what was going on.

"Shh…it's okay," Saera's voice entered my ears. She had to shove the balding doctor aside before I saw her. "You're hurt, but you're already starting to heal, just try to relax."

"We have to get her into Subterra," Harp said, "now!" I couldn't see him, but Harp's commanding voice was distinctive enough. Saera had told me I was healing, so why did I sense the urgency in Harp's tone? The stretcher started moving again, and I noticed we were heading toward the Hymag. Traveling inside the Hymag, which could reach speeds up to a thousand miles per hour, would get us to Subterra in a couple of minutes.

"Kyran, call ahead and make sure the bioprinter is available," Harp said.

The edges of my vision blurred as I tried to make sense of Harp's words. I tried to search out Saera's eyes in the hope of finding answers, but she looked straight ahead as she helped maneuver the stretcher. I felt sure that Saera wouldn't have lied to me when she said I was healing, but then my injuries weren't all that was wrong with me. I still had that device stuck in the back of my head, and Harp's mention of the bioprinter sent a shiver down my spine. As I tried to juggle my thoughts, my mind was getting fuzzier, and memories I couldn't place seemed to rack my brain. In the end, I couldn't keep my eyes from closing.

My eyes shot open again, and I wasn't in the cavern anymore. I was lying in a Hymag box, but I couldn't tell if we were moving. The pain I had felt before had retreated, leaving a dull hum of discomfort in its wake. I was sure drugs had helped in creating the sensation. I saw Saera and Harp, although their faces were kind of blurry. The sight of Harp reminded me of what he had said before: "Make sure the bioprinter is available." The word became a repetitive mantra inside my head, and I didn't like the way it forced my stomach into knots.

Images of a strange-looking tube entered my brain, but I couldn't tell if these were memories or a dream. The thing resembled something from the history files stuck in my head. In the olden days, they would stick the dead in a coffin and bury them in the ground—and I lay inside.

The glass shell of the tube made it possible for me to see the men and women wearing protective suits as they bustled around the room. Hard white light fell on me from the ceiling. I blinked to see similar tubes standing on both sides of mine, but only the left one was also occupied.

The man inside it lay still as robotic arms poked and prodded his body. As I watched the machines working, it reminded me of how lasers could graft a tattoo into the skin, except instead of adding ink, this thing seemed to be adding muscle and skin tissue. The man's mouth stood up in a contorted manner, baring teeth as if stuck in a scream, but I couldn't hear him. His eyes were open wide, and tears slid down his temple.

As fear started to rise inside me, my tube started to hum. I wanted to get up, crawl out of this torture device, and run until I got home, but all I could do was watch the lid slide over me until it locked into place. Lights flashed, and the humming got louder, while the robotic arms hovered over me. My heart pounded in my chest like a wild animal demanding a way out. I couldn't breathe, and darkness edged around my vision. I welcomed these signs that I was about to pass out. At least then I wouldn't feel the pain, and after I would wake up, I wouldn't remember what had happened. I wouldn't remember that I had chosen to do this and that it had been the biggest mistake I had ever made. I should have listened to Reece, and I should have told Saera the truth. All I wanted was to go home.

The moment my eyes shot open, I realized it had all been a dream. The men and women in protective suits were gone, and so was the bright light. The room was dimly lit, which was fine by me. My vision was blurry from the tears filling my eyes. I blinked and felt a trail of drops roll down my temple, and it reminded me of the man in the tube. I shuddered at the thought.

Even with my vision blurred, I searched the room as much as I could, and found Saera sitting in a chair next to the bed I was lying on. I blinked to check that it was really her, and then tried to speak before I realized my throat felt as dry as the wastelands outside the dome.

The hoarse sound I made was enough to draw Saera's attention. She pulled her chair closer so our faces were inches apart, and she wiped a strand of hair from my forehead.

"They gave you something to relax your muscles," she said in a low voice as she reached for a cup and held it to my mouth. Cool water eased some of the dryness from my throat.

"How did we do?" I asked in a raspy voice. Saera shrugged in a noncommittal way.

"Not sure," she said, "Kyran said he got the data out, but after we'd gotten you back to the base, everything went so fast. Doc said he couldn't help you there, and so we rushed you back to Subterra. We've only been here for about an hour."

I tried to move, but nothing seemed to work. The drugs must have also kept the pain away, because I didn't feel much of anything, except for discomfort in my throat and the tears rolling down my cheek.

"Where is here?" I asked as my eyes roamed the sparse, little room.

"One of the primary medical facilities back home where the doctor works when he isn't patching up us rebels in the hideout underneath Umbras."

"The others," I said and swallowed. The feeling in my throat had improved with the help of the water, but it didn't seem wise to say too much. Saera smiled and pointed a thumb over her shoulder toward the door.

"They're all sitting in the hall waiting to get you home."

The smile didn't hold up for long, and she shifted in her seat before she realized she was still holding the cup of water in her hand, and she placed it on the table beside the bed. Our eyes met for a moment, and she opened her mouth as if to speak, but then closed it.

"What?" I asked. She looked at a spot on the wall behind me for a moment as if she needed to find the courage to say what she wanted to say, and then she cleared her throat.

"It's that thing stuck in your head. It's kind of dislodged. They are preparing to remove it," she said.

"Oh," I said. A sense of dread rushed through me, and it felt as if someone had sat down on my chest, making it hard to breathe.

Saera placed a hand on my chin and directed my gaze to hers.

"You'll be fine," she said. The conviction in her voice made me feel better, but it didn't erase the lingering nightmare of lying in that tube and Harp's words.

Behind Saera, a door opened, and as if on cue, Harp stepped into the room. He stood tall as ever as he crossed the floor with his hands behind his back.

As he approached the bed, I thought he looked older. The touches of gray hair streaking his temples seemed more notable, although the lighting in the room might have had something to do with it.

Saera stood from her chair to face him.

"What is taking so long?" she asked, sounding bewildered.

"They're ready for her," Harp replied as he directed his gaze toward the door and nodded. The door opened and two figures wearing masks walked in. At first, they reminded me of the men and women wearing protective suits, but then I noticed the balding doctor's protruding belly. It was comforting to know that there was someone behind that mask that I had met. The doctor and his companion took up positions at the front and rear of my bed, and I felt the jolt as the bed was set in motion.

Saera stayed by my side as they rolled me from one room to the next. The contrast between the two rooms was huge. Screens covered the walls, showing all kinds of colorful images. Desks were full of different sorts of devices and computers running the screens. Bright lights filled my eyes, and I closed them. I opened them again when I felt the bed come to a halt, but as I did, I wished I hadn't.

A long, circular glass tube filled my vision. The doctors who had pushed my bed stood there, pressing buttons and activating lights on the machine. My heart jumped into overdrive, drumming a warning signal inside my chest. The glass lid slid backward in an invitation for its next victim. More alarms went off in my head as the balding doctor moved around the tube and stood at the head of my bed. They couldn't seriously consider putting me in there. Fear took control of my body, sending tremors up and down my limbs.

"Wait…" I managed to say, but any other words remained stuck in my throat as I tried to catch my breath.

Saera stepped closer—worry written across her face. She placed a hand on my shoulder and spoke my name in a calming voice. I ignored her, my gaze set on the glass coffin. They couldn't expect me to go in there, because I wouldn't survive it. Every primal instinct in my body fired to life, trying to get it to move.

"No!" I said and tried to scream when my limbs wouldn't budge, but all that exited my mouth was a frustrated groan. Somewhere at my side, a machine started to beep at an irregular and frantic rhythm.

People scrambled around me, but I had only eyes for the tube that I was sure was going to kill me, until a face blocked my view.

A young boy stood by my side, watching me with curious eyes. As our gazes locked, his mouth lifted into a generous smile. The sight of him made me gasp. Besides his generous smile, his dark eyes held a sense of wonder that I didn't even know existed in this world. As if the answer to every question ever asked resided inside this boy's mind.

At my side, the beeping sound settled into a steady beat, and I felt the fear fade into the background. The boy looked up and nodded at Harp, who I hadn't even noticed standing behind him.

"Can she handle it if they remove the device?" Saera asked. I barely made out her whispered words, but the boy's smile grew wider as he turned to face her. He nodded, and Saera responded with a tentative smile of her own.

Then the boy returned his attention to me. It felt as if I knew the kid, and some memory buried deep inside my mind would probably confirm it, but at this point, I couldn't find it. The boy placed a hand on my chest. Even through the fabric of the sheets, I felt the heat seeping through my skin and into my bones. All my nerves seemed to calm at once and pulled me into a deep sleep.

Chapter twenty-eight

Maece

I awoke in a dark room, but I instantly knew where I was. Mostly it was the familiar smells of the blanket and pillow that betrayed my location. They had taken me home a few hours after the procedure that had been an apparent success.

I must have been out of it because I don't remember much after shouting at my doctor. All I knew was that I had to get out of that medical facility with one of those bioprinters so near. I wasn't going to spend one more minute inside that place. The irrational fear that they'd place me inside that coffin again without my consent had made me lash out at the poor man. A hazy memory of Reece and Riffy dragging me from my room was all that was left after that.

As I lay in my own bed, I inhaled, deeply drawing in the scents through my nose. It fired the synapses in my brain, sending tiny pinpricks running up and down my scalp. The device in the back of my head was gone, and now my brain had reclaimed the memories that had eluded me for so long.

As if they resembled a living, breathing entity, those memories murmured with a soft hum in the back of my head, ready to step forward if needed. That single inhalation of familiar scents brought everything back—everything I wanted to know, needed to know, or should have remembered filled my head. I had come home in every sense of the word.

I opened my eyes to scan the room. A grimy teddy bear sitting on the bedside table raised a smile to my lips. My old dresser stood propped against the wall along with a couple of stone figurines on top that had remained where I had left them two years ago, and a washbasin hung on another wall. A small figure sitting in the middle of my room caught my attention, and I sat up. As the blanket slid from my body, I realized I wasn't wearing any clothes, and I pulled fabric up over my chest.

The young boy sitting in the middle of my room, who I now remembered by name as Spiro, had his eyes closed, and it didn't appear as if he had peeked. He was the same kid who had stood by my bed before they had stuck me inside that bioprinter. It was as if the information I needed sat stored inside a filing cabinet, and I only needed to open a drawer to fetch it in order to recognize one of my closest friends.

Blue light edged inside the room through the window from a streetlight outside. It created a blue halo as it fell over the child-like shape sitting on the ground in the middle of the room. With his bald head and round face, Spiro looked almost angelic in the blue light. He sat with his legs crossed and his back straight while his hands rested on his knees.

As I watched him, I sensed his calmness reaching out around him and felt its tingle on my skin. He didn't even open his eyes as he spoke, "It is said that it is not polite to stare."

"Yet you have never said it," I replied. A smile grew on the boy's face, and I felt his joy fill the room.

"It is good to have you back," Spiro said.

"It's good to be back," I replied. Although I didn't feel entirely sure about it, I added something else. "It is good to see you."

Spiro had been the reason for me to infiltrate the Tenebrae Enforcer Department in the first place. It had seemed like the right thing to do at the time, but now I wasn't so sure. He had convinced me that there wouldn't be any other way, and Harp had agreed with him. At the time, I didn't understand why Harp was so adamant to send me on this mission or why Spiro had chosen me. There wasn't anything special about me, but after Spiro had expressed that the situation was even direr than I could imagine, I had relented. It seemed he had been right all along.

Like Saera and me, Spiro had been one of the kids Harp had rescued from the power plants. But unlike us, Spiro had a neuro-device implanted in the back of his head from when he was a baby. Touching that Hymag line might have rendered the device useless, but it still sat lodged in the back of his head.

At first glance, he still resembled that twelve-year-old kid, but when interacting with him, the way he spoke and the knowledge he held, a person immediately knew he was different.

"You're feeling better now your memories have returned," Spiro said.

Even though it wasn't a question, I replied, "I am."

He considered it a form of politeness to engage in normal conversation even though he had no need for it. That device lodged in the back of his head hadn't just screwed with his internal systems—after an electro-magnetic shock had disabled the device, the change had enhanced him. Disabling the device resulted in his synapses firing at inhuman speeds inside his brain, using his neurons for efficient, lightning-fast communication not only within his own head but also with the minds of others. He knew what I would say before I had even thought of voicing it.

His eyes opened and caught mine. The blue light coming from outside enhanced the color of his eyes and almost made them sparkle even though he peered at me through narrow slits. Spiro's Asian heritage had blessed him with a face that reminded me of a porcelain doll.

I felt his mind reach out to me, and even though he had been doing it for as long as I had known him, it felt strange to me now. As if somehow the connection had been deepened.

You know more than most, but not all. It'll take time, and I'll help you along the path.

Spiro's words echoed inside my head, though his mouth hadn't moved. It was as if Harp was talking to me over the communications channel.

"The fog clouding your mind will soon lift," he

said aloud. "It will take effort for it not to overwhelm you."

This had been the risk from the start. Spiro had predicted as much. His gift had given him the ability to see, understand, and do more with his brain than any other human had ever managed.

I had always suspected he had the ability to see into the future, although he had never admitted it. Considering this now would force me to withdraw that conclusion. It wasn't as much as seeing into the future as predicting it by ways of a complicated equation that involved the past, present, and logical reasoning.

He knew what ArtRep was up to, but his present being would never allow his physical form to be violated by another neuron device ever again. To retrieve the information the Subterran government wanted about the threat that ArtRep posed, he needed Sulos's plan, and his condition wouldn't allow him to do this on his own. That was why he had approached Harp and how I had gotten involved.

From the start, Spiro had informed me of the risks. He had explained about the memory loss and that he felt confident it could be reversed. To his credit, he had never promised that my memories would return, and although that had scared me at the time, I'd respected his honesty. He would have never asked me to do this if he hadn't thought it necessary.

I trusted Spiro's judgment—still did and that's why I had to take the risk. I had to find a way to figure out ArtRep's endgame, and getting our hands on enforcers gear had seemed the only way, even if it meant my brain could fry or my memories were lost forever. Too many people had died working at those plants or enforcing the law, and now the fate of the entire planet hung in the balance. At least we had figured out their plans, and now it was up to us to do something about it.

Spiro lifted from his seat on the ground in an almost snakelike motion.

"Your sister would like to see you," he said, "but you will have to be patient. It will take time for her to understand."

It wasn't hard to read between the lines what he meant, and he didn't need to project it inside my head. By doing what we had, Spiro, Harp, and I had lied to her, but mostly me. It had been my idea to fake my death.

The only way for us to have had any kind of hope to breach the ArtRep systems was to get our hands on enforcer technology. Only with the heads-up would our tech guys be able to extract the information we needed. If we hadn't, we still wouldn't have known what Sulos was up to. I had known it could take years for my mind to adjust to the neuron device, let alone being able to resist it. Our early projections had been at least five years, and I wanted Saera and the others to be able to move on with their lives. I didn't want them to worry about their crazy friend and sister who might or might not survive.

Fortunately, I had been lucky enough that Harp had met Kyran. Without him and his tinkering from within TED's systems, I would probably still be sitting in that chair inside Memory Junction.

"Saera," I said. The word left my mouth in close to whispered silence. My stomach turned at the thought of having to explain what I had done. She still thought I had been caught by accident or some stupidity on my part.

Mere seconds later, I heard footfalls in the hallway outside the room. I glanced at Spiro, and he read my concerns either from my face or from the words forming inside my head.

"Pain can be a companion of truth," he said, "as can trust, honor, and love."

I shook my head at his vague remark that once would have cracked me up, but now Spiro's strange way of expressing himself seemed to make more sense to me.

A moment later Saera appeared in the doorway. Spiro took a slight bow and turned. He stopped to rest a hand on Saera's arm. She looked down at him and nodded at the smile he offered.

"Don't worry," he said to her. "Your sister is in no danger of starting to talk like a fortune cookie." Saera grinned at Spiro's reply to the question that hadn't been asked but for sure had lingered in her thoughts.

The reference to the old Chinese custom had, of course, originated from Reece, and it had resonated with the rest of us. We had all used the phrase around Spiro, and sometimes I had wondered if he took it as an insult, but as I sensed his reaction, I knew he enjoyed the comparison and saw it as a term of endearment.

As Spiro left the room, I sat up on the bed but held the blanket draped over my naked body. Saera hesitated by the door. Left alone with me, her musings over Spiro's reaction quickly faded, and I sensed the fear that ran through her body. I could almost taste it.

In a way, it seemed as if I was wearing the heads-up device and I could still scan her vitals. It made for a strange sensation and would surely take some time to get used to, but Spiro had warned me of the changes my body could go through after the device had been removed from the back of my head.

"You know you don't have to be scared of me, right," I said. With eyes wide from shock, she stared at me but remained frozen in her spot.

"I'm not afraid…" she started to say but stumbled on the words. I cocked my head and narrowed my eyes at her. At that, she threw up her arms in exasperation. "All right…maybe a little."

"Because you think there's a possibility I'm not me anymore," I said.

Saera nodded her head and added, "And because of this." She waved a finger between us and grimaced. "I'm not sure I'm comfortable with you reading my mind."

"I can't read your mind," I said with a smile tugging at the corners of my lips.

"The kid seems to be doing that just fine and"— she hesitated—"you both had a similar device stuck in your heads."

"You don't have to worry about me doing that," I said, sounded convincing even to myself. "Besides, he had that thing working inside his head for twelve years, and me only two, and come to think of it, he still has it stuck in his head, so…"

The fact was that I didn't know to what extent what had happened had changed me or might still change me. I had noticed some heightened senses, but those were minor, like distinguishing all the different smells inside this room. Somehow the scent from the piece of soap sitting on my washbasin reached me where I sat. And although I had always been able to read Saera's body language, it came easier to me now. I even noticed the reaction of her pupils, but nothing came close to what I had witnessed over the years by watching Spiro.

Saera seemed to consider my reply before she said, "Well, you better not, because I can't have you know all my dirty secrets."

"I already know all your dirty secrets," I said as a grin spread across my face.

"I might have acquired some new ones while you were gone," she replied with a sheepish look on her face. I instantly knew where her mind had drifted, and I truly hoped I wouldn't inherit Spiro's gift, because I could live without the details of Saera's love life.

"It's weird," Saera concluded and crossed the short distance from the door to my bed. She sat down at the foot of the bed and gave me a strange look that edged on the border of being either thoughtful or suspicious.

"What?" I asked, unable to hold her gaze.

"So…" she said, but then she paused. Cocking her head to the side, she continued. "Everything is back in its place now?" She tipped a finger to her own head and then gestured at mine.

I feigned thinking about it. It wasn't as if my mind had been flooded with all the things I had forgotten, but I felt confident that if needed, the right memories would surface. With a mischievous grin plastered on my face, I said, "So you've finally made a pass at Kelle."

Saera frowned, probably not expecting the off-topic comment, but then even in this bluish-lit room, I could tell her face flushed red. Before I had left, Kelle had only been with us for a few years. She must have been fifteen or sixteen when Harp showed up with her on our doorstep. Right from the start, it had been obvious that Saera was smitten by the brooding young girl. But Kelle wasn't one to be easily won over. She had some serious trust issues and probably still did. I didn't think even Reece, who managed to bond with her first and who has since become a close friend, knows Kelle's entire story. As I watched Saera, I had a feeling she must have found out by now.

I stretched out my arm to reach for the small table beside my bed. A reading lamp and the grimy-looking teddy bear sat on top of it. As before, my grin widened into a smile at the sight of the stuffed animal that had been the first memory to breach the wall built by the device that had been planted inside my head.

Holding the blanket around my naked body in place, I grabbed the bear. Saera watched me in silence as my fingers traced the toy's back and found the secret compartment. I pulled out the fine silver bracelet that had been sitting in its hiding spot ever since I'd been gone.

"I believe this was how you initially intended to win her over," I said. Saera's eyes widened at the sight of the piece of jewelry she had entrusted to me for safekeeping. The thin band had belonged to her mother, who had received it from Saera's dad after he had found it at the plant he worked at. It hadn't looked like much at first—all brown and smudged, but Saera's dad had polished the old jewelry for weeks before he presented it to his wife as a birthday gift.

It was the only token Saera had left to remind her of her parents, and the fact that she'd been willing to give it to Kelle told me enough about how much she cared about her.

Smiling brightly, she took the bracelet and held it as if it had been made of glass. After a moment of staring at it, she glanced up, and the bluish light filtering inside the room reflected in her moist eyes. She scooted closer and threw her arms around me.

Apparently, I had given her enough proof that I had returned to my old self again as she held me tight and said, "Good to have you back, sis."

It felt good to hug her again and to be hugged myself. It had been too long, and I couldn't wait to see the others again. Unable to reply, I tightened my grip and relished the idea of being home with my family again.

"Oh, can I play," a mischievous sounding voice exclaimed.

Chapter twenty-nine

Maece

Reece stood by the door, leaning against its post with a wicked smile on his face. Saera released her grip and half turned to face him. I didn't know if it had been Saera's expression or something else, but Reece softened his tone.

"Harp has gone ahead to meet with the Subterran council, and he would like us there if you're able."

He did a decent job at holding a lopsided grin on his face, but I could easily read the concern from his eyes. Memories flooded my brain as if someone had left a tap running. I shifted my gaze and saw Saera watching Reece with a smile on her face. The way her face lit up reminded me of us goofing around on the streets of Subterra, getting into all kinds of mischief. I hoped I wouldn't be the one to put another dent in that smile—not again.

The information Harp and Kyran had fed Saera and me had all been true. The abuse of the Subterran people in the plants, how ArtRep used Subterrans as enforcers and that we needed a way to remove those neuro regulators. The thing was that Harp had known about most of this information before he had set us off on finding it.

Our team hadn't been part of the initial investigation that had gained the council's support for Harp years ago. Along with the council's endorsement also came the approval of the Subterran government, although they would never admit it. It was only when signs appeared that something bigger was going on that Harp had recruited Reece and myself. Riffy, Kelle, and Saera were never involved, and Reece and I were sworn to secrecy.

I swallowed hard at the thought of having to explain things to Saera. She was going to be so pissed.

"I myself would rather jump off a cliff, but if you're up for it, I'm willing to sacrifice myself and tag along," Reece continued.

"Sounds to me like you were summoned yourself, so don't pretend you're doing us any favors," Saera replied before she turned to me. "What do ya say, you up for an evening stroll?" The smile was still plastered on her face, and I blew out a breath in the knowledge that Saera might find out some of the finer details sooner than I thought. I just hoped she wouldn't find out about the part that I had volunteered to become an enforcer—at least not tonight, so soon after we had all just found each other again.

"Sure," I said and turned to Reece. "Any idea what they want?"

"I was hoping it would be about the fact that we've just broadcasted ArtRep's dirty little secrets on every feed across the planet," he said as he raised a hand to rub at the back of his neck.

"But?" Saera asked.

"I'm not sure," Reece replied. "It all seems too quiet, and Riffy and Kelle have been searching the feeds but have found nothing yet."

"That doesn't have to mean anything," Saera said. "We always have trouble updating the feeds down here. The connection is lousy, and if there's a problem at a relay station, it could take days for information from up above to reach us."

Saera was right: it could take days for information to travel, but I had a feeling that wasn't the case this time. Something in my gut told me things were off.

"Well, if the data does find its way to us down here, I'm sure the council won't be happy about it," Reece said, "and they won't be happy with us." His words could have been interpreted as serious, but the grin on his face told me he was hoping for just that.

The council was just a front that was supposed to hide the fact that government officials had any dealings with the so-called rebels. In their eyes, we were just puppets on their strings, and that was exactly how they intended to make us feel—so, in Reece's eyes, there were never enough ways to irritate them.

Saera turned back to face me and shrugged. The crooked smile on her face was one of resignation. She didn't care about the council and their fits—she never had. She lifted the hand holding the bracelet and whispered, "Thank you." Then she got up and walked to the door where Reece blocked her way out.

He shifted clumsily on his feet as if he had no control over his body. His eyes darted from me to Saera and back again. It wasn't hard to identify his reason for the discomfort that he showed. Reece was afraid that I had told Saera about volunteering to become an enforcer and divulging that he had known about it.

I shook my head at him, hoping that he would understand that I hadn't told Saera even though I should have. Our eyes locked, and he raised his eyebrows before he released the breath he'd been holding. I frowned at him for being so obvious, but Saera hadn't noticed as she addressed me over her shoulder. "See you out there, okay?"

"Okay," I replied. With that, she exited my room, and I glared at Reece.

He was still standing near the door with his back against the wall this time. With the edge of the blanket clutched in my fist as I held it before my chest, I tilted my head. He stared at his feet for the longest time, unwilling to face me as if this moment hadn't been awkward enough.

It hadn't been easy to break things off with Reece before I had left. He hadn't been happy about it, but we had talked it through, and at the time he seemed to have accepted it. If I'd been honest with myself back then, calling the break-up *not easy* would have been the understatement of the year.

Because in my time frame it only seemed to have happened a week ago—it still hurt. While my own memories hadn't been wiped from my brain, only suppressed, the enforcer memories did appear to be gone. This shouldn't have been the case, and I wondered if Kyran had a hand in that, but figuring that out could wait.

"So," Reece said as he shifted from one foot to the other. "You're back."

"I'm back," I said, not sure what else to say.

"And I guess you haven't told Saera the truth yet," he said as he looked over his shoulder in the direction where Saera had gone.

"I woke up like five minutes ago." My remark triggered a tug at his lips and morphed into a grin.

"I'll give you that for now, but don't expect much time to adjust, because the rest of the gang is waiting out there, and I think they might want some answers," he said as he pointed with a thumb over his shoulder.

"And you won't take pity on me and tell them what you know," I said.

"And what—take the brunt of Saera's wrath?" he said. "I don't think so." Reece took a step to close the gap between us but then hesitated before he stopped altogether. He stuffed his hands in his pockets and said, "I think we're gonna need some time to talk this through—all of us." The expression on his face had gone serious, and it reminded me of the time that I told him what Harp and I had planned. That night he had held that same concern in his eyes, and it was just as hard to look at now as it had then.

As if a switch flipped inside his head, Reece dropped the concerned expression, and the big smile that frequently lit up his face appeared. I slightly shook my head in amazement even though I knew this to be Reece's signature method of handling the hard stuff.

With a shrug, he said, "First we deal with the council. Then you, me, and the rest of the kids are going for a drink. And after we get totally wasted, we'll talk things out."

I let out a chuckle and said, "Great plan."

"Of course," he said. "My plans are always great, unlike the plans of some of us." His words were said in a playful tone, but I still felt the sting at his affirmation that my plan might have been less than bright. My feelings must have shown on my face, because he shifted uncomfortably but composed himself quickly.

"Get your lazy ass out of bed," he said. "We have a council to meet."

Reece crossed his arms over his chest and eyed me expectantly. I raised an eyebrow at him and tilted my head questionably. He just stood there without any intention of moving.

"Reece," I said and gestured at the door. He looked over his shoulder as if someone might have appeared there before his gaze shifted back to me.

"What?" he asked.

"I would like to get dressed," I said, but I couldn't help a smile from forming on my lips.

"As do I," he said matter-of-factly.

"Get out of my room, Reece," I said in a firm, but still playful voice.

Grinning, he said, "A guy can try, right." With a chuckle, he turned on his heels and moved to the door.

"Reece," I said and noticed the uncertainty in my own voice. Reece stopped at the door and turned to face me. His expression had gone serious again, and I felt grateful that he still knew me so well. "Did I do the right thing?"

The question seemed odd, even to myself. Intellectually, I knew I had done the right thing. Trying to stop the abuse of our people by ArtRep had the number-one priority in my book—but did it really? I couldn't help wondering if, in my quest to help strangers, I had let down the people who cared most about me. That was probably why I sought Reece's approval—again. He had given it to me once, just before I'd left, but so much must have happened in the time that I was gone. *Would he have given me that approval had he known what he knew now?*

He straightened and looked me in the eyes as he said, "You did what you thought was right, and even though I wasn't happy about it then, and I'm not happy about it now, I support your decision." His words came close to what he had said to me back then, and I felt the sting in my eyes as tears threatened.

"The others will understand—just as I have," he added. "Don't worry. We're all just glad you're back."

"Are you…" I started to say but hesitated as I suddenly felt unsure of what it was what I wanted to ask. My eyes shifted down to the sheet draped over me. I wasn't sure if I wanted to know if he'd been angry with me, although he didn't show it. But if not, did that mean he was over of whatever we had once shared? It was hard to remind myself that for him it had been two years because it didn't feel to me as if that much time had passed.

As I looked up, Reece stared at me with an intensity that might have been able to burn right into my soul and the pain that sat behind his eyes was evident. He shook his head and stepped closer until he was standing next to me. I resisted the urge to look away and tilted my head to face him.

Placing a tender hand on my cheek, he bent down to kiss the top of my head.

"We don't have to sort all of this out now," he said in a soft tone. "We have time."

I held my breath for as long as his touch lasted and closed my eyes to savor the feeling, but before I knew it, the moment had passed, and Reece straightened.

"But we're gonna be okay, right?" I asked. My breath caught as I looked up at him. He gave me a gentle smile that was nothing like the all-or-nothing charm offensive that he usually threw around. It was a kind smile, but his eyes revealed something that didn't felt reassuring. An overwhelming sensation of loss fell over me as Reece turned and walked out.

I stared at the doorway long after Reece had disappeared, unable to get past the sensation that I had broken something and not just with Reece. I just hoped the damage wouldn't be permanent.

Chapter thirty

Maece

Relieved to be back in my own formfitting black pants, I adjusted the belt. I stared at my reflection in the mirror on top of my dresser for a while as my gaze remained fixed on the black and gray ink that dawned across my dark skin. The sleeveless shirt revealed the intricate drawing of feathers neatly packed together to form the wings that started at the base of my neck to run down my arms and, from what I remember, down my back.

The depicted wings of a protector, or, as Reece liked to call it, an angel, were chosen by the others as my own personal tattoo. We all had these markings chosen by the others to remind us what we meant to them. *Some protector I had turned out to be.*

I sighed and then slipped into my old jacket. It seemed I had lost some weight judging by the hole I had to use in the belt, but I had also gained some muscle. My favorite jacket felt tight around the arms, and that bummed me out.

After leaving my room, I stepped into the general living quarters of our meager home and was met by

Riffy's arms wrapping around me in a tight hug. Back at the medical facility, I had known everyone was there, but my memories seemed a bit fuzzy, and it all happened in such a rush—so this was the warm welcome I had hoped for.

"Hey Riff," I said as I hugged him back, "you've gotten big." Riffy had always been bigger in size than most kids his age. It seemed his body had developed some method of self-preservation, holding on to all the carbs and proteins it could manage. These past two years had been good to my little friend.

Reece sat on a table in the middle of the room. He'd never been able to sit on a chair like a normal person. He nodded in my direction as Kelle got up from the couch where she was sitting with Saera.

Kelle's robotic arm twitched as she approached. The prosthesis sat hidden underneath her long-sleeved jacket and the glove she wore on her right hand. If you hadn't known it, you would never guess about the severed arm just below her elbow. It even showed her being nervous as the artificial digits flexed.

Like before, she hesitated, but unlike inside that hallway in the ArtRep building, this wasn't because of a lack of trust. She was nervous because of something else. The eyes that searched for reassurance with Saera as Kelle looked over her shoulder betrayed her. Kelle had never been one to be nervous about things; her preferred emotion was anger, and it tended to reflect in her eyes. As I watched her, I saw none of that anger, although her expression looked to be as stoic as always.

I felt the urge to take away Kelle's insecurities and crossed the room with my arms in an open invitation. The young woman had to stand on her tiptoes, and I had to bend down for her to wrap her arms around my neck, but it fit as it had always done.

"Hey, stranger," I said as I briefly lifted her off the ground.

"Hey," she said as she extricated herself from my grip. I placed the flat of my hand on top of her head and enjoyed the tingle that her cropped hair created on my fingertips. Kelle was only a few years younger than the rest of us, but her timid demeanor had always left her to be the baby of our group. Although I knew her quite capable of handling herself, that didn't quench the urge to protect her.

Kelle's face had turned a shade of pink, but before I could comment on it, Reece spoke up.

"Ahh," he said, "this is so touching, and I could watch it for hours if we weren't supposed to be downtown like…fifteen minutes ago."

I shot him a glare and felt relieved to see the mischievous gleam had returned to his eyes. He shot me a wink, and I couldn't help grinning. Our ties went deep, and I felt our connection at that moment and not just with Reece. It didn't diminish the sensation that I had screwed up, and I knew that I would still have to deal with the aftermath, but I also felt certain that it wouldn't tear us apart.

"He's right," Saera said as she stood. "Let's get this council thing over with, and then we celebrate."

Our eyes met as she spoke that last word, and her face spoke of a reason to celebrate. The others concurred her statement, and it made this warm feeling swell in my chest that on the one hand felt so familiar and on the other no more than a distant memory.

They all filed out of the room, and I paused a moment to glance around. Not much had changed in the past two years inside the tiny apartment. The main living room held the same sparse pieces of furniture as the day that we'd moved in. The same old couch and a basic block of concrete that served as a table surrounded by several smaller blocks that could be used for sitting. My room had also remained the same, and so I figured the same must hold for the rooms inhabited by the others.

Harp had arranged this home for us several years ago so we could stay together and keep an eye on each other. The place was part of a bigger complex that, like most Subterran buildings on the outskirts of the city, had been carved out of stone. Neighbors lived left and right from us, but also above and below. Fortunately, most of them kept to themselves and so did we—well, unless Reece and Riffy did something stupid to attract their attention, but mostly we kept to ourselves.

I almost started to feel as if I'd never left, but then I heard Saera's voice pipe up behind me.

"Maecy," she said in a soft voice, "you comin'?"

The sad look in her eyes as I turned to face her where she stood by the door told me it was wrong of me to feel that. Instead of my personal memories, this time it had been the enforcer memories that eluded me and made me feel that I hadn't missed a thing. I hadn't missed my family, but that wasn't true for them. It wasn't true for Saera. I could see it in her eyes, and I hadn't even told the truth yet about how and what.

"Yeah," I replied and moved toward her.

"You okay?" she asked as I stopped by her side.

A genuine smile crept across my face because, besides the fact Saera and I would have to have a serious talk, I did feel okay.

"Better than okay actually," I said.

Saera gave me a once-over and nodded in satisfaction.

"C'mon then, we're late," she said and grabbed an arm forcing me to follow.

The city's location deep underground didn't allow Subterrans to construct buildings as high as the structures on the surface, nor would the people living there want homes like that. Houses were simple in design, usually square with a maximum of four or five floors. Residences at the edge of the city were mostly carved right from the stone, and this allowed for additional floors, but for the most part, people preferred to live next to each other instead of above and below one another.

For the occasion, the council had chosen to convene at the Department of Nutriment. Like most government buildings, this one stood alone without any neighboring buildings and, fortunately for us, not that far from our own home.

Official meetings usually took place inside the Government Center Tower. The Center Tower wasn't nearly as big as the ArtRep buildings in Tenebrae, but it was the largest building in Subterra. This wasn't an official meeting, though. This was a highly classified meeting between the rebel leadership and some folks who happened to be part of the Subterran government. So that was probably the reason they had summoned us to the Department of Nutriment.

My eyes swept the street as we crossed from one side to the other. It seemed my internal clock had gone a bit haywire, because I felt wide awake as if it were the early afternoon, but from the lack of activity on the streets, it had to be the late hours of the night. Unlike Tenebrae and its prominent view of the sun hanging high up in the sky, Subterra had no natural phenomena to track time.

"Dude, you sound like one of the vent exhausts up in Tenebrae," Reece said as he patted Riffy on the back. The two of them walked a couple of steps ahead of the rest of us, and Riffy seemed to have a little trouble keeping pace.

From my peripheral vision, I could see a faint smile forming on Saera's face as she walked by my side. I couldn't blame her. It wasn't easy to keep a straight face at Reece's and Riffy's antics. Kelle, though, walked on Saera's other side and wore the same stoic expression she always had plastered across her face.

"I'll race you up the steps," Reece said and took off in a jog.

Riffy groaned and shouted after him, "I don't want to…" His words trailed off, and as if Reece had some invisible hold on him, he started to tread the steps in pursuit of his friend.

As the three of us followed, it was easy to tell Riffy would never make it to the top in one go. The steps that would lead us into an open square in front of the Department of Nutriment were wide, and there were at least a hundred of them. At the top of the stairs, two massive statues looked down on us. Although beautifully carved out of lava stone, I had always hated the kneeling figures. The look of despair on their faces and their submissive postures reminded me too much of the bow-down attitude our government had held over the years toward our Tenebrae neighbors, and I wondered if the information we had released upon the world would change anything in that regard.

The thought gave me pause as I gazed around to take in my surroundings. There should have been more activity going on around us besides the empty streets that filled my vision. A few bars seemed to be open for business as lights from the establishments filtered out through the windows. The voices of a couple late-night drinkers bounced off the walls behind us as they stepped out into the street.

"Is it just me or is it way too quiet out here?" I said and shifted my gaze to Saera. She looked around as if she'd only first noticed.

"There still hasn't been anything on the news feeds yet," Kelle replied, hinting that she knew exactly what I was talking about.

"I'd have guessed it would have stirred more of a ruckus," I added.

"Like I said before, it could be a delayed transmission," Saera said as she caught up with the conversation. If the news about the Subterrans-turned-enforcers had broken along with the poor conditions at the power plants and the reasoning behind it, it would have brought people onto the streets. They would have marched down to the Government Center Tower and demanded an explanation.

"Maybe," I said in reply to Saera but again had that sinking feeling there would be more to it.

As we reached the top of the stairs, I glanced over my shoulder to see how Riffy fared, but instead of falling on the figure of my oversized little friend who lagged behind, my eyes fell on the intricately constructed path, walkways, and buildings that made up the metropolitan area of Subterra. Hymag lines provided travel to the smaller settlements either deeper underground or near the surface. Those lines also transported some of the workforce that lived here but worked at the mushroom and fungi farms or at the remaining Subterra-controlled power plants.

In a way, Subterra was the complete opposite from the Combined Districts of Tenebrae. There they had to add to the landscape if they wanted a place to live. Here, one would have to carve away at the stone until only what was needed remained. Something else that set the two people apart was that Subterrans had never felt the need to place a facade over the depressing gray features of their homes. In that, I had to hand it to the people of Umbras. At least they tried to make something out of nothing, even if it did turn out to be a mirage. Perhaps something like that would have helped some to remain hopeful.

Heavy, almost exaggerated panting pulled me from my thoughts. Riffy stood by my side, where he bent over and found support by resting his hand on his knees.

Reece gave him an encouraging pat on the back, but then said, "Man, you suck at climbing stairs."

Riffy just shook his head, unable to say anything as he gulped in air.

"Don't let him get to you, Riff," I said as I laid a hand on his shoulder. He gazed up from his bent over position and gave me the sweetest look of appreciation.

"Don't pity him," Reece said firmly, but with enough teasing mischief in his voice. "What if next time in the field he has to cover your back?"

"I think he had our backs just fine last time," Saera chimed in.

"Oh, don't you get me started," Reece added.

Saera retorted, and Riffy added a breathy reply as I watched. Relief, warmth, and so many more emotions filled my heart, feelings I couldn't even imagine a few days ago, and I felt grateful to have them back.

At my side, Kelle tapped my arm. I glanced down to meet the young woman's placid expression. It might not have shown on her face, but her eyes spoke volumes and projected a joy that didn't seem to translate through the rest of her body.

"We're already late," she said in a way that

reminded me way too much of Harp, but she was right.

"Guys…guys," I said loud enough to drown out the other's banter. They all looked at me appalled until I pointed a finger in the direction of the building that held the Department of Nutriment.

The building had the same look and feel as the rest of the buildings in this city—a straightforward gray structure with black square holes that served as windows and several steps that led up to an entryway. A Hymag stood parked at the side of the building on its own private platform.

Considering it was night, it seemed obvious that none of the windows were illuminated. Besides, the lights might have alerted someone to the meeting being held at an ungodly hour—a meeting between members of the Subterran government and the rebel leadership, which in the eyes of Tenebrae might be considered treason.

"All right, all right," Reece muttered before he shrugged and plastered that big smile of his across his face. "Everyone relaxed now?"

With that, he turned and started across the small, open square that led to the Department of Nutriment building.

Inside, a man in a finely tailored suit nearly hidden underneath a long black coat guided us along a couple of hallways until he opened a double door and let us into a spacious room.

A path lined with chairs on either side of the aisle led to a small stage. A woman and two men sat at a table on top of the stage. From the moment we entered the room, every movement seemed to have stopped, and all eyes focused on us. From behind the table, the man sitting in the middle stood and gestured to us.

"Please, come join us," he said. He pointed at the chairs placed in front of the stage. I noticed Harp sitting in one of those chairs turning so he could see us.

As we approached, he glanced at the time device on his wrist to let us know that we were late. Catching the not-so-subtle gesture, Reece said, "Sorry we're late. We had a little trouble finding the place."

Harp shook his head in disapproval but didn't say anything. Kyran, who was sitting at Harp's side, avoided our gazes and kept staring straight ahead. As I passed him, I understood why. Apparently, Kyran was having trouble keeping a straight face.

"I'm glad you could make it," the woman at the table on the stage said, but she didn't look glad. Before we managed to sit down, she stood up and started to introduce herself, and I decided to remain standing. I didn't like the fact that they were sitting up there looking down on us and sitting down would make that worse.

"My name is Elise Henkel, second alderman to the city of Subterra," she said. Of course, we all recognized the middle-aged woman with her too long white hair trapped in a ponytail.

The woman had been second alderman for as long as I could remember, and her hair had been white for nearly that long. The years showed on her face as she introduced the others.

"This is Luther Wear." She pointed at the man in the middle, who, by then, had sat down again. He sported a weird-looking comb-over that seemed unnatural. His round cheeks flushed red under the scrutiny of our probing eyes. A third man sat on the far right, and according to Elise, his name was Monroe. She didn't mention if this was his first or last name, only that both men were third in the line of aldermen.

Monroe looked impressive with his broad shoulders and seemed to demand my attention. His skin had the same dark color as mine, and it stood out against the soft green of his suit. I remembered Saera mentioning his name and also seeing him once in one of the bars where I was having a drink with Reece.

In my mind, it didn't seem that long ago, but it must have been years since I visited that bar with Reece. At the time, I had thought it odd, an alderman spending his time at a local drinking hole as he sat alone at his table. Our eyes had met a few times, and they'd held the same intensity as they did now. I had lost track of him a short while before Harp had shown up at that same bar. As the memory resurfaced, I wondered if it had been a coincidence that Harp had shown up at a place he rarely visited at almost the same time this alderman had left. Back then, it would never have occurred to me that the two men might have a connection, but now and because Saera had mentioned their conversation, it seemed obvious that there had to be something going on between Harp and alderman Monroe.

"We have carefully reviewed the information retrieved from the ArtRep offices and have come to a decision," Henkel said, pulling me back to the briefing.

"Unfortunately," Monroe said. Henkel paused and regarded the man with a disapproving look. Monroe, on the other hand, ignored her. He demonstratively crossed his arms over his chest and turned his head away from Henkel.

"The decision has been made," Henkel said in an authoritative voice, "and we have chosen to take Harand Sulos's offer."

My jaw just about unhinged itself as my mouth fell open.

"Excuse me?" Reece exclaimed, sounding incredulous. Beside me, heads shifted from left to right and eyes holding the same shocked surprised locked. All of us looked at each other in amazement, except for Harp. He sat unmoving, his eyes gazing up at the stage where they held Henkel's. For a moment, I thought she might be able to hold his gaze, but a second later, her eyes flickered to the tabletop.

"We will refrain from taking any form of action against the efforts of the Combined Districts of Tenebrae to create a new world for our future kind."

"You are willing to let our people suffer," Reece said, "just so a few can outlive that destructive sun out there." He pointed a finger at the ceiling of the building as if anyone could see the dying star.

"But we've broadcast the…" I started to say, but the words died off before I could finish the sentence. One look at Harp's rigid expression told me enough.

His jaw flexed as he ground his teeth.

"They cut off our access to the feed before we finished," he said with venom in his voice. Reece cursed, and Saera followed his comments with her own colorful string of words.

Up on the stage, Henkel bowed down and whispered something into Wear's ear. As Henkel pulled away, Wear stood and nervously patted the weird-looking hair on top of his head. He lifted his hands as if to soothe us.

"Harand Sulos has the power to destroy this world with all its inhabitants, and he's threatened to do so by this time next year, while he'll be able to live out his life in peace," Wear said as his face flushed red again.

"Sulos is dead," Saera called out.

"No, he's not," I said more to myself, but sensed Saera watching me. Harp shifted his head slightly and nodded in my direction.

"Indeed, he is not," he said in confirmation. The definitive answer came from Henkel, but I didn't need the white-haired woman to explain to me that she had talked to the man through long-distance communication and that Saera had killed the wrong man. Well, maybe not. Sulos was a man with access to a vast range of technology and, of course, bioprinters.

Turning to Saera, who had turned a sickening pale, I said, "Artificial representation."

Her eyes found mine, but my words didn't register. I grabbed her shoulders and shook her slightly. Kelle stepped in beside her and gazed up at us with a concerned look on her face.

"You didn't kill the wrong person," I said, "just a printed copy that Sulos operated from a distance." I paused a moment to gauge her reaction. Kelle wrapped an arm around Saera's waist, and that helped.

"AR," she said.

"Right," I replied. She nodded as if she understood, but I had a feeling the information needed some time to sink in.

Henkel had been talking while I had busied myself with Saera, and I just caught the last part of what she was saying.

"As many as possible will be accommodated, and the remaining numbers can live out their lives on this planet," she said. "This is no different from how it has always been."

"Except some of us will have to work themselves to death so a few can live in luxury," I said. I could almost taste the venom in my voice. Henkel had been right about one thing—none of this seemed to alter the eventual fate of these workers, although the meaning of these lives had changed significantly. They weren't just working to keep the cities from falling apart or to keep the shields up to protect us from the increasing temperatures of a dying sun. Neither did they work to run the mushroom farms or any of the other energy-consuming undertakings. They had been working harder than ever inside those power plants to accommodate the pleasures of the fortunate.

This would not sit well with the men and women

working the power plants if this were to come out.

"I wonder how the people will react to this news," I added.

This time Henkel's face flushed red, as did Wear's. She pounded a fist on the table and shot me a fierce look.

"The council has made its decision, and you are bound to obey that decision," she said and paused to emphasize her point. She locked eyes with Harp, and this time she did hold his gaze. "You have taken an oath to serve the people of Subterra, and I am holding you to that."

"Exactly," Reece exclaimed, "an oath to the people and they have a right to know about this."

"Reece," Harp said in a sharp tone. Reece looked taken aback as his gaze turned to Harp. As their eyes met, Harp spoke in an even, but rather threatening tone.

"We will do as we are told." It wasn't hard to read the defiance in Reece's blue eyes and a muscle in his jaw flexed. The moment seemed endless, but as if by some silent communication, Reece relented and his gaze shifted to the ground.

"Remember that," Henkel said as her voice cut through the tension, "or else you might find yourself in a detention facility." Her eyes were still on Harp as she added, "I'm sure you'll manage to keep your people in check."

Harp nodded while he held her gaze, and seemingly satisfied, Henkel straightened. She spared us one more glance and then turned on her heels and strutted off the stage. Wear quickly followed, but

Monroe remained seated.

As the footsteps of the departing aldermen faded, Monroe raised himself from his seat. I shifted my gaze between the remaining alderman and Harp as the others just stood aghast. There seemed to be some form of silent communication going on between the two men, and from the look in Harp's eyes, it wasn't that hard to decipher what was being said.

I told you so! radiated from Harp's posture, and an accusing gaze held Monroe frozen to his spot. Monroe didn't look nearly as impressive as he had before. In fact, he looked rather small under Harp's scrutiny, even though he towered over him from up on the stage.

I took a step forward, not sure what it was that I wanted to do, but Harp stopped me from whatever it was with his hard glare. His commanding eyes didn't get to me like they used to, but I still obeyed—albeit without taking my eyes off him. As Harp's gaze softened, it felt like quite an achievement.

"Later," he said, and at that single word, I took a step back.

With a curt nod, Monroe excused himself and left in the same direction the other aldermen had.

As soon as he had left, an explosion of sound burst from those of us left standing at the base of the stage.

"I'd say I'd be surprised," Reece said, "but I'm not."

"What just happened?" Riffy said.

"I'm heading back to the base," Kyran said as he

turned to Harp. "I think I might have just figured out what those weird numbers we've found in the ArtRep mainframe mean."

Harp narrowed his eyes before he asked, "The currency trail?"

Kyran absently nodded while his unfocused eyes stared off into space. The wheels inside his mind must have been spinning at high speed if the thoughtful expression on his face was any indication.

"Well," Saera said impatiently, "if it's not energy, then what is it?"

Kyran snapped out of it and faced Harp again.

"I'll need to check this, but I think they're people," he said.

"Tickets, more likely," Reece said, catching on. Along with the rest of us, I turned my gaze to Reece except my eyes didn't hold the questions like Riffy's did.

"Tickets, accommodations, land, who knows," Kyran said, "but I'll find out."

"They've sold us out?" Kelle said, sounding disgusted. "The government sold us out for a seat on a vessel that that will bring them to Sulos's new world?"

I looked at the young woman standing next to Saera, her eyes intently focused on Harp. It wasn't hard to recognize the anger bordering on hatred that radiated from those eyes. Saera must have noticed, because she placed a hand on Kelle's shoulder.

We all knew how Kelle felt. We've all been there. All of us were born within the confines of those power plants whose workers had been abused by

Sulos for decades. And now it might have been our own people, our government, that was willing to condone this treatment.

Deciding someone would have to be the voice of reason, I said, "We need to be sure before we start pointing fingers."

"Agreed," Harp said. He gave me an approving nod before he turned to Kyran. "Find out who," Harp said, "and keep it between us for now."

Kyran eyed Harp for a moment and then gave him a nod. Without another word, Kyran stepped away from our group and left. I watched as he crossed the room and went on his way back to the rebel hideout underneath the City of Umbras.

Voices coursed on and over each other, all exclaiming the lack of understanding of what had just happened.

"I take it we're not going to stand for this," Saera said. Her gaze sought out Harp's, expecting a reply. He moved his hands behind his back and straightened his shoulders. His eyes shifted from Riffy to Reece, over to Saera and Kelle, before they landed on me. A sly smile tugged at the corner of his mouth.

"It seems the council has no knowledge of what the word *rebel* actually means," he said.

"Perhaps we should reeducate them," Reece said.

"I agree," Saera said. "What's the plan?" All eyes returned to face Harp until Kelle spoke up, "How about we talk about this over food and drinks."

"Oh, I second that," Riffy said as his eyes went wide. "I'm hungry."

"You're always hungry," Reece said and patted

Riffy on the back.

Harp grinned before actually exposing us to one of his rare smiles. "Food and drinks," he said, "sounds good. Besides, I think it's time we gave Maece a proper welcome home."

His gaze shifted to me, and I felt my cheeks flush as I diverted my eyes.

"Oh, Maecy is feeling embarrassed," Reece said in a whiny voice. Saera, who stood closer to him, kicked him in the shins. I grinned at the satisfied look she gave me.

"I think we're all in agreement," Harp said and turned to leave.

"You already have a plan, don't you?" Reece called out after Harp. "On how to deal with Sulos."

"I always have a plan," Harp said without turning back.

"Is this the plan where we charge the Tenebrae power plants and free our people or the one where we commandeer a ship and kick Sulos out of his new world?" Reece said. Reece, being Reece, had kept himself from sounding serious, but that didn't mean he believed Harp was incapable of initiating any one of those plans, and neither did I.

"Knowing Harp, he'll probably wanna do both," I said under my breath. Reece shifted his head a little, and I knew he had heard me.

"But you do expect this plan to work?" Reece added in a playful tone. Harp didn't answer. Instead, he lifted a hand from behind his back and showed us his middle finger.

Reece grinned as he faced us. I shook my head at

seeing the mischief in his eyes. He hadn't changed at all over the years. As he noticed me watching him, he stepped closer and my body tensed. By the time he took my hand, I was holding my breath. He squeezed my fingers lightly before he said,

"Come on." The moment would have been anticlimactic if it weren't for the heartfelt smile and the wink that followed. Despite the ease that as of late came with reading the faces of the people around me, it seemed my own insecurities didn't allow me to delve into the meaning of Reece's gesture. As quickly as the moment had come, it was gone when Reece released my hand and threw an arm around Riffy to tug him along.

I started to follow as Saera threw an arm around my shoulders and stopped.

"Despite all the crap we just witnessed, of which I haven't even processed everything," Saera said with a broad grin on her face, "I'm really glad you're back." She pulled me in for a hug, and I gladly accepted.

Over Saera's shoulder, I noticed Kelle watching us with a contented grin on her face. It wasn't a smile exactly, but it was a step up for Kelle, and I had a feeling I'd be seeing more of this less brooding version of her.

Saera released me from her hug but kept an arm draped around my shoulder.

"Listen," she said as she grabbed Kelle with her free hand and tugged us along to follow the others. "I'm gonna need your help."

"Oh," I said, not sure where this was going to go.

"Have you noticed Riffy around Ty, lately?" she asked. Before I could say that I hadn't seen them together since I've gotten back, she added, "No, of course, you haven't, but I'm gonna need your help because Kelle is no fun in this department."

"Here we go," Kelle muttered as she rolled her eyes, but she couldn't keep herself from shooting Saera an adoring look. I raised an eyebrow as Saera tightened her hold around my neck.

"I'm telling you, those two are into each other. They just need a little incentive," Saera said.

As I listened to Saera's rambling, Reece and Riffy walked ahead of us as they followed Harp close on his heels. The banter between them started up again as well, and I knew they deliberately tried to get on Harp's nerves—at least, I was sure that was Reece's aim.

"Must have been a lot more peaceful sitting inside Memory Junction," Kelle said. I gazed at her as she added, "Compared to this lot." Her tone was serious, but the tiniest of twitches around her mouth betrayed that her words weren't meant as such. I looked ahead to see the guys walk down the hall and couldn't stop myself from grinning.

"Peaceful can be overrated," I said, "as long as it comes to you guys." Saera beamed at me, and I moved my hand behind her to grip her shoulder as we followed the guys to what I presumed to be one of Reece's favorite drinking holes.

Recall

M. VAN

Thanks for picking up this book and I hope you've enjoyed it.

As an independent author, getting a review or rating on any site is a pretty big deal. It helps us to keep the story going.

So, if you had fun with this book, I would really appreciate it if you left a review on Amazon, Goodreads or anywhere else you'd like. Thanks again.

Other books
by M. Van

The Wheels and Zombies series

Ash: A novella in the Wheels and Zombies series

Brooklyn, Wheels and Zombies

Aground

Wheels' End

Stand-alone novel

Behind the Glass

www.ingramcontent.com/pod-product-compliance
Lightning Source LLC
Chambersburg PA
CBHW050538260626
47157CB00002B/353